CRAFTY CAT
and the
CRAFTY CAMP CRISIS

CAT
AND THE
CRAFTY CAMP
CRISIS

Charise Mericle Harper

:01

First Second
New York

There is a spot on the world.

Really?
Where?
How big is it?
Does it look bad?

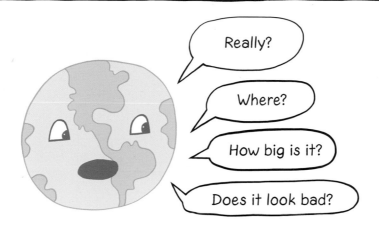

Don't worry. It's a good spot.
A spot where amazing things are happening,
and it's right behind this door. Let's look.

BIRDIE'S ROOM

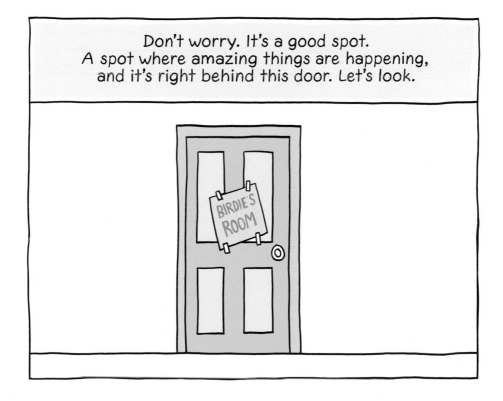

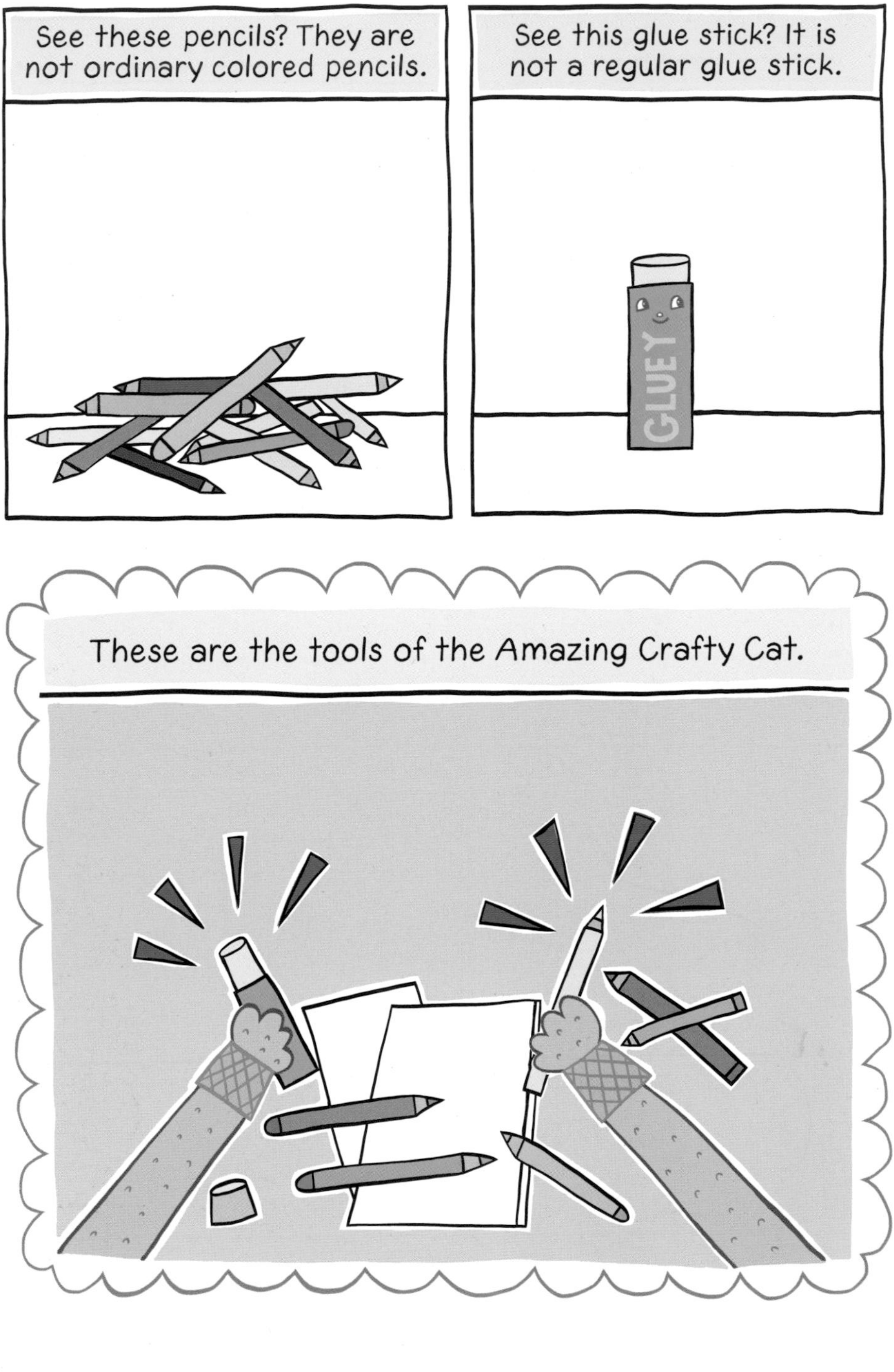
See these pencils? They are not ordinary colored pencils.
See this glue stick? It is not a regular glue stick.
GLUEY
These are the tools of the Amazing Crafty Cat.

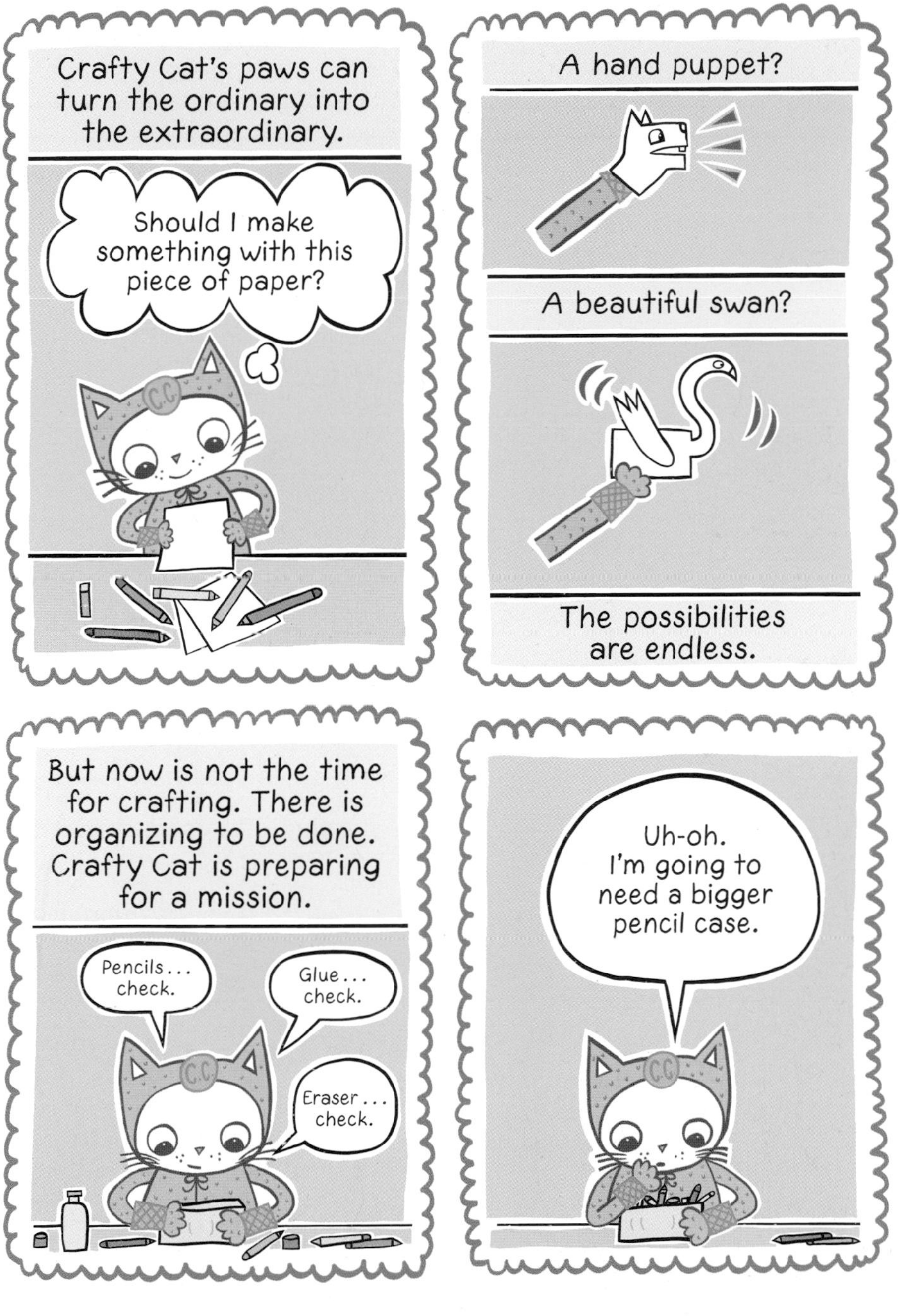
Crafty Cat's paws can turn the ordinary into the extraordinary.
Should I make something with this piece of paper?
A hand puppet?
A beautiful swan?
The possibilities are endless.
But now is not the time for crafting. There is organizing to be done. Crafty Cat is preparing for a mission.
Pencils... check.
Glue... check.
Eraser... check.
Uh-oh. I'm going to need a bigger pencil case.

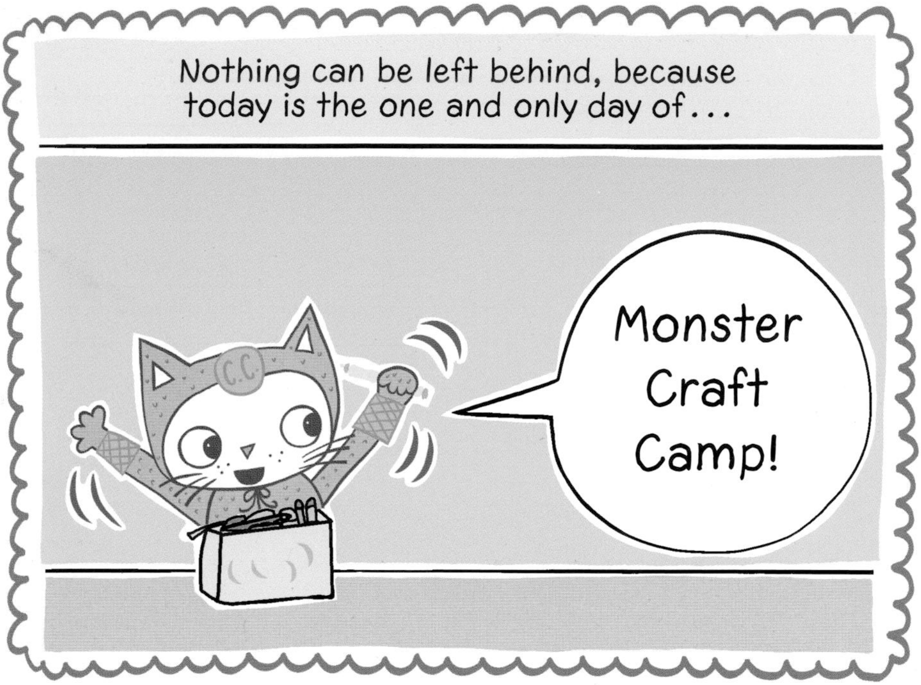
Nothing can be left behind, because today is the one and only day of...
Monster Craft Camp!

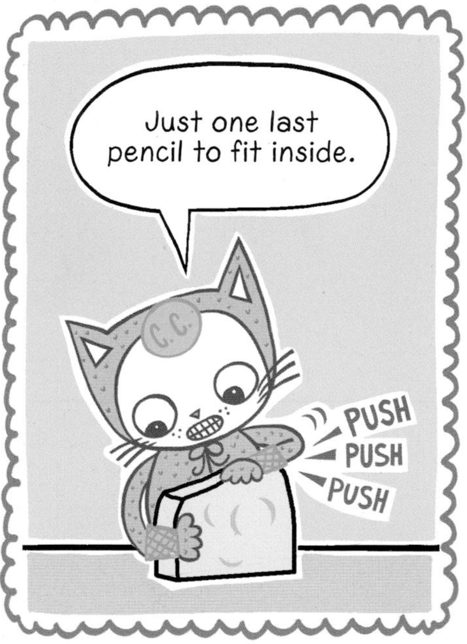
Just one last pencil to fit inside.
PUSH
PUSH
PUSH

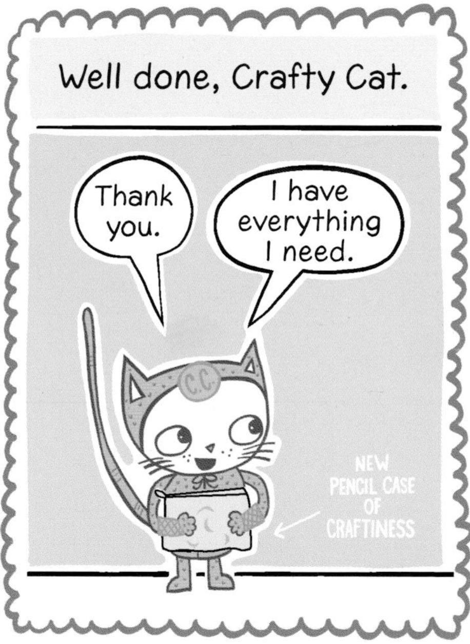
Well done, Crafty Cat.
Thank you.
I have everything I need.
NEW PENCIL CASE OF CRAFTINESS

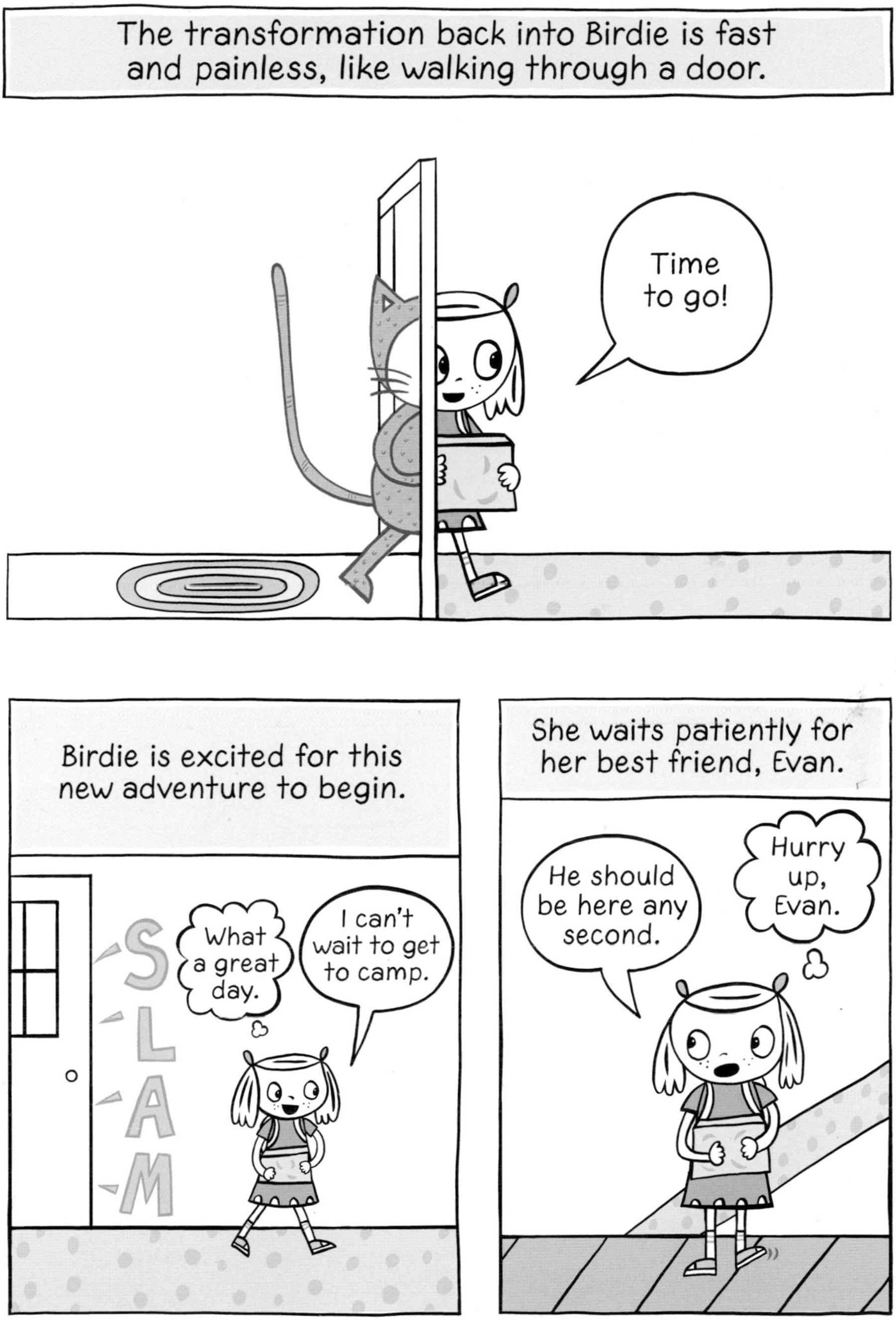
The transformation back into Birdie is fast and painless, like walking through a door.
Time to go!
Birdie is excited for this new adventure to begin.
SLAM
What a great day.
I can't wait to get to camp.
She waits patiently for her best friend, Evan.
He should be here any second.
Hurry up, Evan.

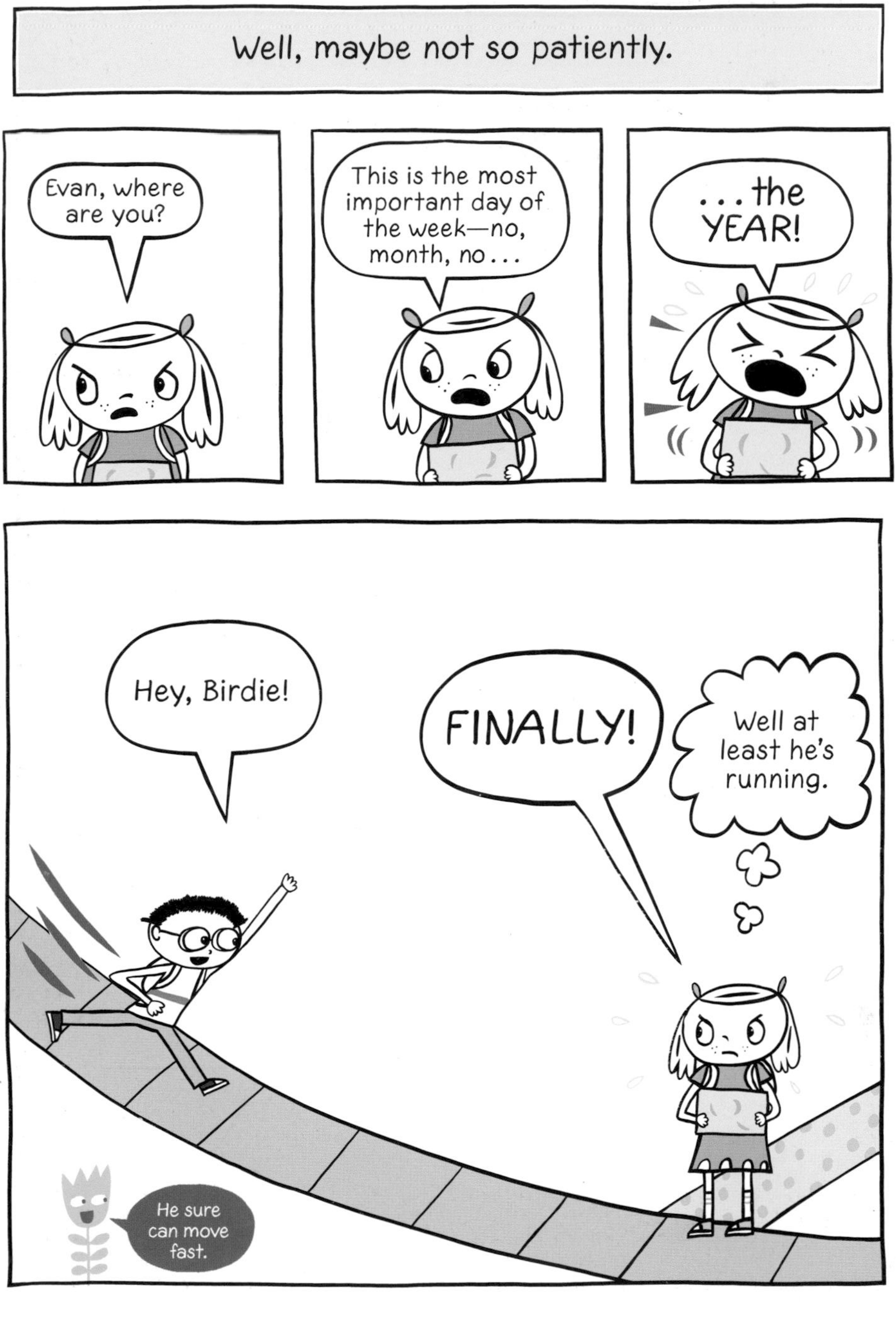
Well, maybe not so patiently.
Evan, where are you?
This is the most important day of the week—no, month, no . . .
. . . the YEAR!
Hey, Birdie!
FINALLY!
Well at least he's running.
He sure can move fast.

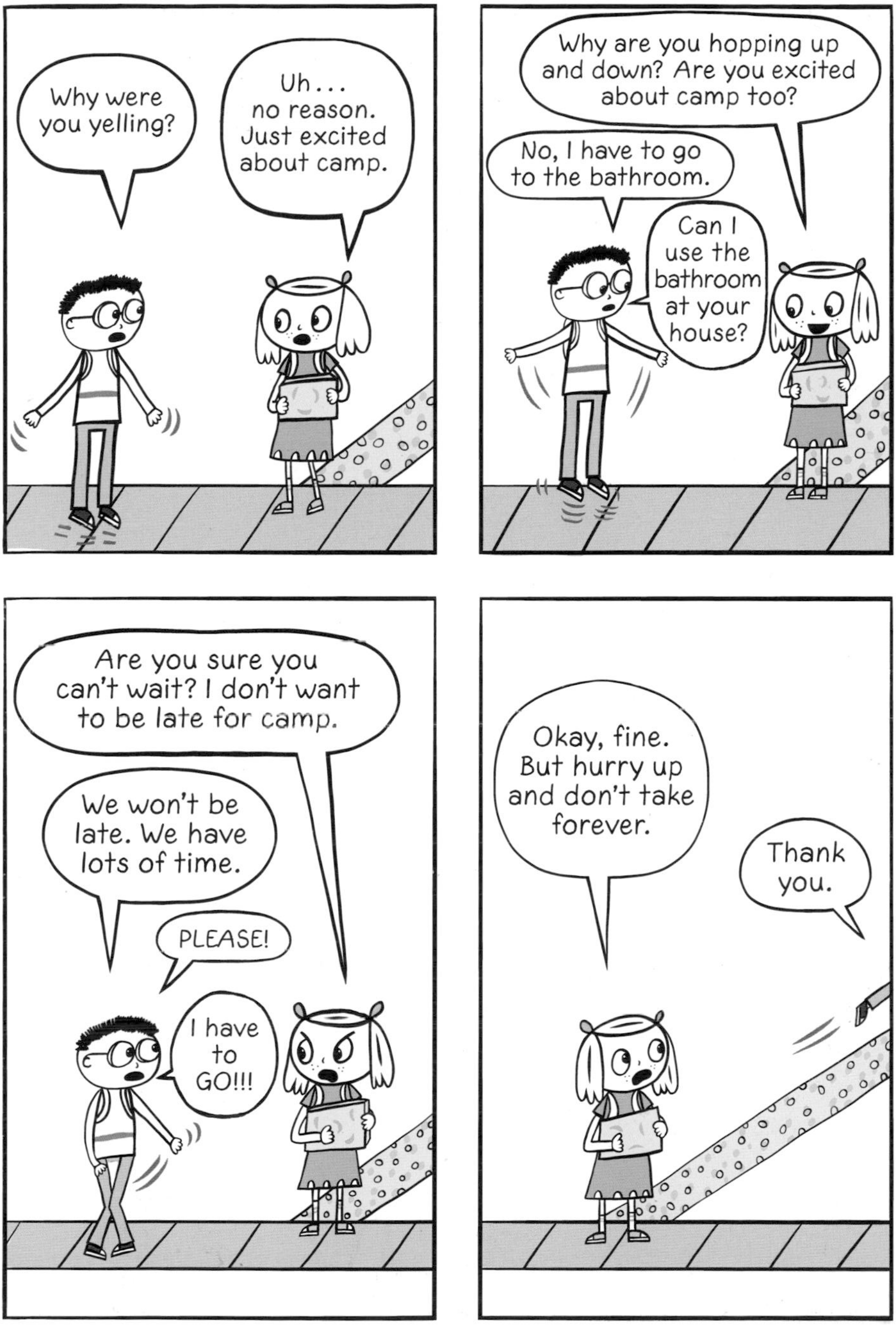
Why were you yelling?
Uh... no reason. Just excited about camp.
Why are you hopping up and down? Are you excited about camp too?
No, I have to go to the bathroom.
Can I use the bathroom at your house?
Are you sure you can't wait? I don't want to be late for camp.
We won't be late. We have lots of time.
PLEASE!
I have to GO!!!
Okay, fine. But hurry up and don't take forever.
Thank you.

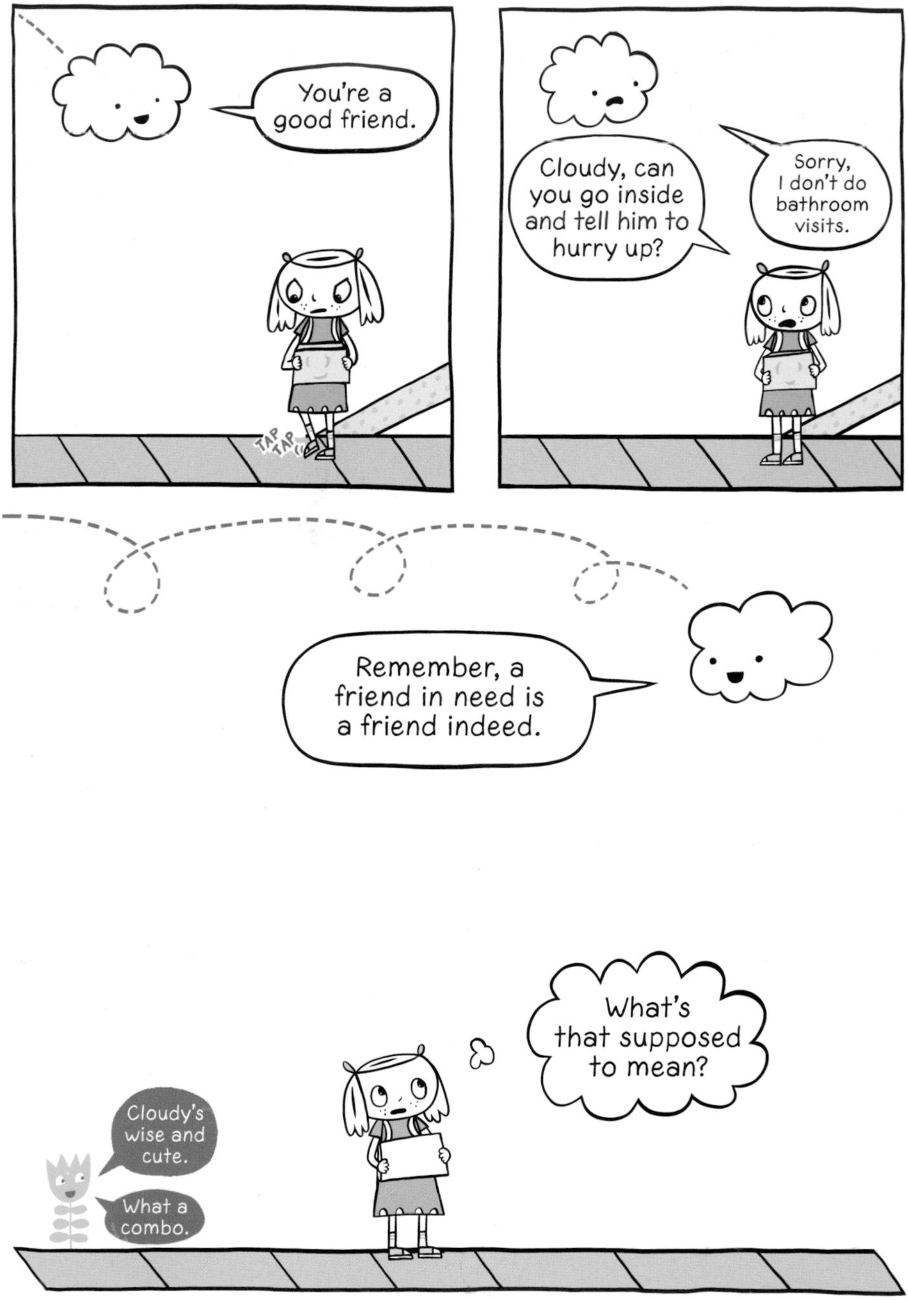
You're a good friend.
Cloudy, can you go inside and tell him to hurry up?
Sorry, I don't do bathroom visits.
Remember, a friend in need is a friend indeed.
What's that supposed to mean?
Cloudy's wise and cute.
What a combo.

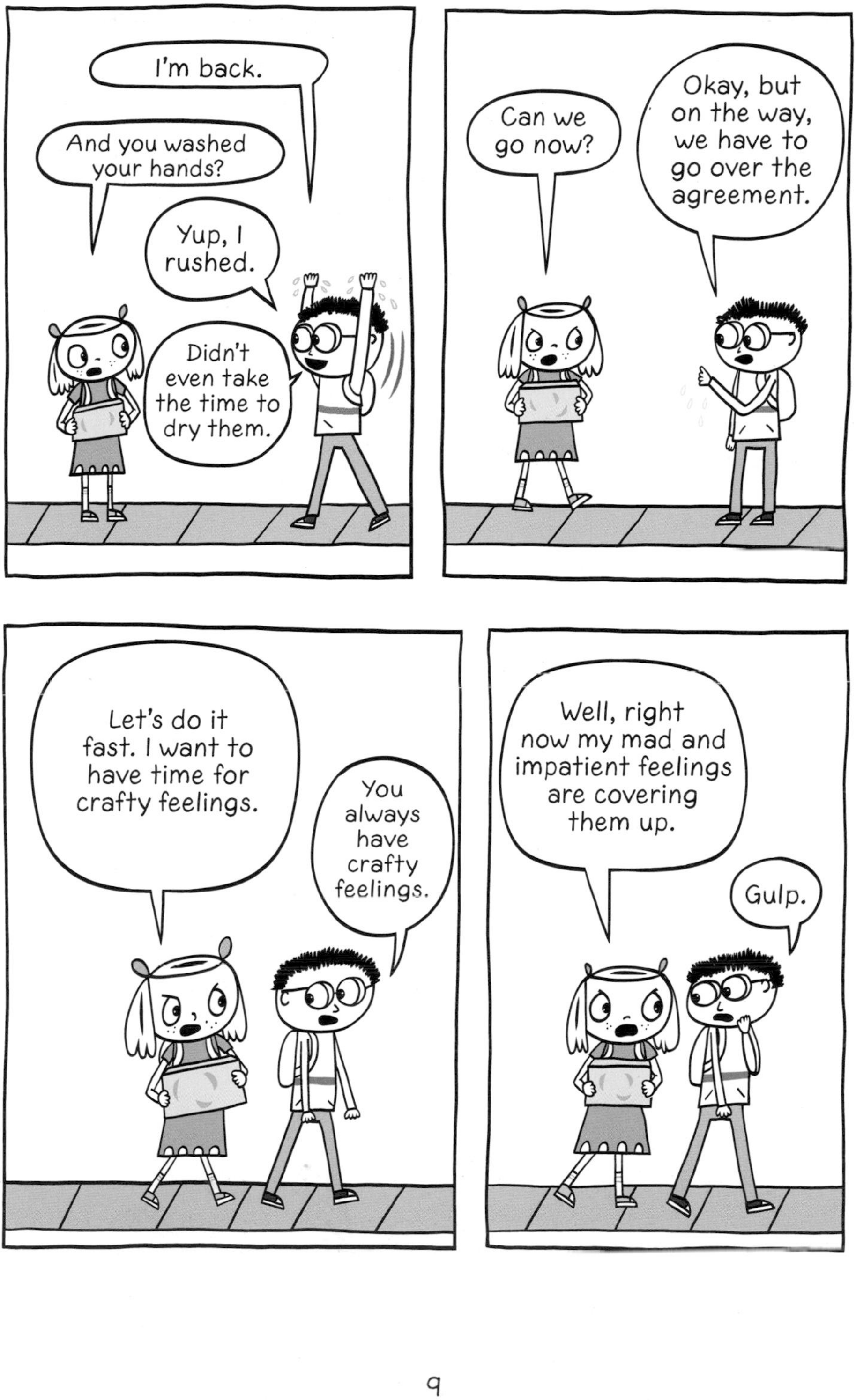
I'm back.
And you washed your hands?
Yup, I rushed.
Didn't even take the time to dry them.
Can we go now?
Okay, but on the way, we have to go over the agreement.
Let's do it fast. I want to have time for crafty feelings.
You always have crafty feelings.
Well, right now my mad and impatient feelings are covering them up.
Gulp.

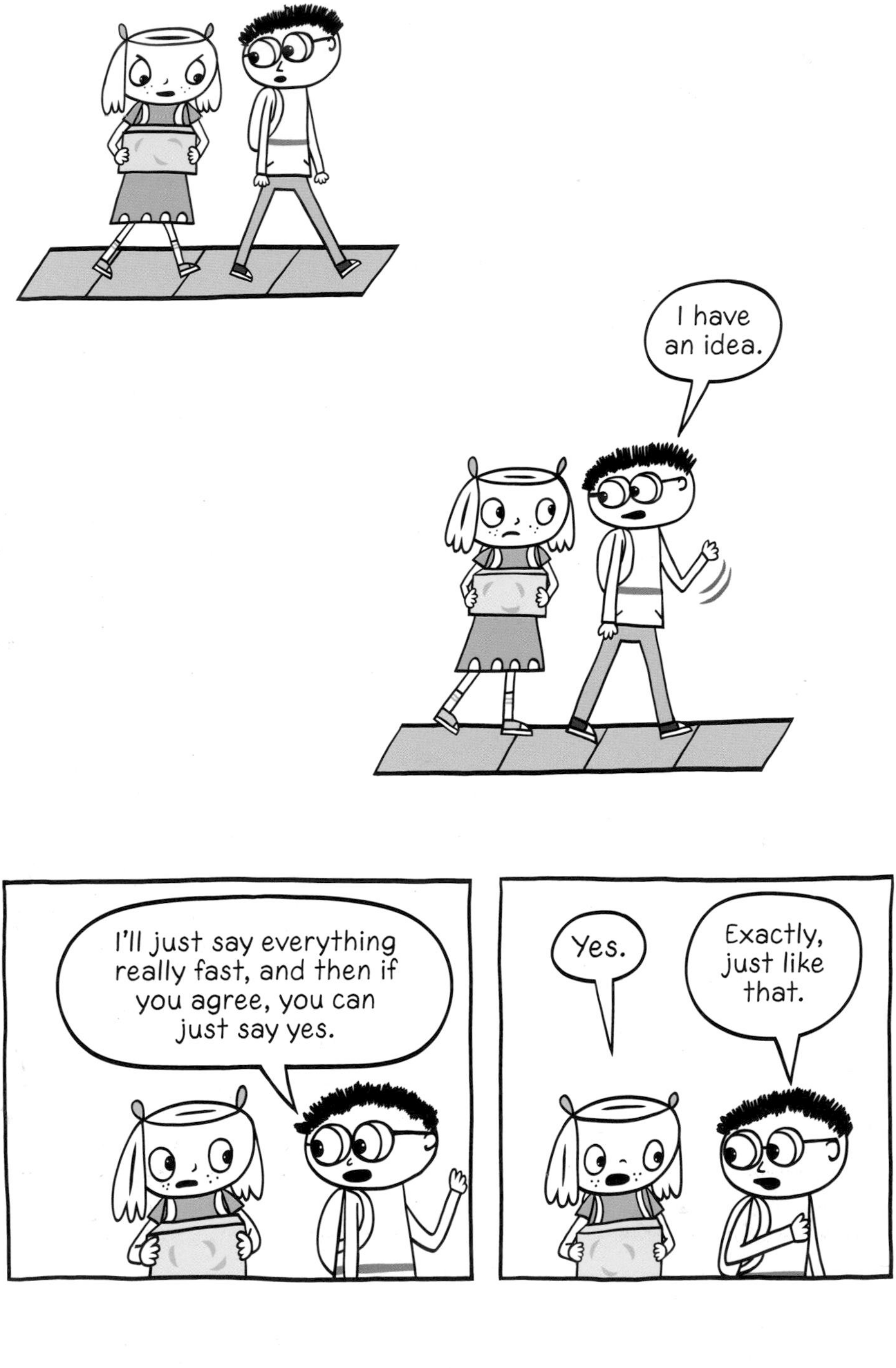
I have an idea.
I'll just say everything really fast, and then if you agree, you can just say yes.
Yes.
Exactly, just like that.

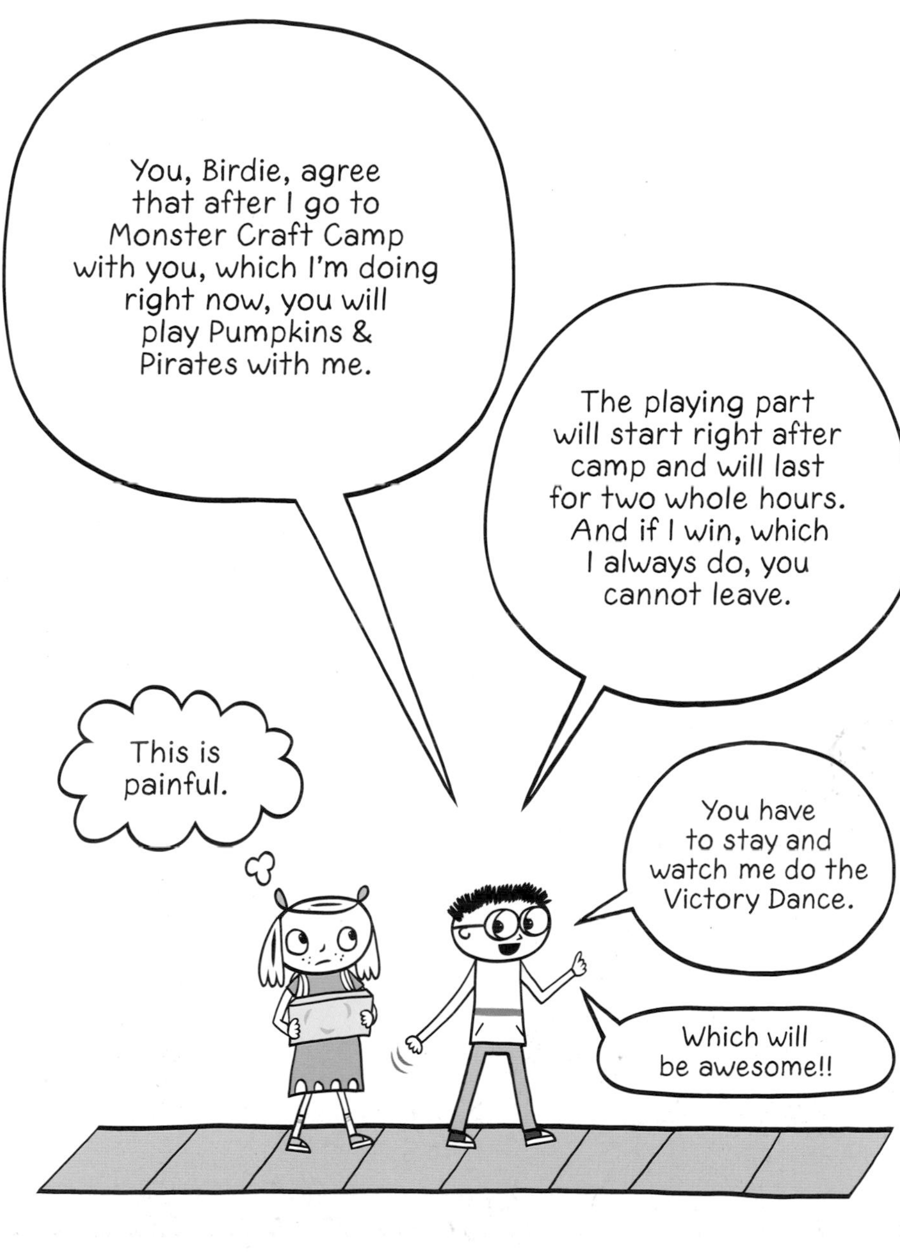
You, Birdie, agree that after I go to Monster Craft Camp with you, which I'm doing right now, you will play Pumpkins & Pirates with me.
The playing part will start right after camp and will last for two whole hours. And if I win, which I always do, you cannot leave.
This is painful.
You have to stay and watch me do the Victory Dance.
Which will be awesome!!

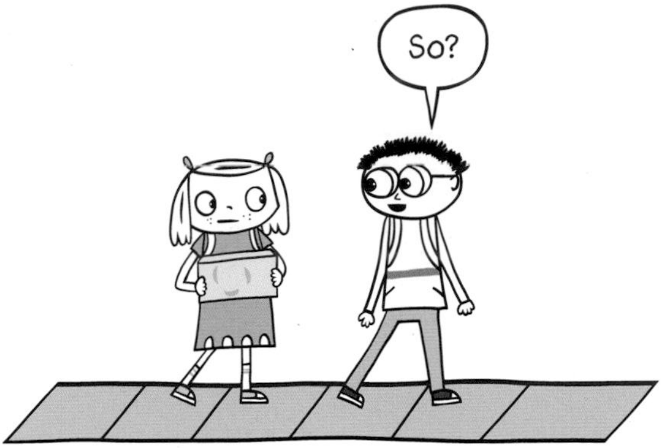
So?

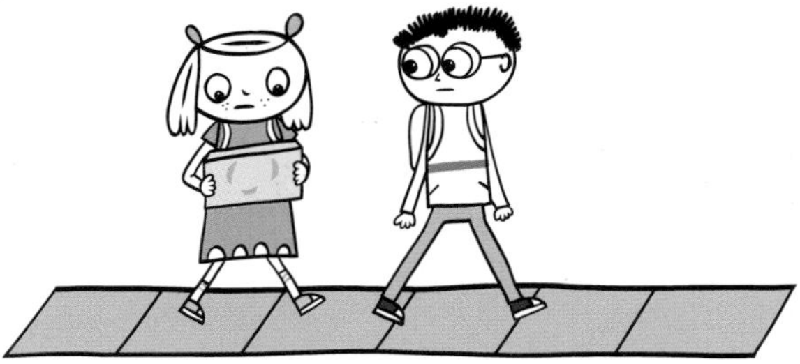

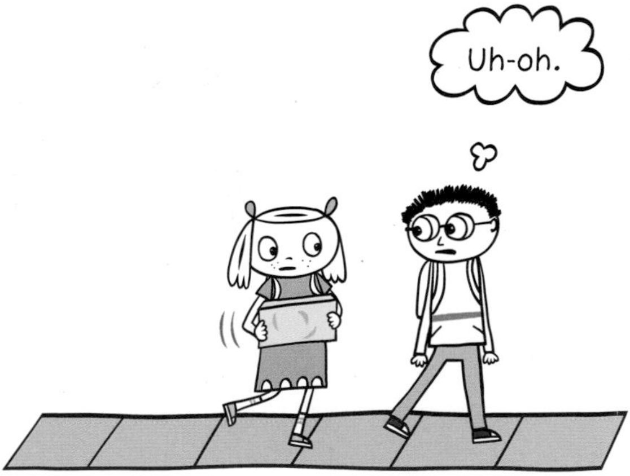
Uh-oh.

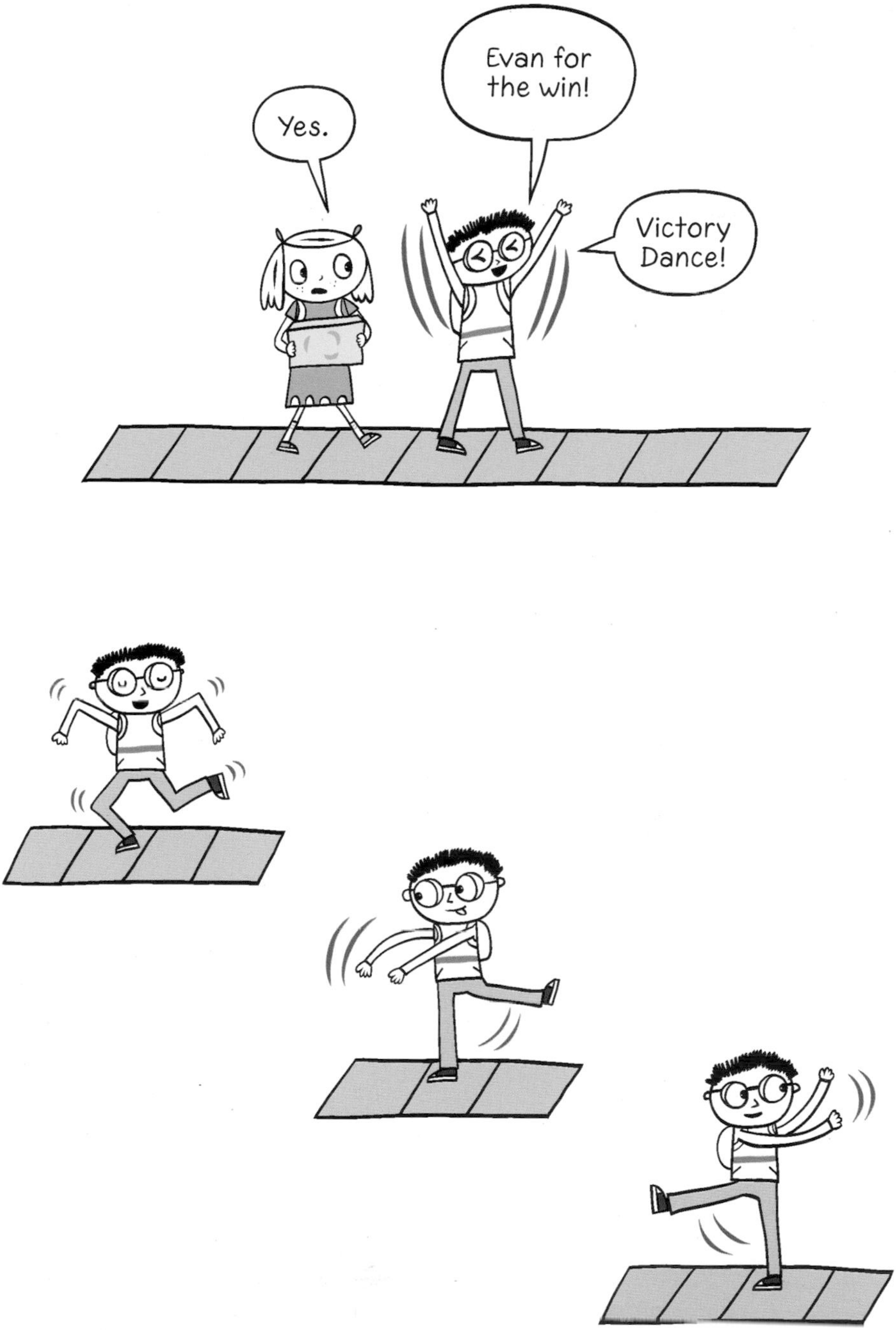
Yes.
Evan for the win!
Victory Dance!

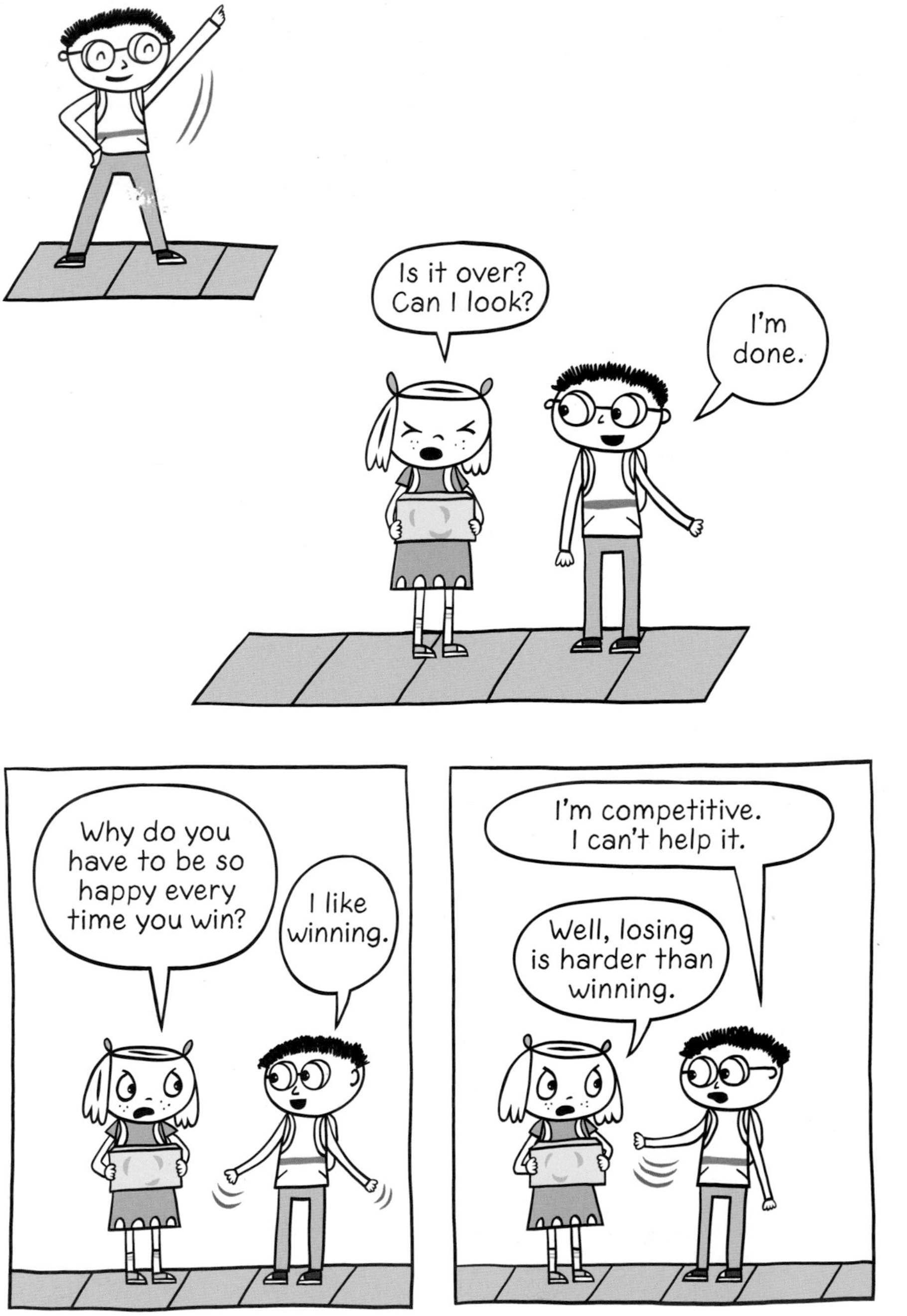
Is it over? Can I look?
I'm done.
Why do you have to be so happy every time you win?
I like winning.
I'm competitive. I can't help it.
Well, losing is harder than winning.

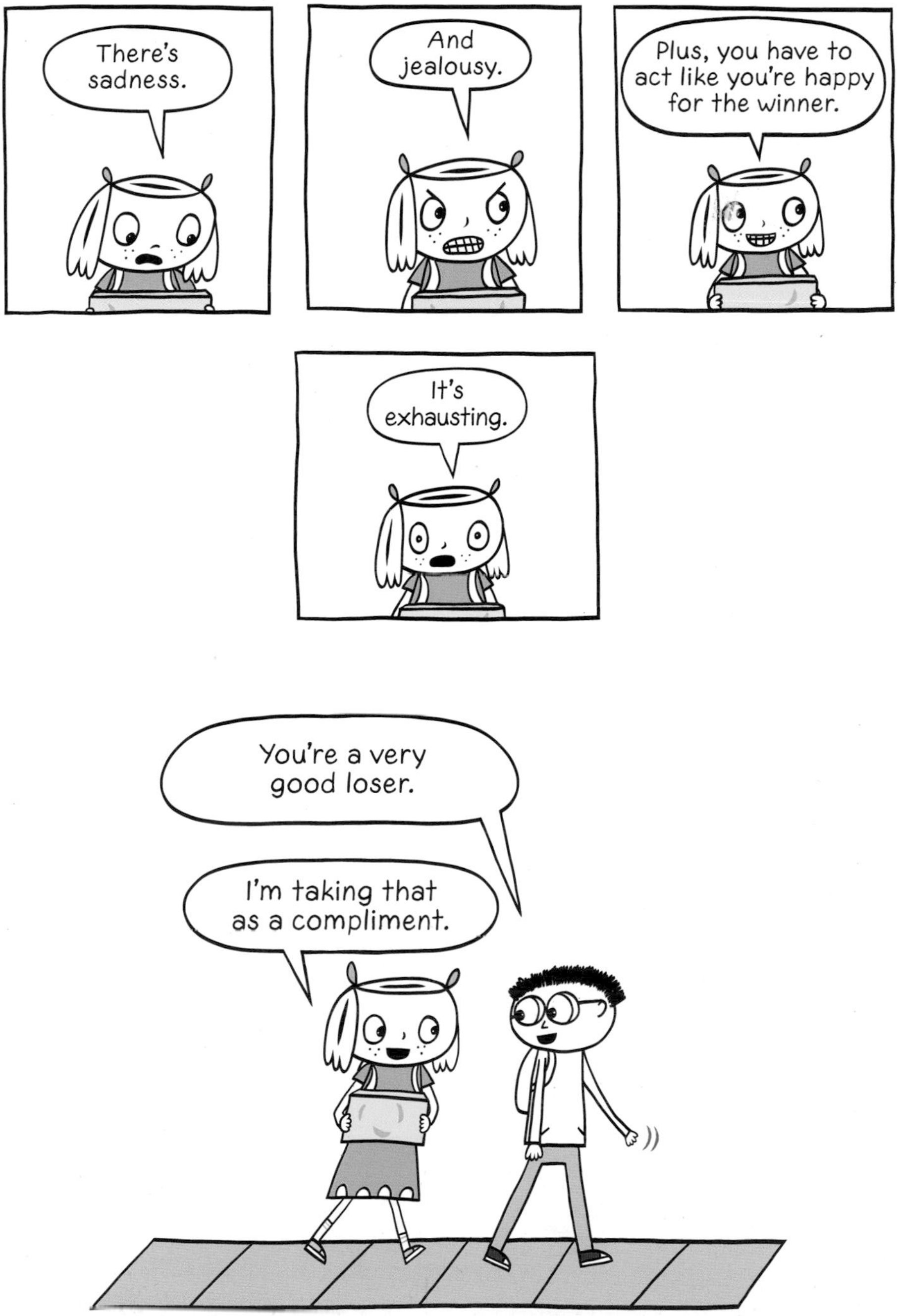
There's sadness.
And jealousy.
Plus, you have to act like you're happy for the winner.
It's exhausting.
You're a very good loser.
I'm taking that as a compliment.

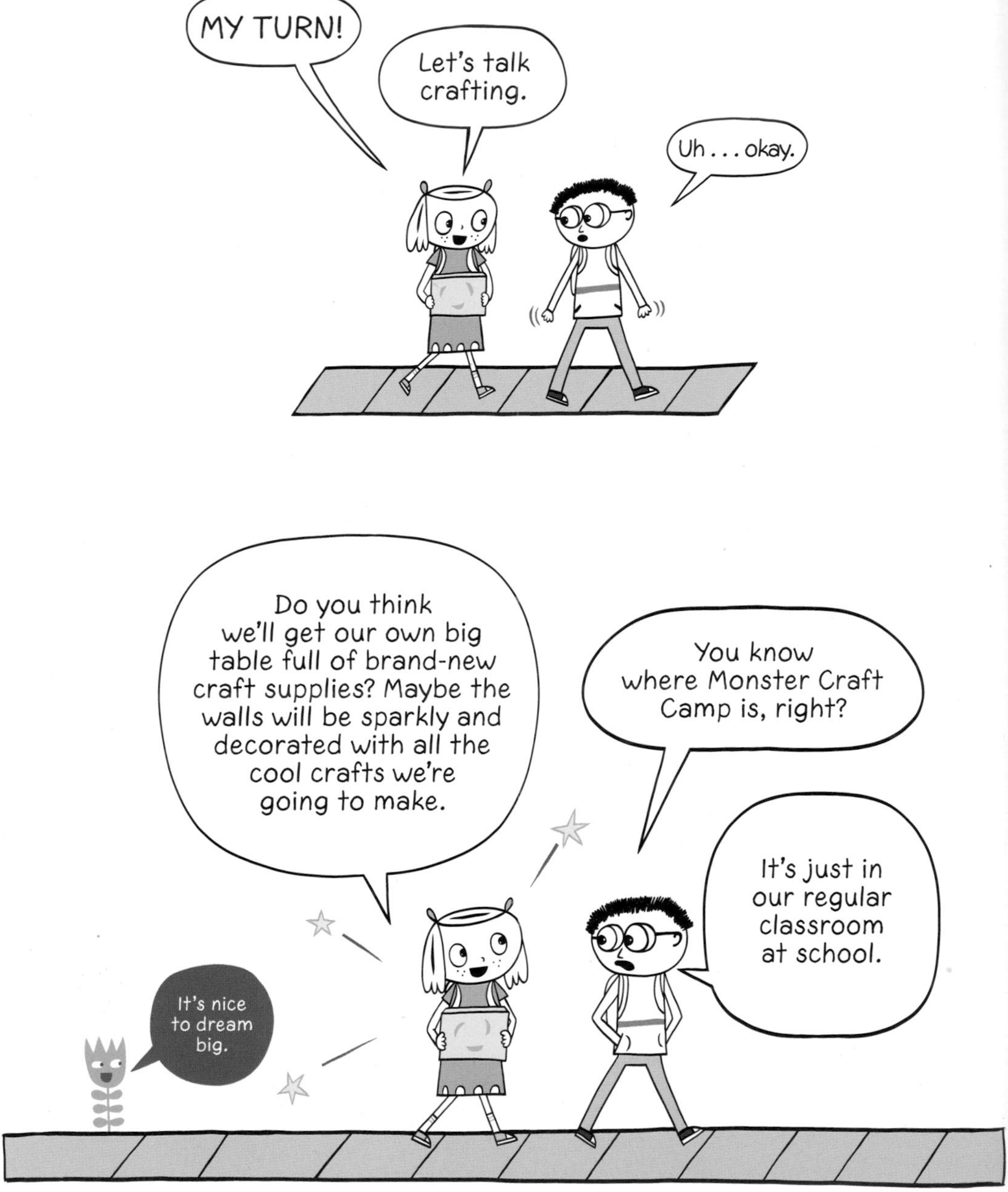
MY TURN!
Let's talk crafting.
Uh . . . okay.
Do you think we'll get our own big table full of brand-new craft supplies? Maybe the walls will be sparkly and decorated with all the cool crafts we're going to make.
You know where Monster Craft Camp is, right?
It's just in our regular classroom at school.
It's nice to dream big.

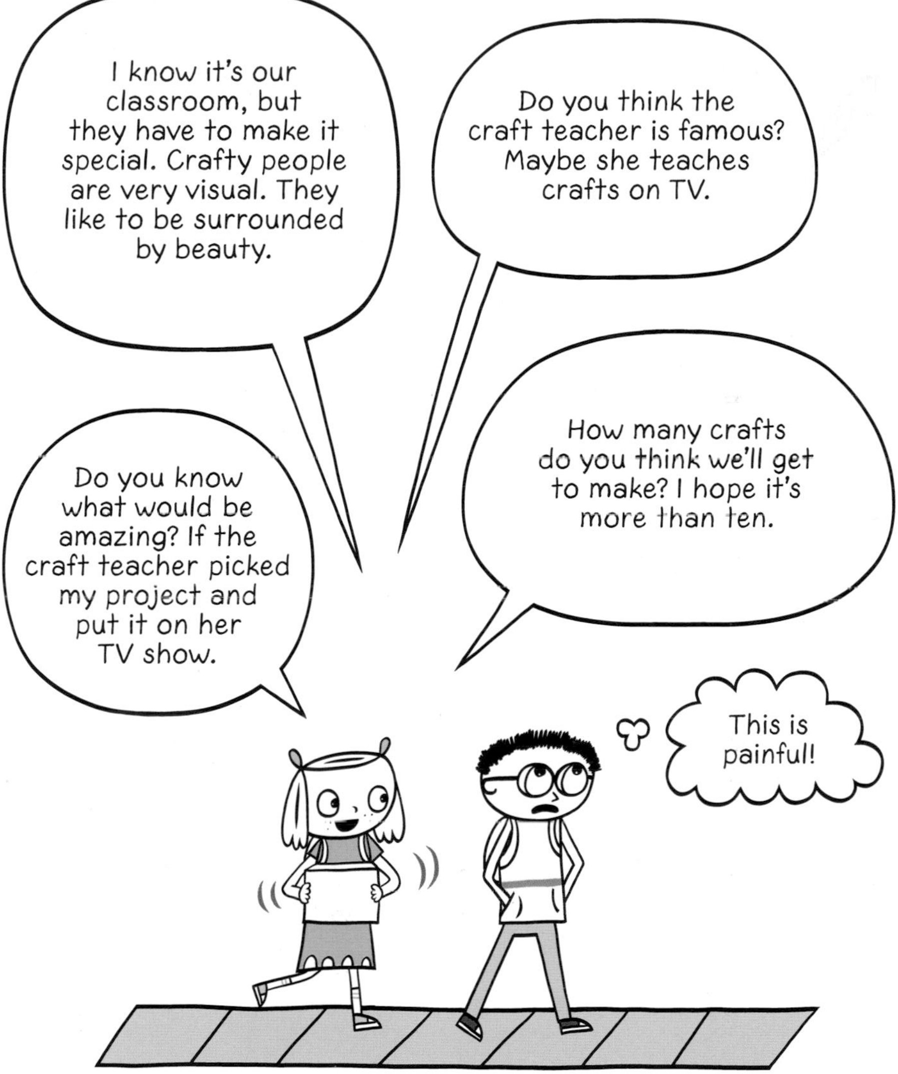
I know it's our classroom, but they have to make it special. Crafty people are very visual. They like to be surrounded by beauty.
Do you think the craft teacher is famous? Maybe she teaches crafts on TV.
Do you know what would be amazing? If the craft teacher picked my project and put it on her TV show.
How many crafts do you think we'll get to make? I hope it's more than ten.
This is painful!

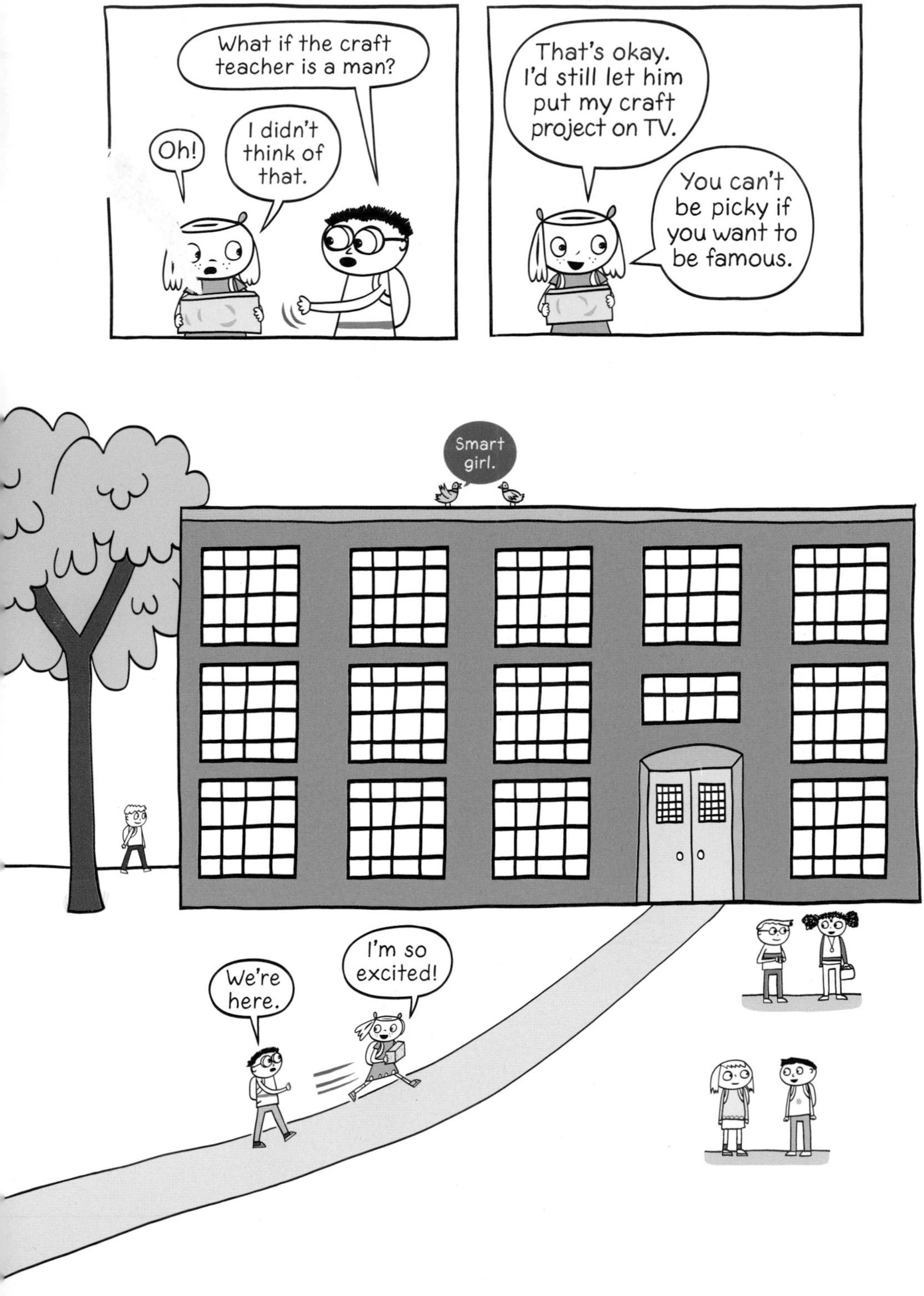
What if the craft teacher is a man?
Oh!
I didn't think of that.
That's okay. I'd still let him put my craft project on TV.
You can't be picky if you want to be famous.
Smart girl.
We're here.
I'm so excited!

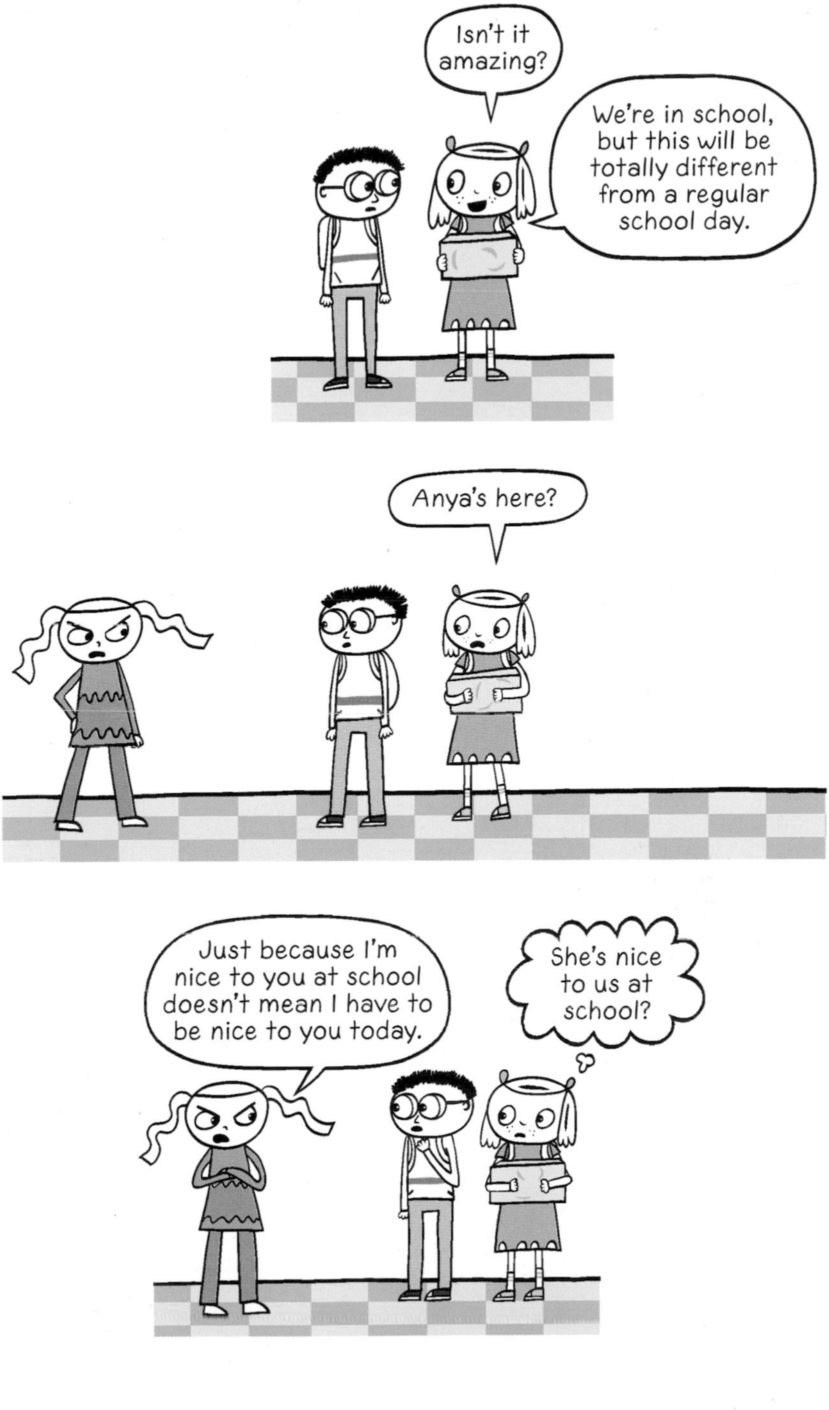
Isn't it amazing?
We're in school, but this will be totally different from a regular school day.
Anya's here?
Just because I'm nice to you at school doesn't mean I have to be nice to you today.
She's nice to us at school?

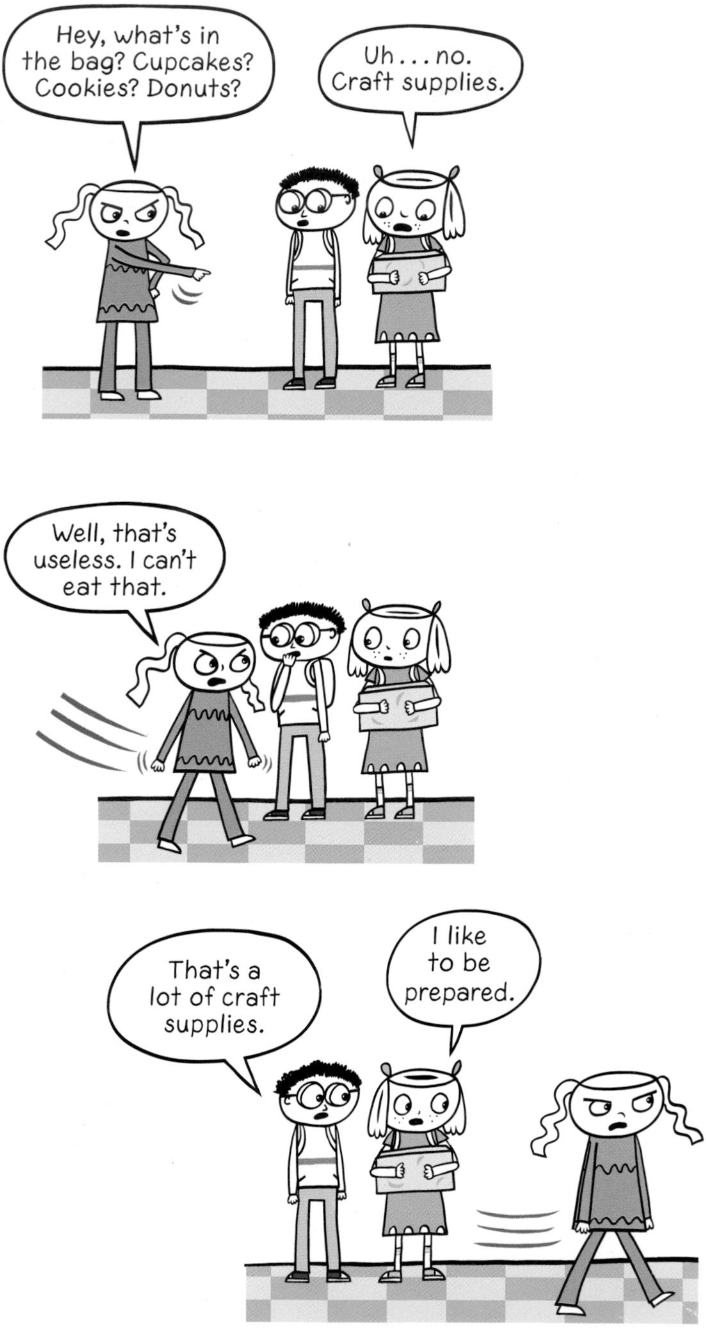
Hey, what's in the bag? Cupcakes? Cookies? Donuts?
Uh . . . no. Craft supplies.
Well, that's useless. I can't eat that.
That's a lot of craft supplies.
I like to be prepared.

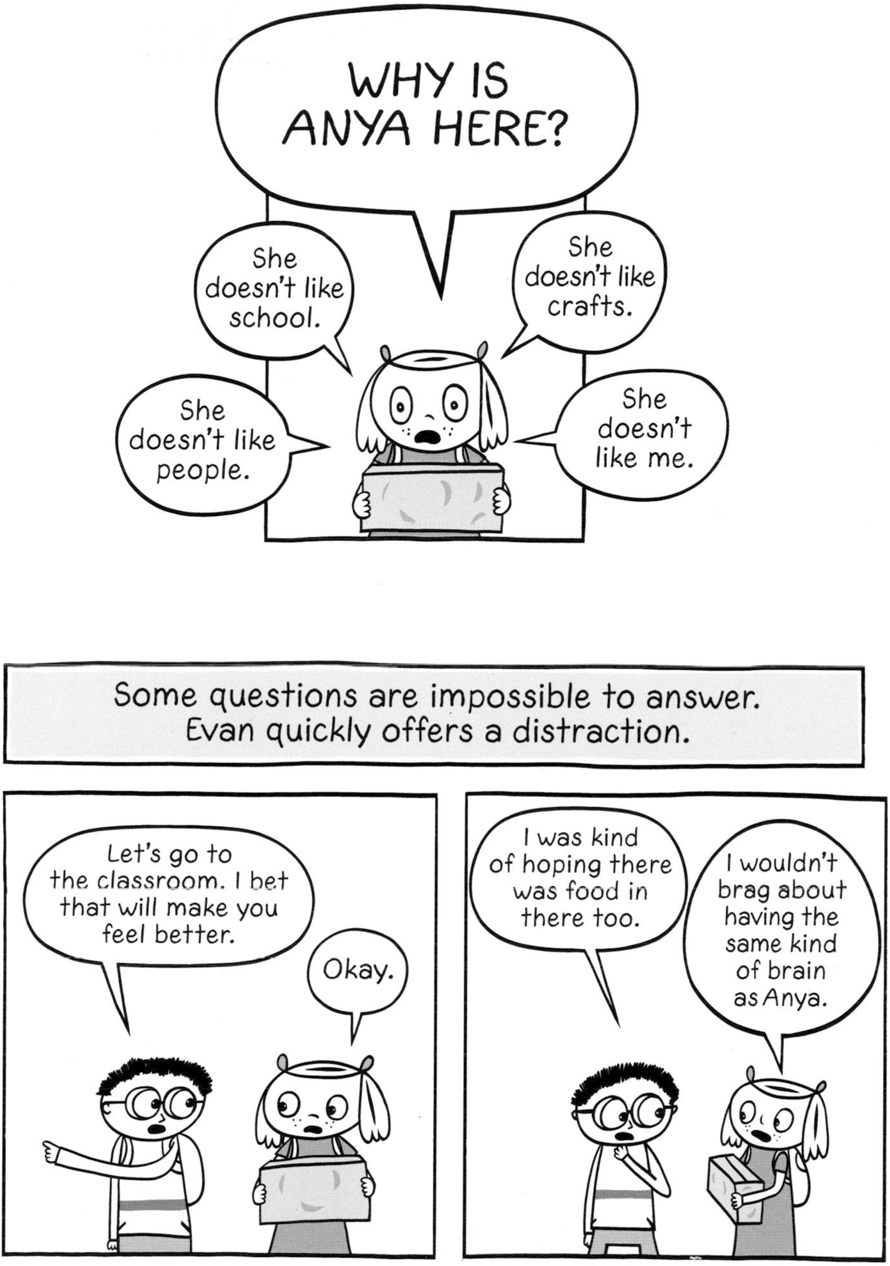
WHY IS ANYA HERE?
She doesn't like school.
She doesn't like crafts.
She doesn't like people.
She doesn't like me.
Some questions are impossible to answer. Evan quickly offers a distraction.
Let's go to the classroom. I bet that will make you feel better.
Okay.
I was kind of hoping there was food in there too.
I wouldn't brag about having the same kind of brain as Anya.

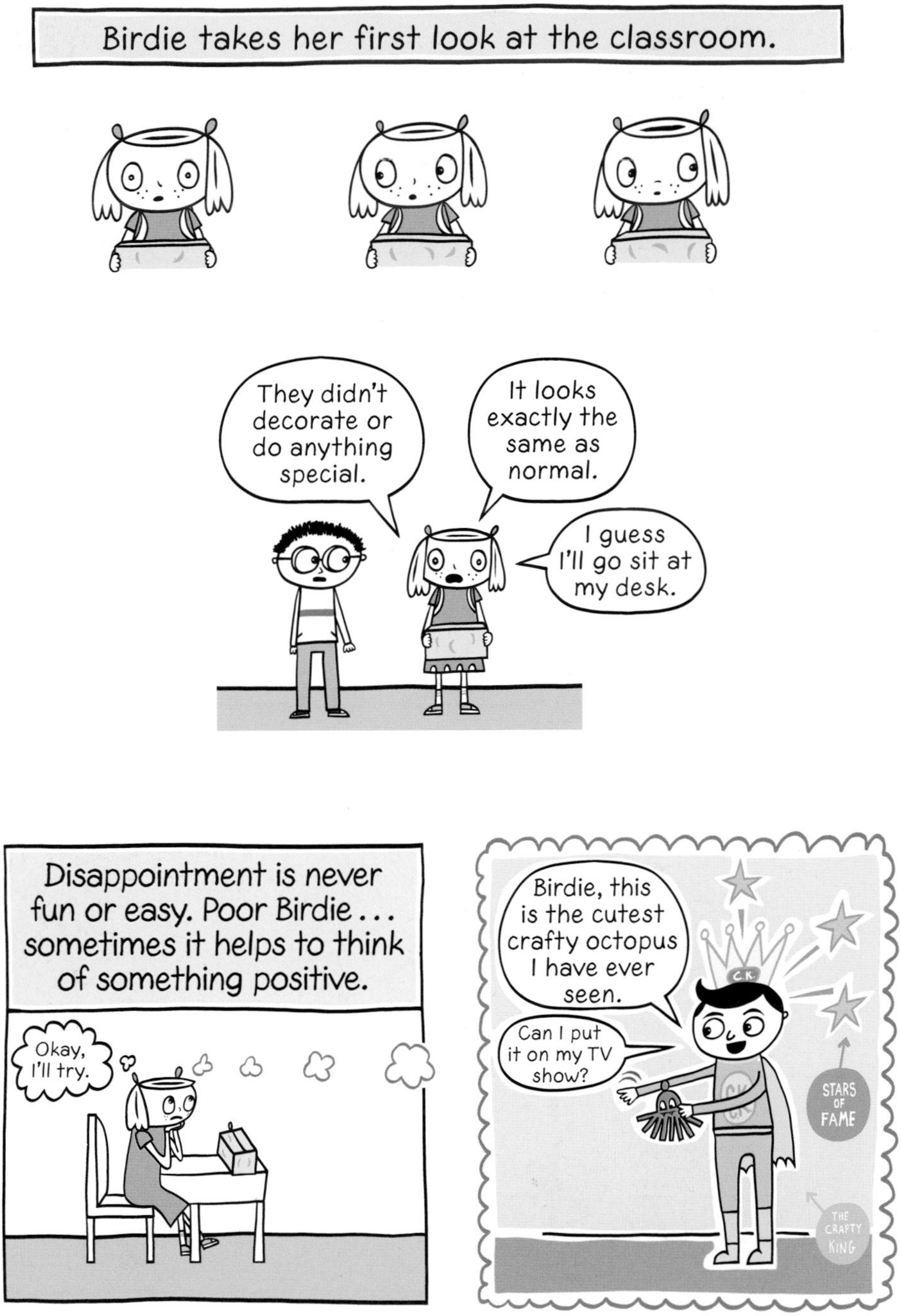
Birdie takes her first look at the classroom.
They didn't decorate or do anything special.
It looks exactly the same as normal.
I guess I'll go sit at my desk.
Disappointment is never fun or easy. Poor Birdie . . . sometimes it helps to think of something positive.
Okay, I'll try.
Birdie, this is the cutest crafty octopus I have ever seen.
Can I put it on my TV show?
C.K.
STARS OF FAME
THE CRAFTY KING

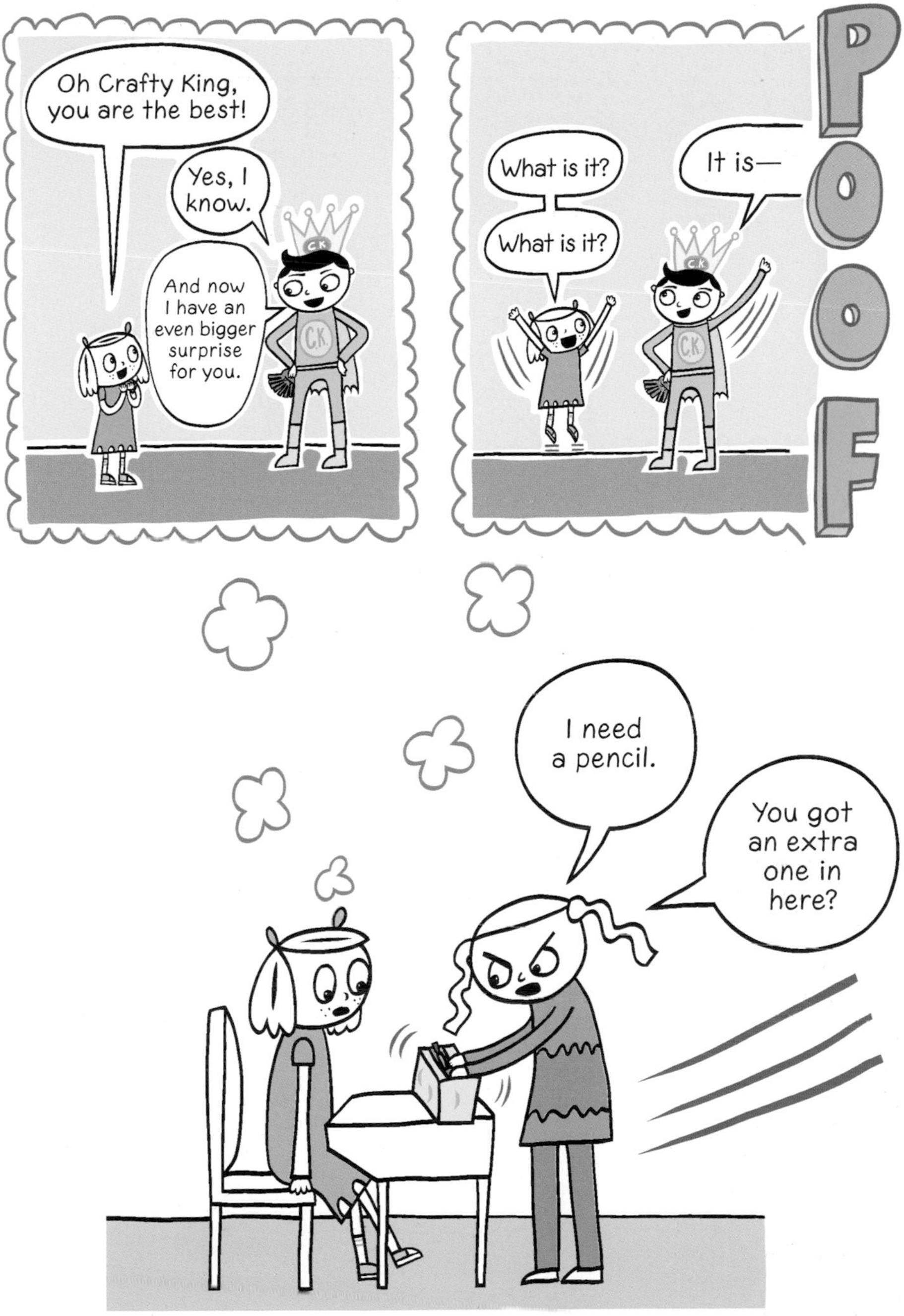
Oh Crafty King, you are the best!
Yes, I know.
And now I have an even bigger surprise for you.
What is it?
What is it?
It is—
POOF
I need a pencil.
You got an extra one in here?

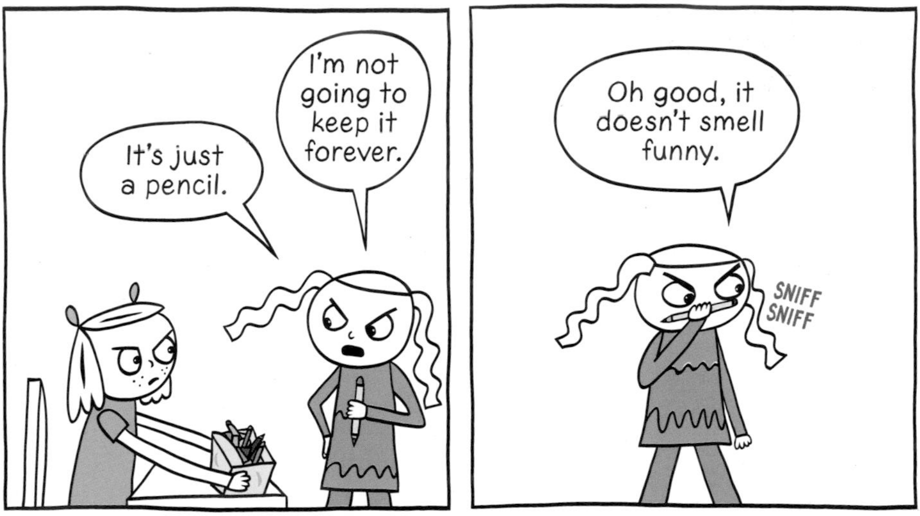
It's just a pencil.
I'm not going to keep it forever.
Oh good, it doesn't smell funny.
SNIFF SNIFF

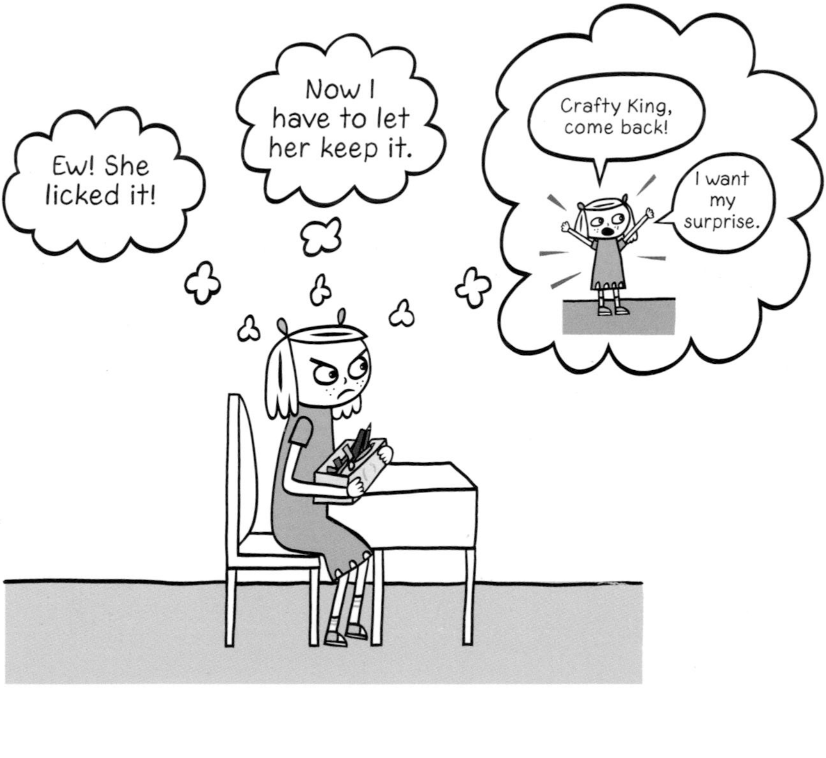
Ew! She licked it!
Now I have to let her keep it.
Crafty King, come back!
I want my surprise.

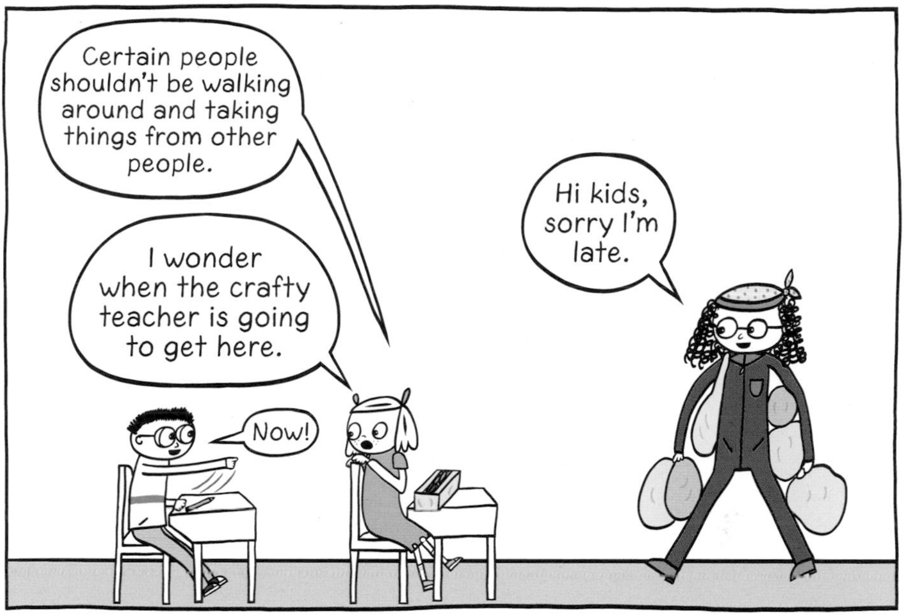
Certain people shouldn't be walking around and taking things from other people.
I wonder when the crafty teacher is going to get here.
Now!
Hi kids, sorry I'm late.

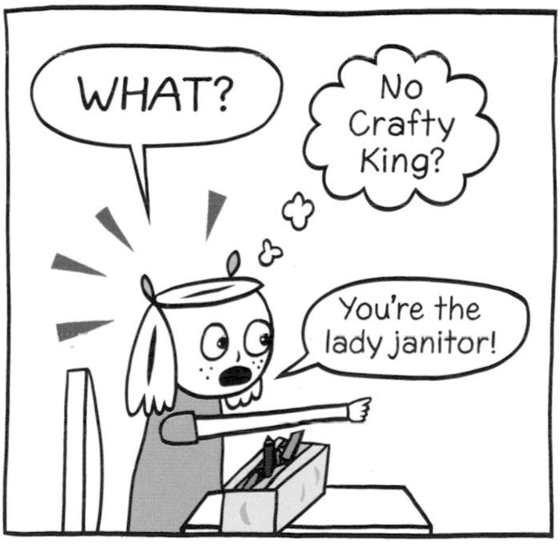
WHAT?
No Crafty King?
You're the lady janitor!

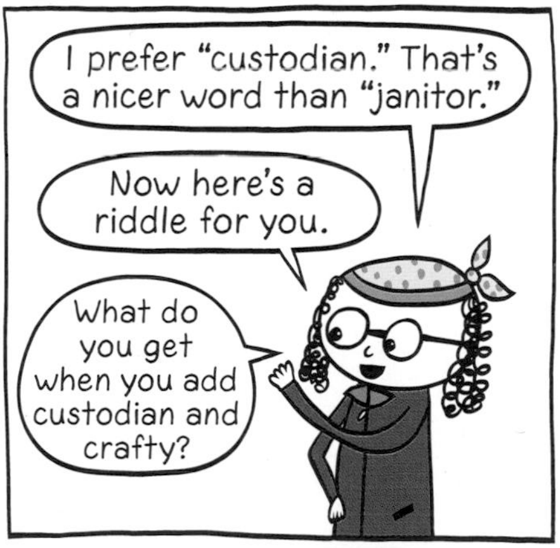
I prefer "custodian." That's a nicer word than "janitor."
Now here's a riddle for you.
What do you get when you add custodian and crafty?

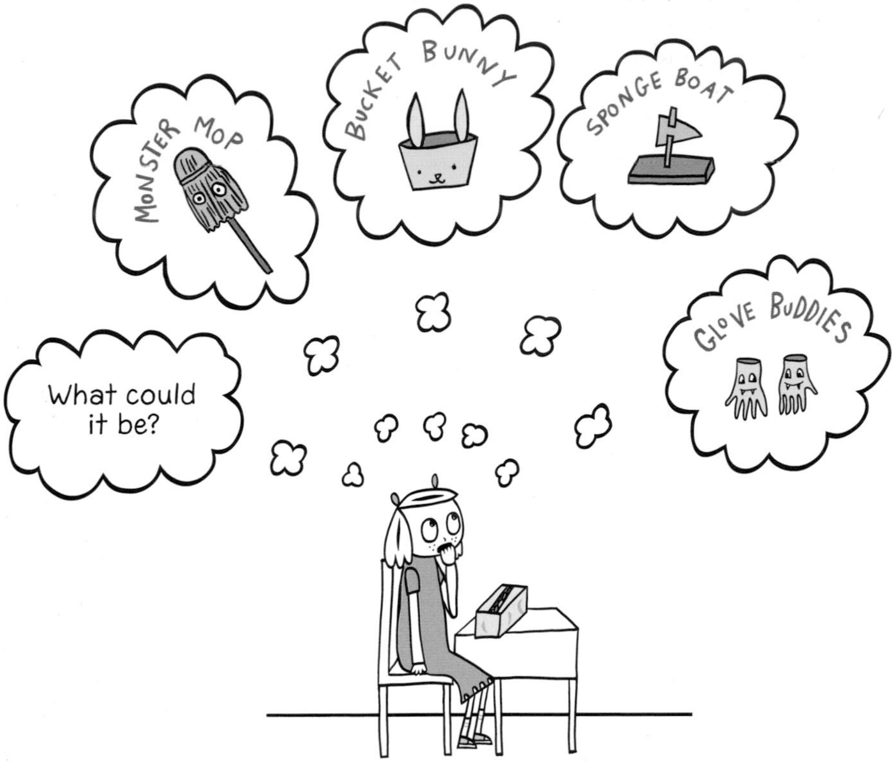
MONSTER MOP
BUCKET BUNNY
SPONGE BOAT
What could it be?
GLOVE BUDDIES

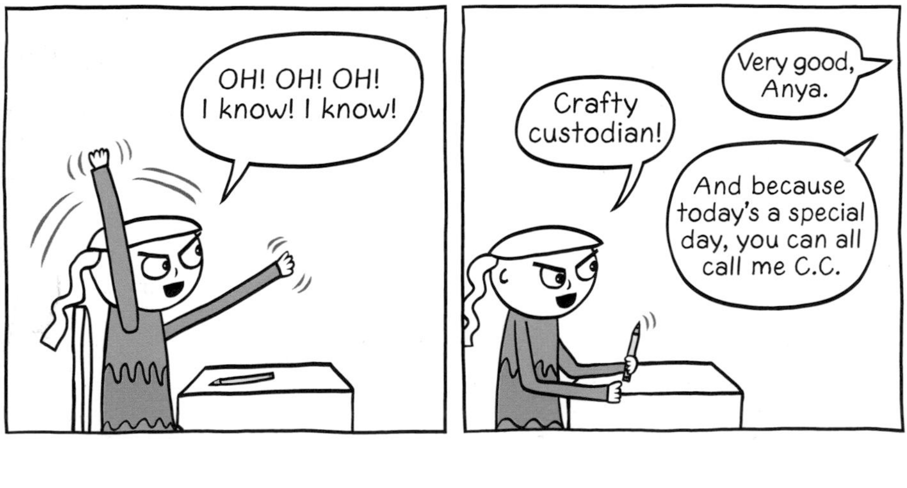
OH! OH! OH! I know! I know!
Crafty custodian!
Very good, Anya.
And because today's a special day, you can all call me C.C.

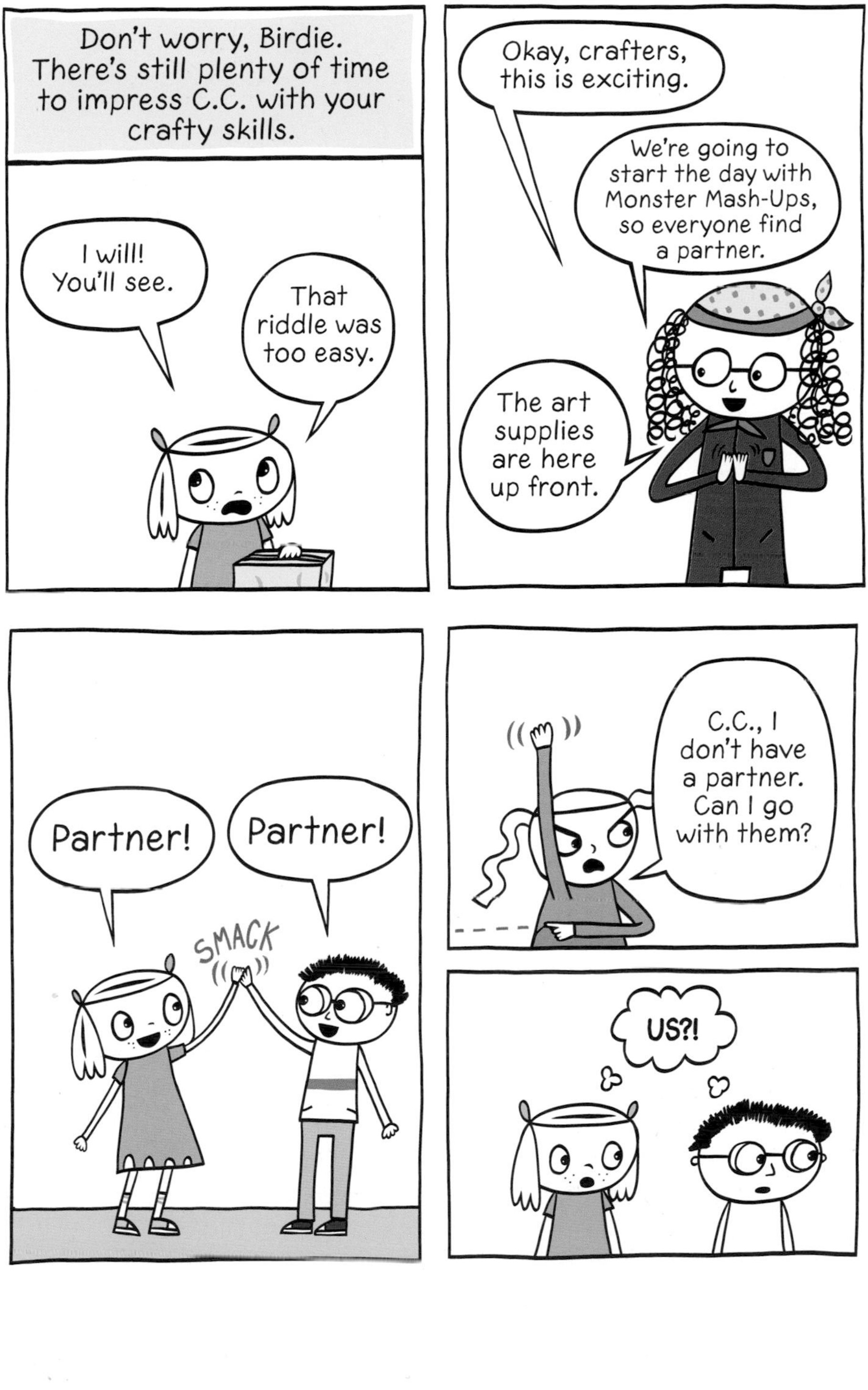

Don't worry, Birdie. There's still plenty of time to impress C.C. with your crafty skills.
I will! You'll see.
That riddle was too easy.
Okay, crafters, this is exciting.
We're going to start the day with Monster Mash-Ups, so everyone find a partner.
The art supplies are here up front.
Partner!
Partner!
SMACK
C.C., I don't have a partner. Can I go with them?
US?!

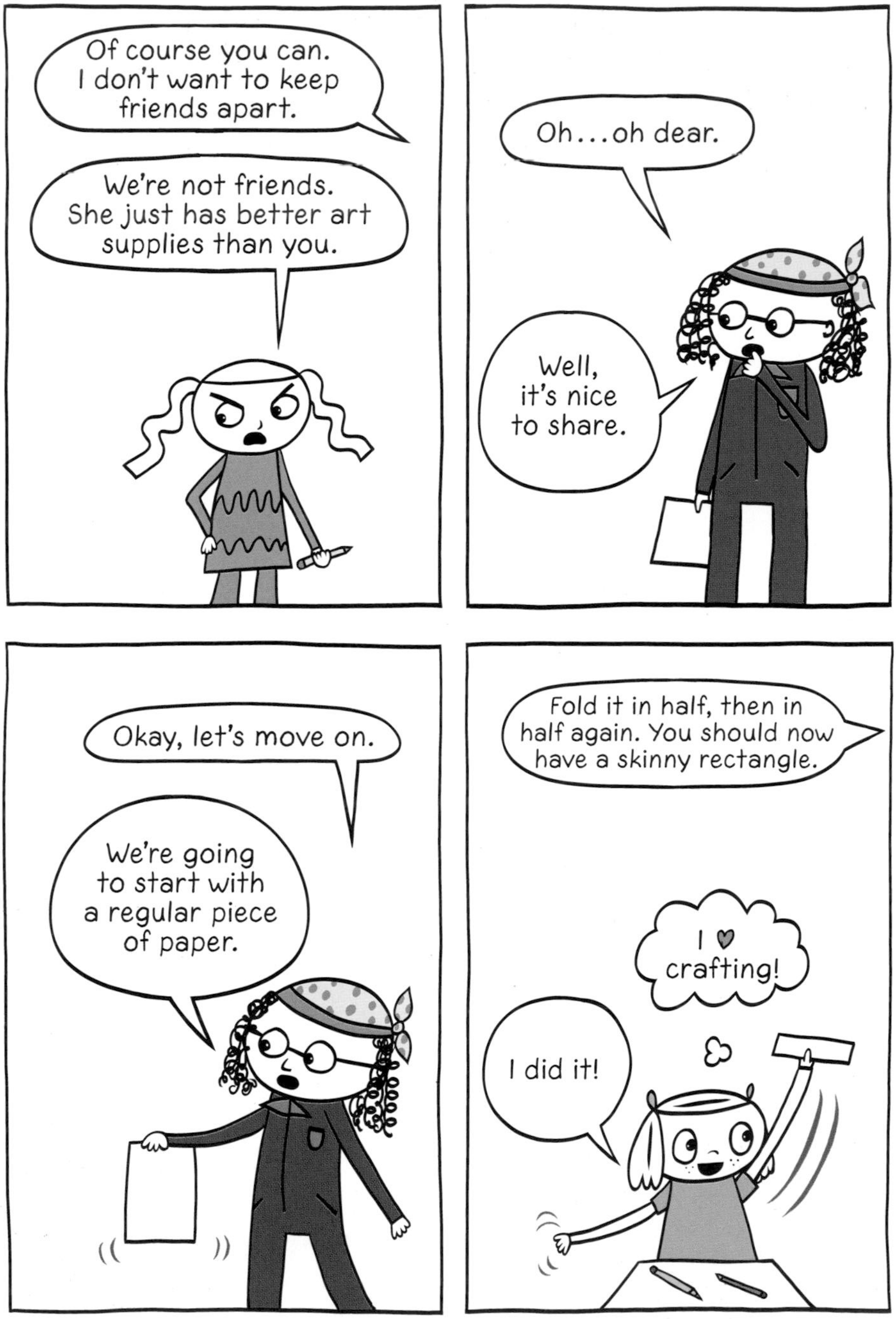
Of course you can. I don't want to keep friends apart.
We're not friends. She just has better art supplies than you.
Oh...oh dear.
Well, it's nice to share.
Okay, let's move on.
We're going to start with a regular piece of paper.
Fold it in half, then in half again. You should now have a skinny rectangle.
I ♡ crafting!
I did it!

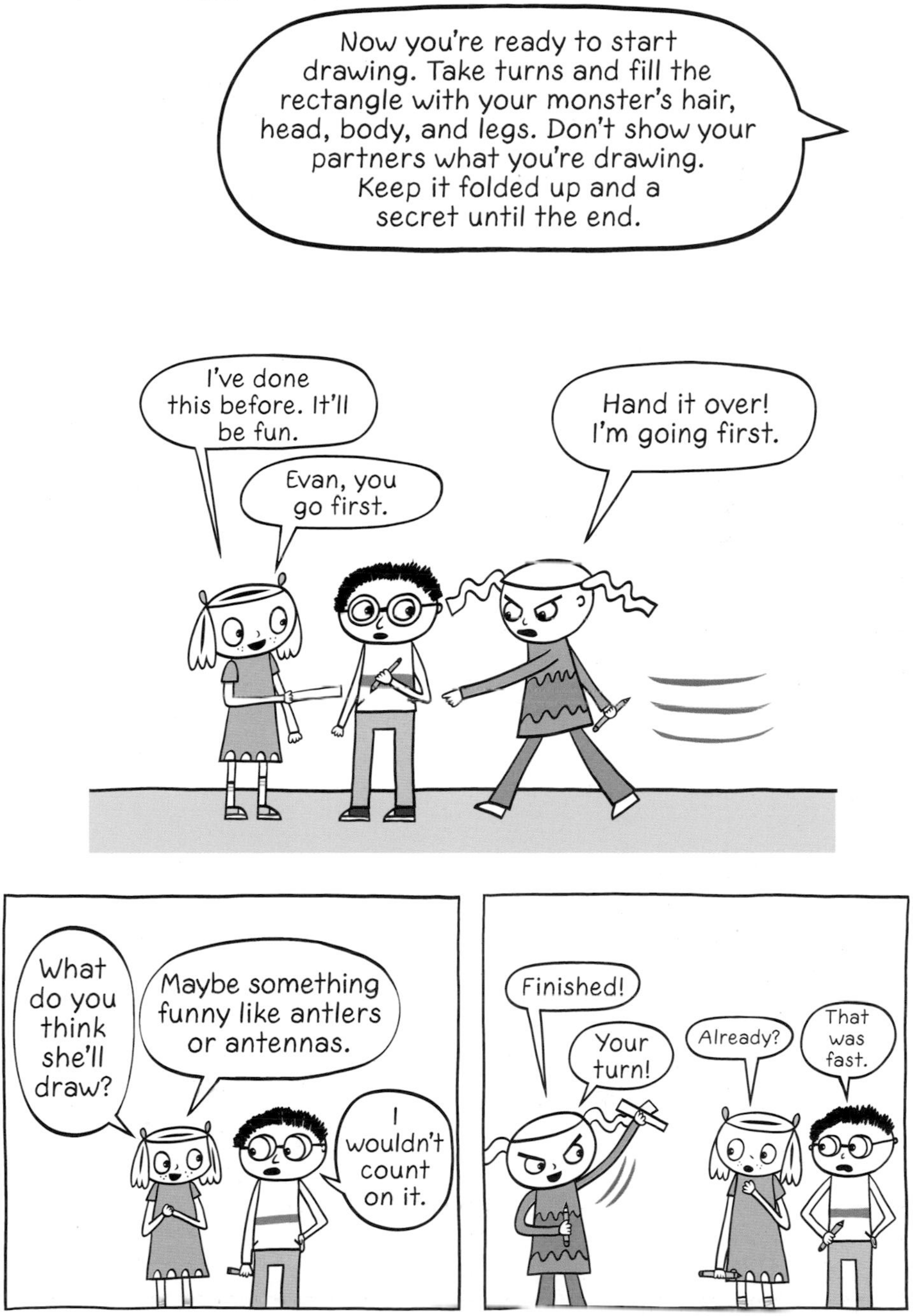
Now you're ready to start drawing. Take turns and fill the rectangle with your monster's hair, head, body, and legs. Don't show your partners what you're drawing. Keep it folded up and a secret until the end.
I've done this before. It'll be fun.
Evan, you go first.
Hand it over! I'm going first.
What do you think she'll draw?
Maybe something funny like antlers or antennas.
I wouldn't count on it.
Finished!
Your turn!
Already?
That was fast.

My turn!
My turn!
My turn!
Birdie thinks hard.
This is a big decision.
Hmm, what kind of head should I draw?

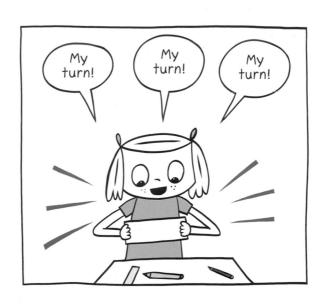

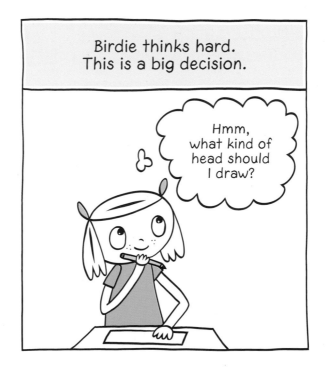

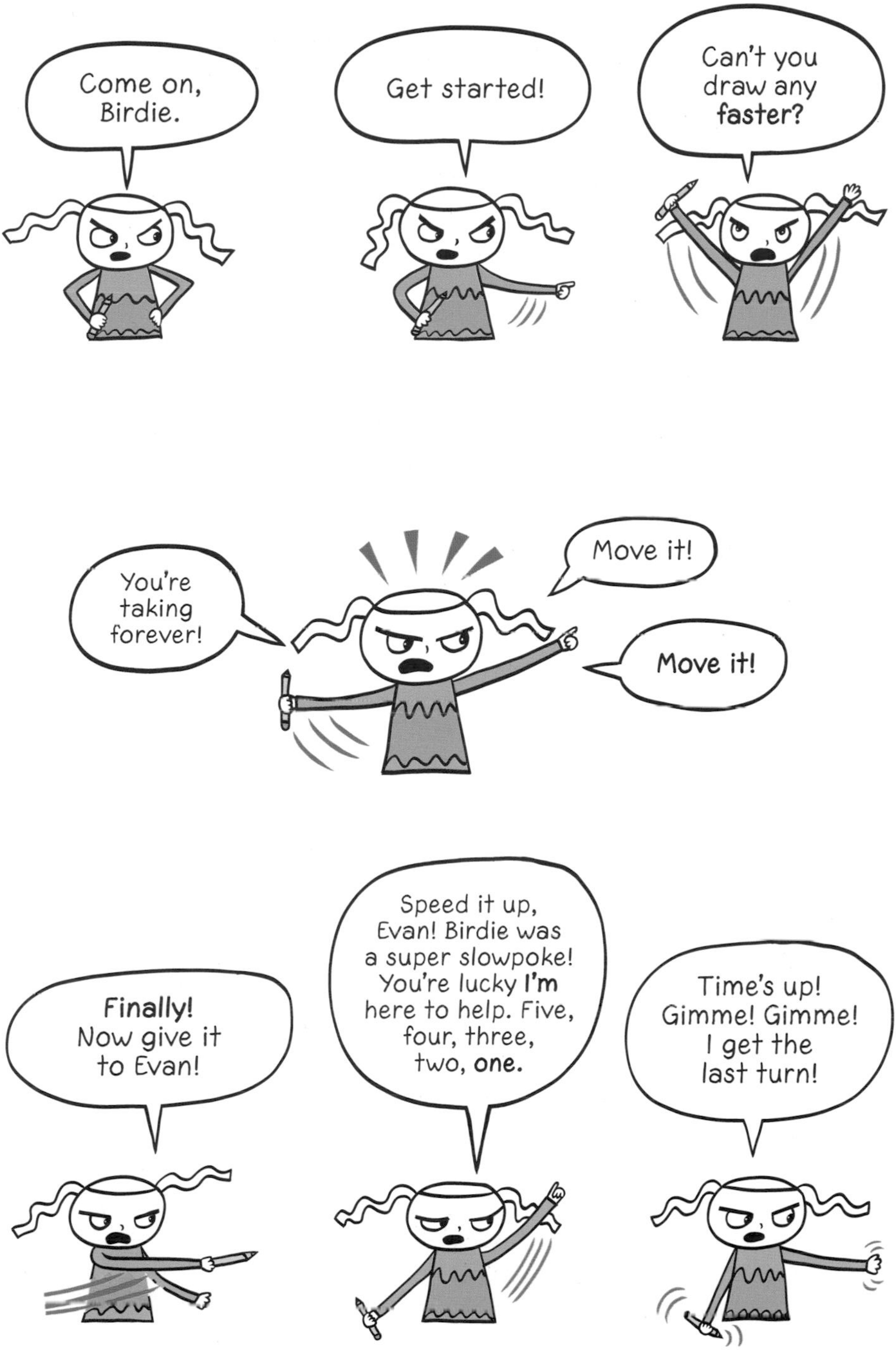

Come on, Birdie.
Get started!
Can't you draw any **faster?**
You're taking forever!
Move it!
Move it!
Finally! Now give it to Evan!
Speed it up, Evan! Birdie was a super slowpoke! You're lucky **I'm** here to help. Five, four, three, two, **one.**
Time's up! Gimme! Gimme! I get the last turn!

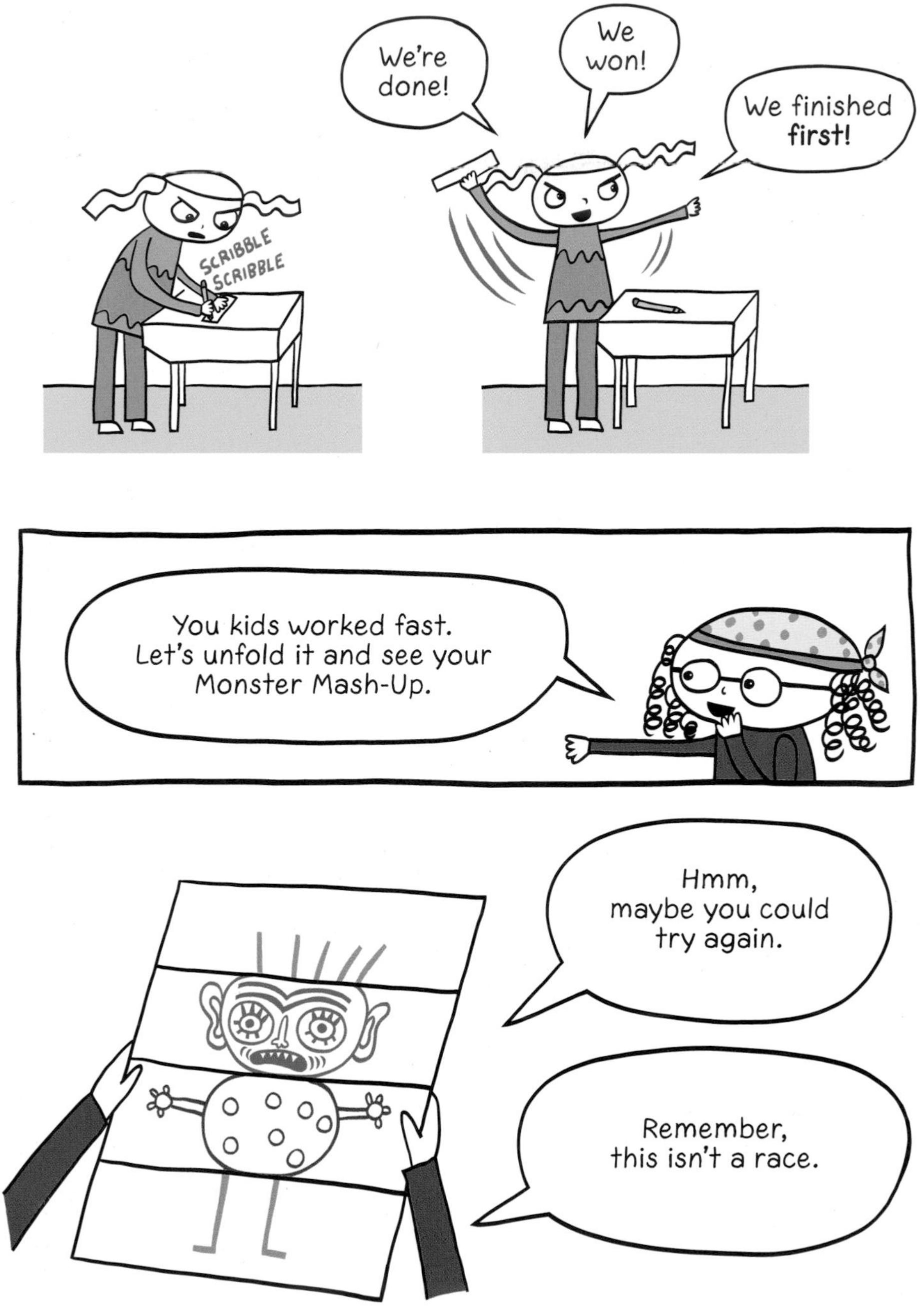
SCRIBBLE SCRIBBLE
We're done!
We won!
We finished **first!**
You kids worked fast. Let's unfold it and see your Monster Mash-Up.
Hmm, maybe you could try again.
Remember, this isn't a race.

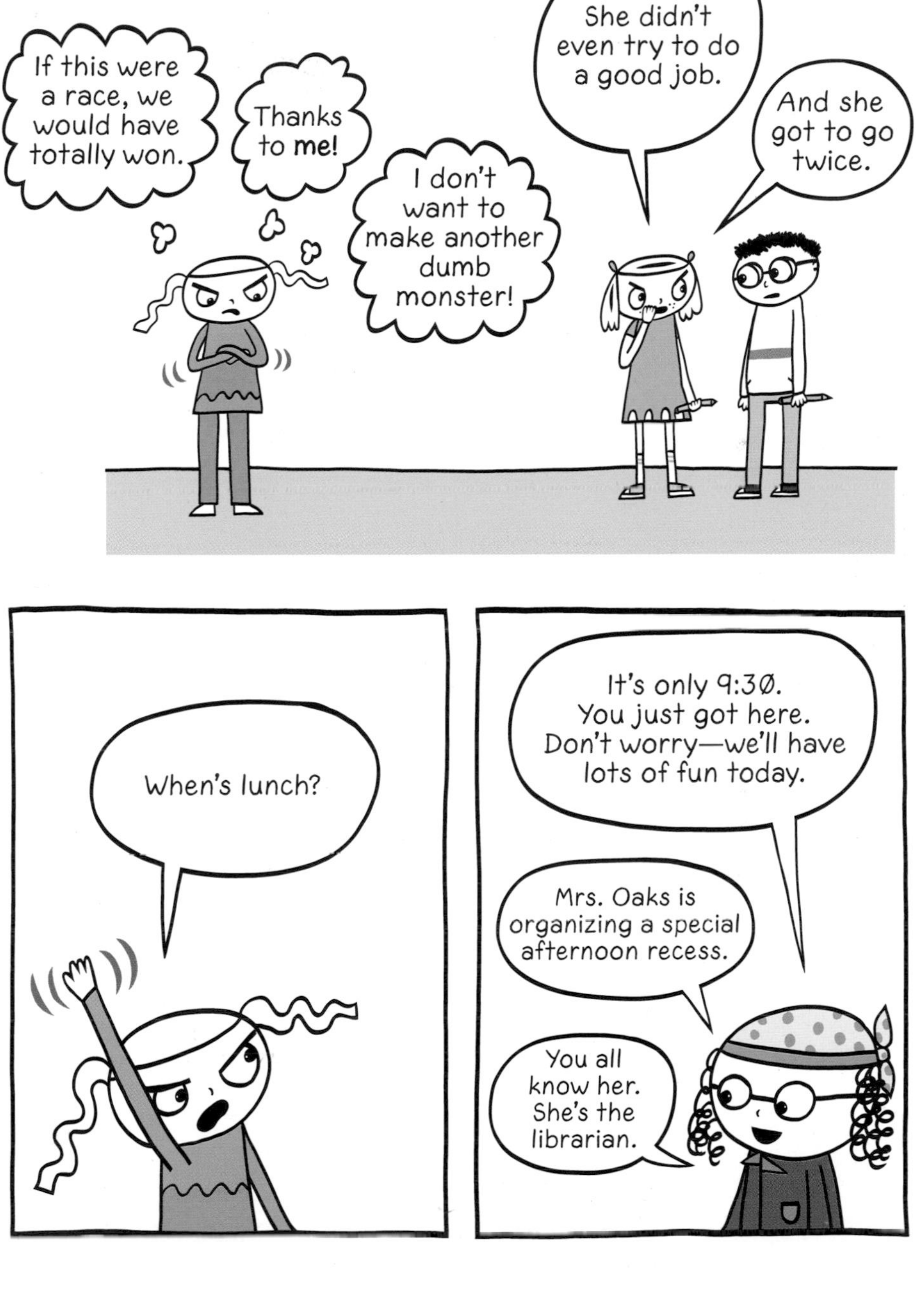
If this were a race, we would have totally won.
Thanks to **me!**
I don't want to make another dumb monster!
She didn't even try to do a good job.
And she got to go twice.
When's lunch?
It's only 9:3Ø. You just got here. Don't worry—we'll have lots of fun today.
Mrs. Oaks is organizing a special afternoon recess.
You all know her. She's the librarian.

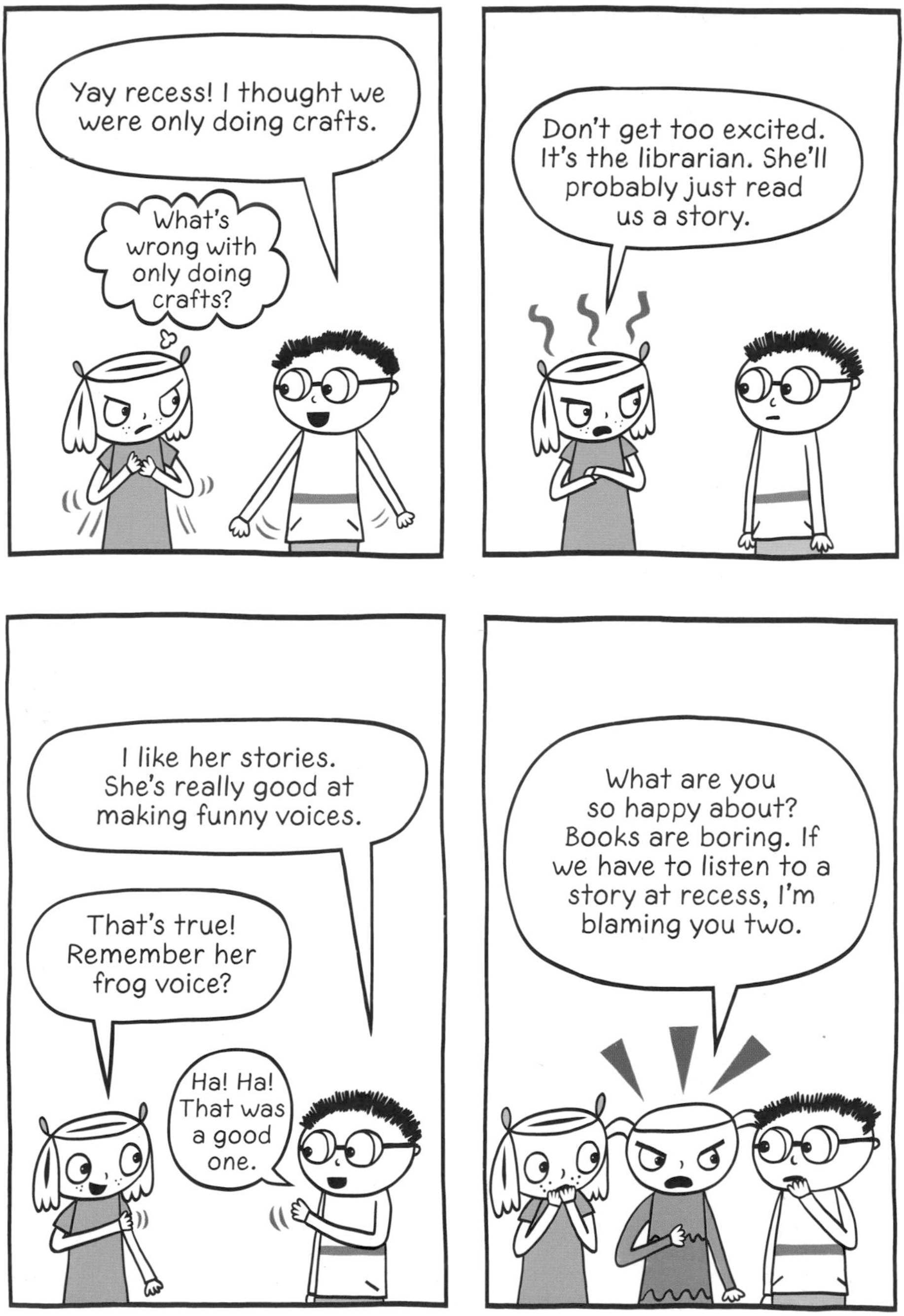
Yay recess! I thought we were only doing crafts.
What's wrong with only doing crafts?
Don't get too excited. It's the librarian. She'll probably just read us a story.
I like her stories. She's really good at making funny voices.
That's true! Remember her frog voice?
Ha! Ha! That was a good one.
What are you so happy about? Books are boring. If we have to listen to a story at recess, I'm blaming you two.

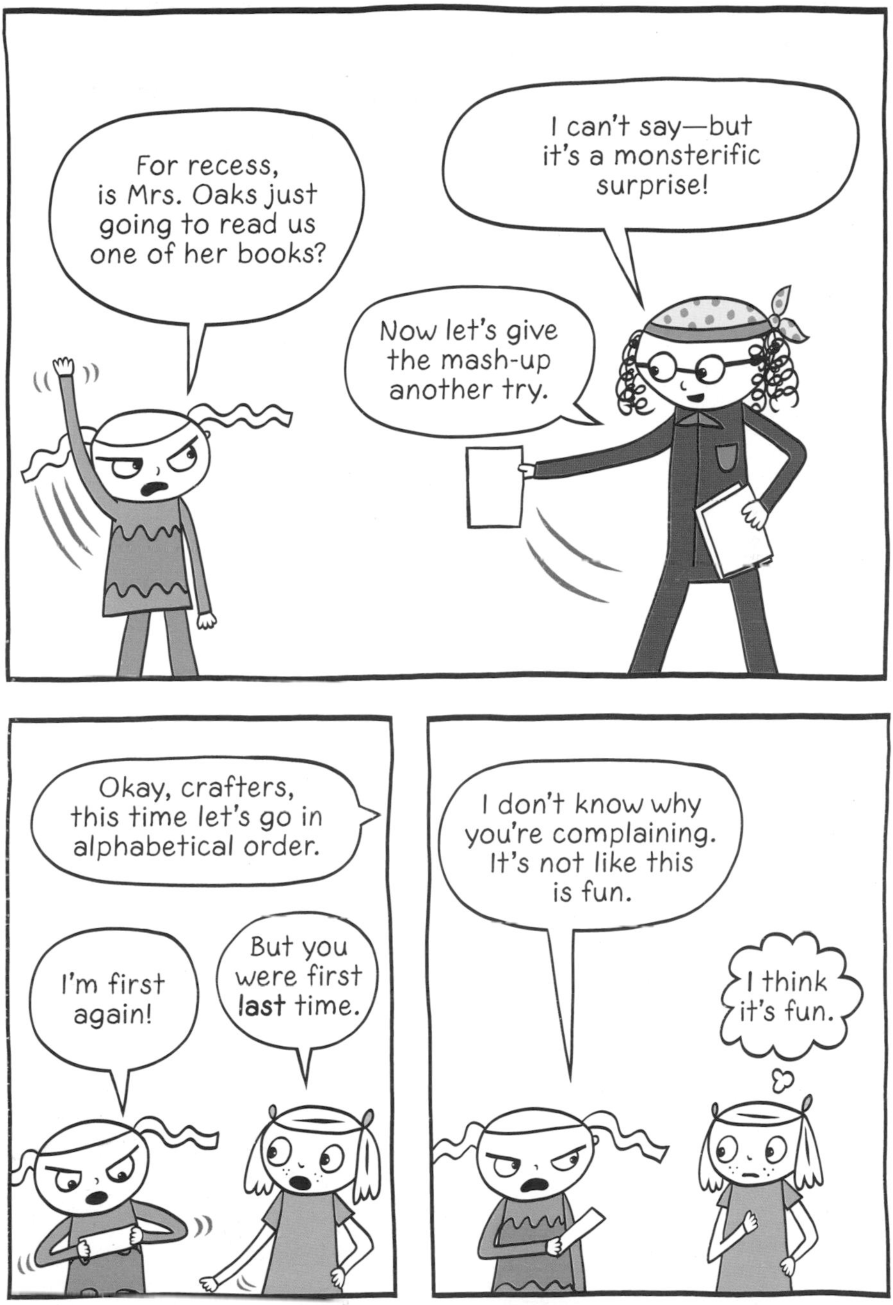
For recess, is Mrs. Oaks just going to read us one of her books?
I can't say—but it's a monsterific surprise!
Now let's give the mash-up another try.
Okay, crafters, this time let's go in alphabetical order.
I'm first again!
But you were first **last** time.
I don't know why you're complaining. It's not like this is fun.
I think it's fun.

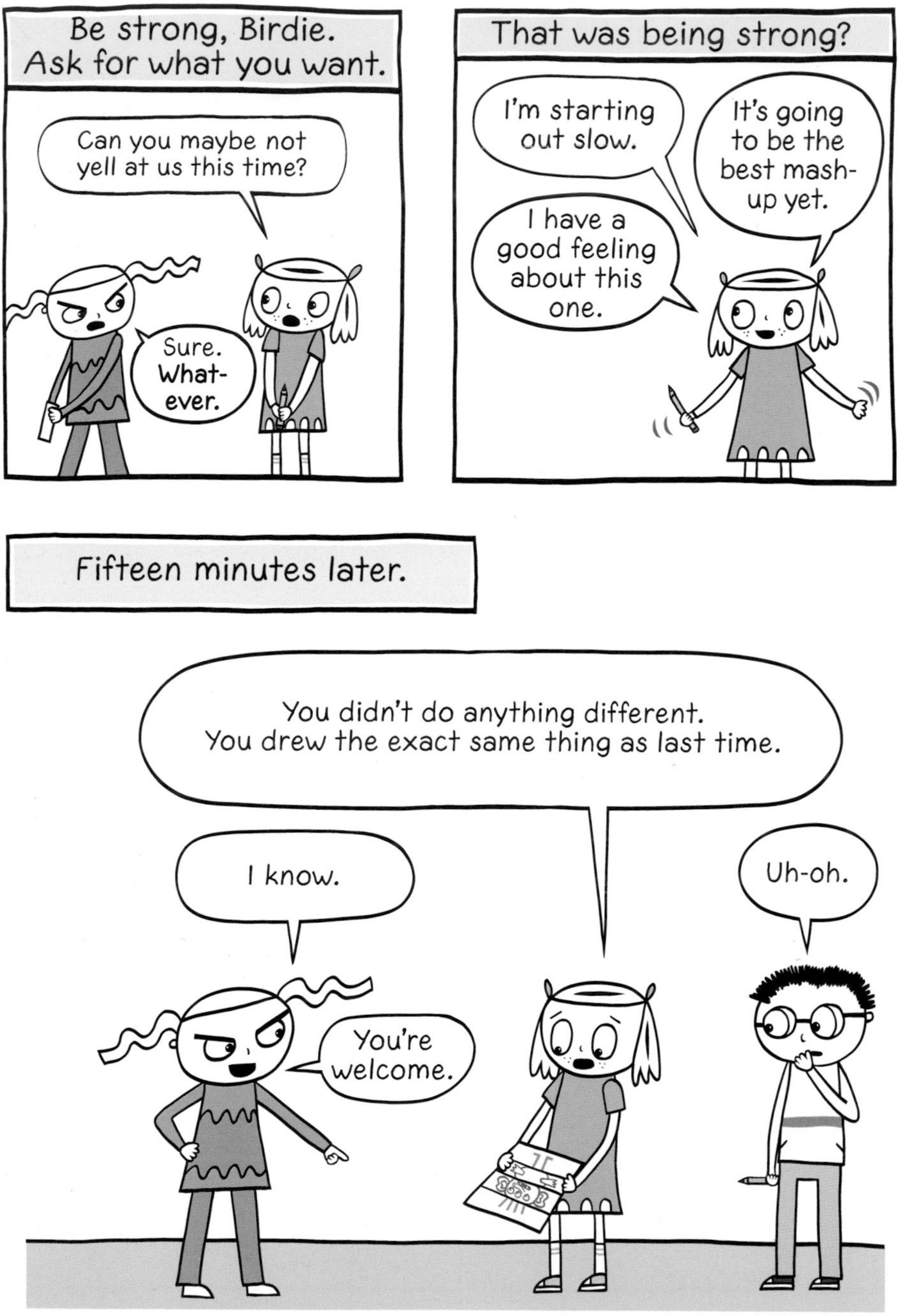
Be strong, Birdie.
Ask for what you want.
Can you maybe not yell at us this time?
Sure. **What-ever.**
That was being strong?
I'm starting out slow.
I have a good feeling about this one.
It's going to be the best mash-up yet.
Fifteen minutes later.
You didn't do anything different.
You drew the exact same thing as last time.
I know.
You're welcome.
Uh-oh.

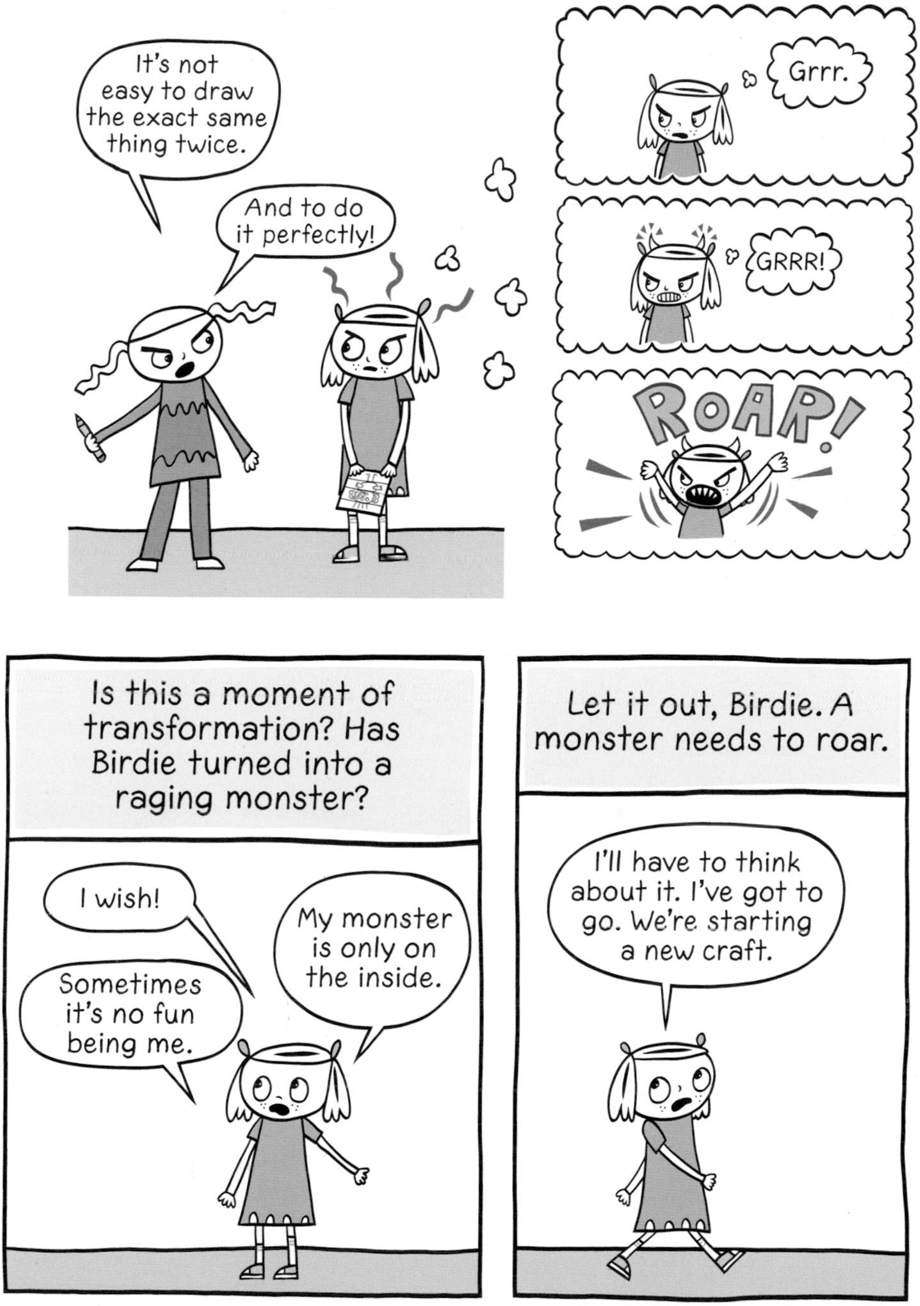
It's not easy to draw the exact same thing twice.
And to do it perfectly!
Grrr.
GRRR!
ROAR!
Is this a moment of transformation? Has Birdie turned into a raging monster?
I wish!
Sometimes it's no fun being me.
My monster is only on the inside.
Let it out, Birdie. A monster needs to roar.
I'll have to think about it. I've got to go. We're starting a new craft.

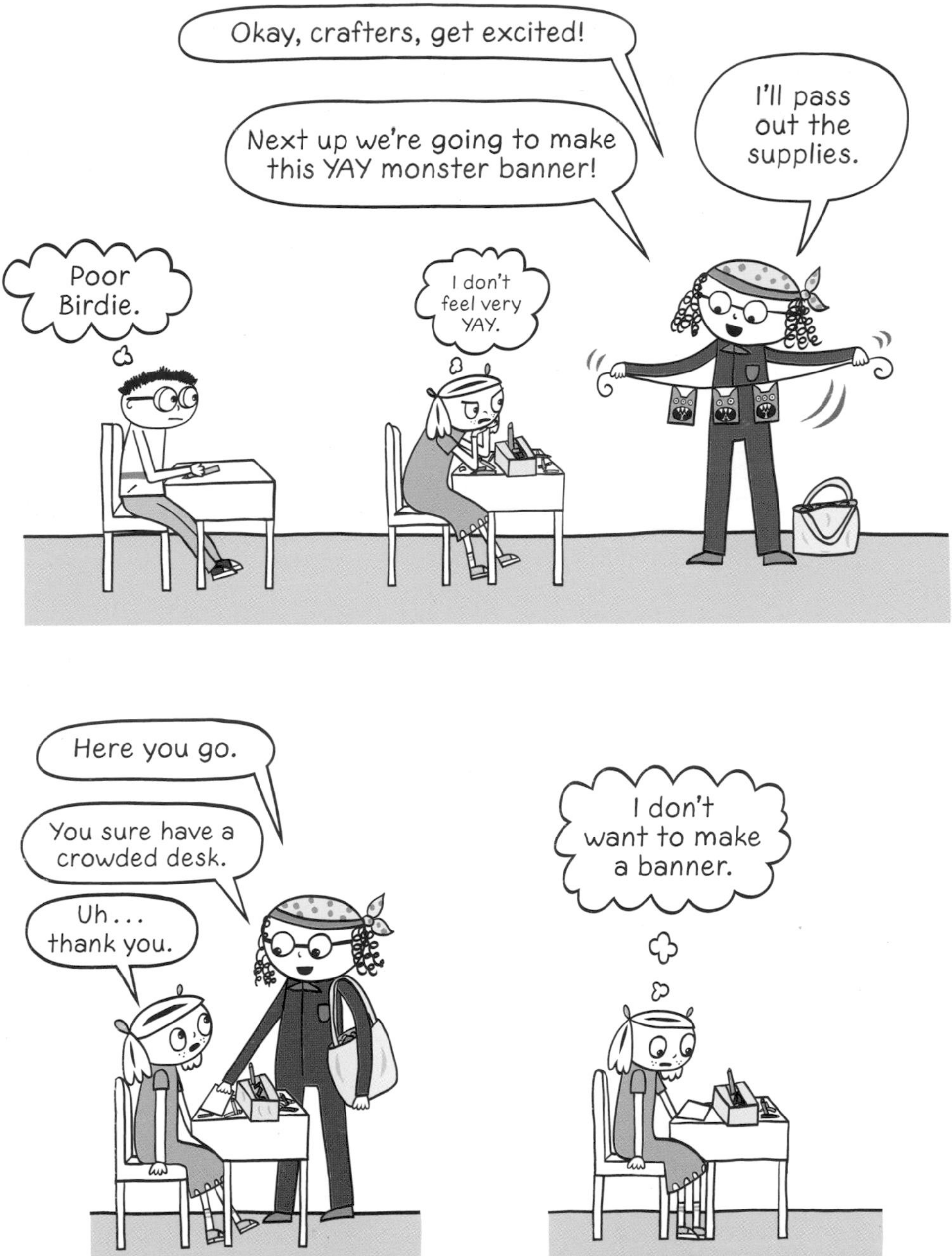
Okay, crafters, get excited!
Next up we're going to make this YAY monster banner!
I'll pass out the supplies.
Poor Birdie.
I don't feel very YAY.
Here you go.
You sure have a crowded desk.
Uh . . . thank you.
I don't want to make a banner.

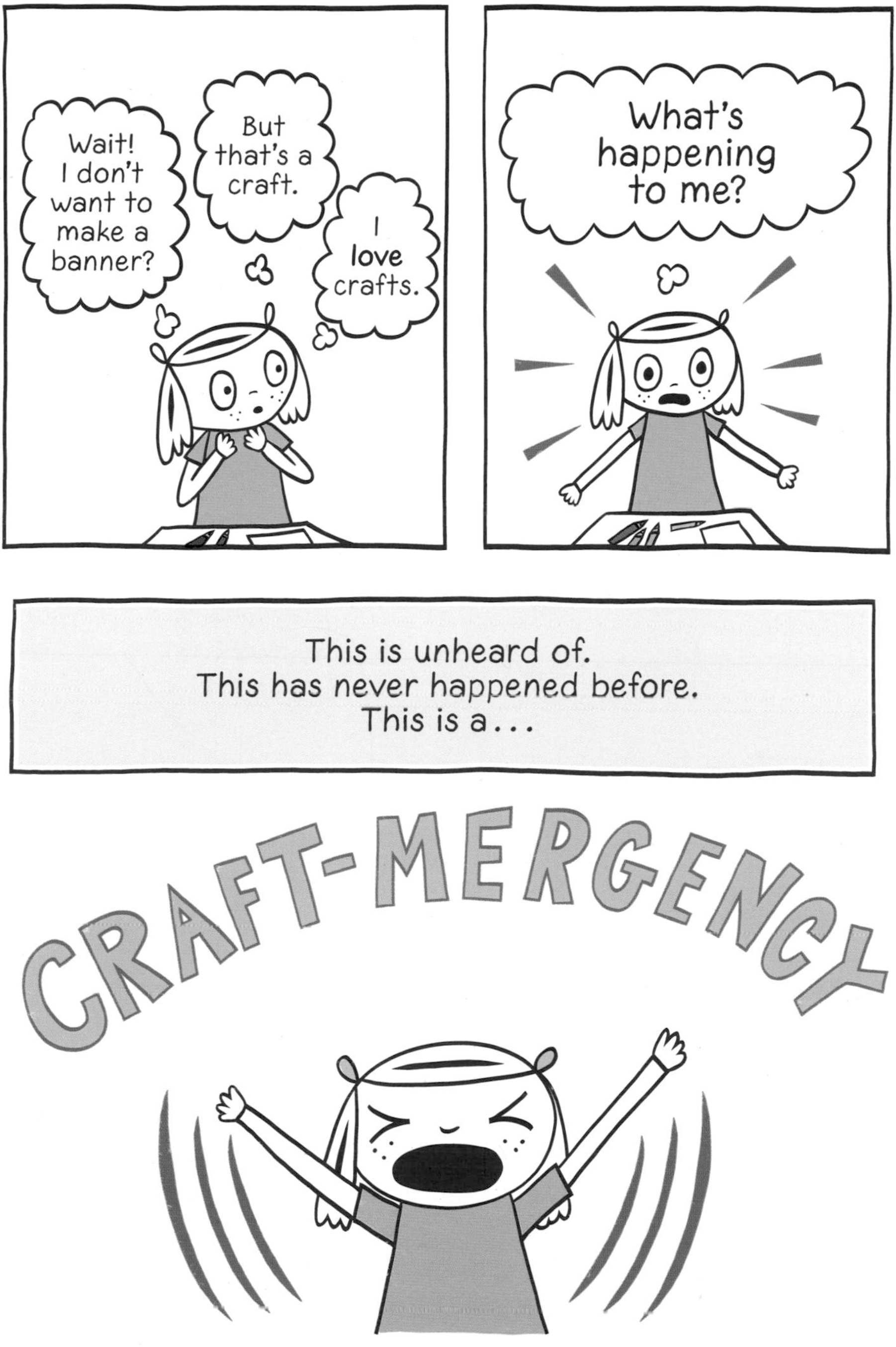
Wait! I don't want to make a banner?
But that's a craft.
I love crafts.
What's happening to me?
This is unheard of.
This has never happened before.
This is a...
CRAFT-MERGENCY

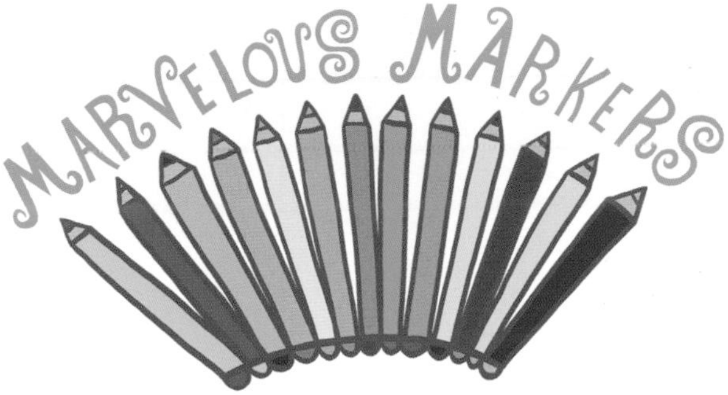
MARVELOUS MARKERS

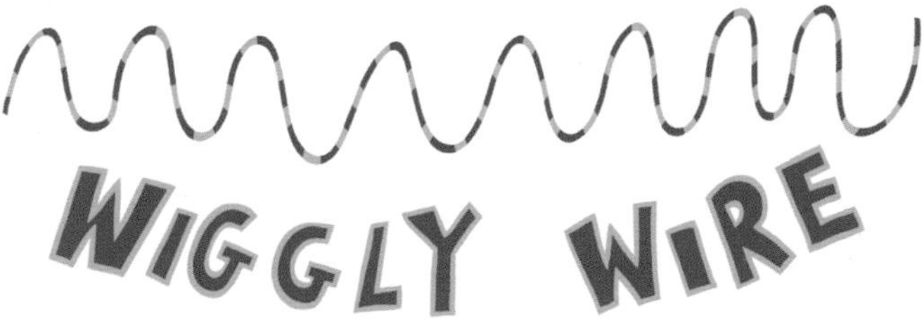
WIGGLY WIRE

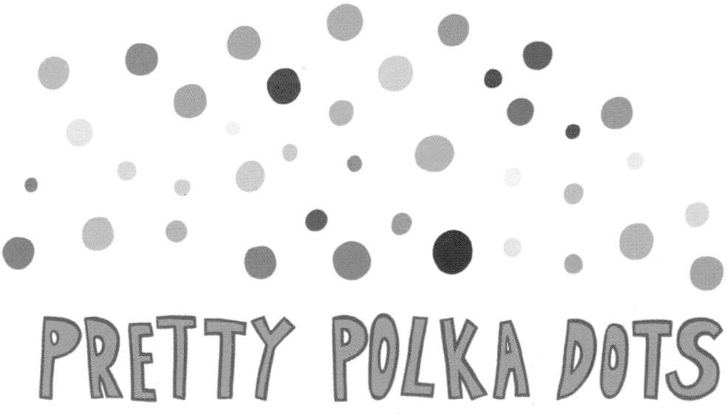
PRETTY POLKA DOTS

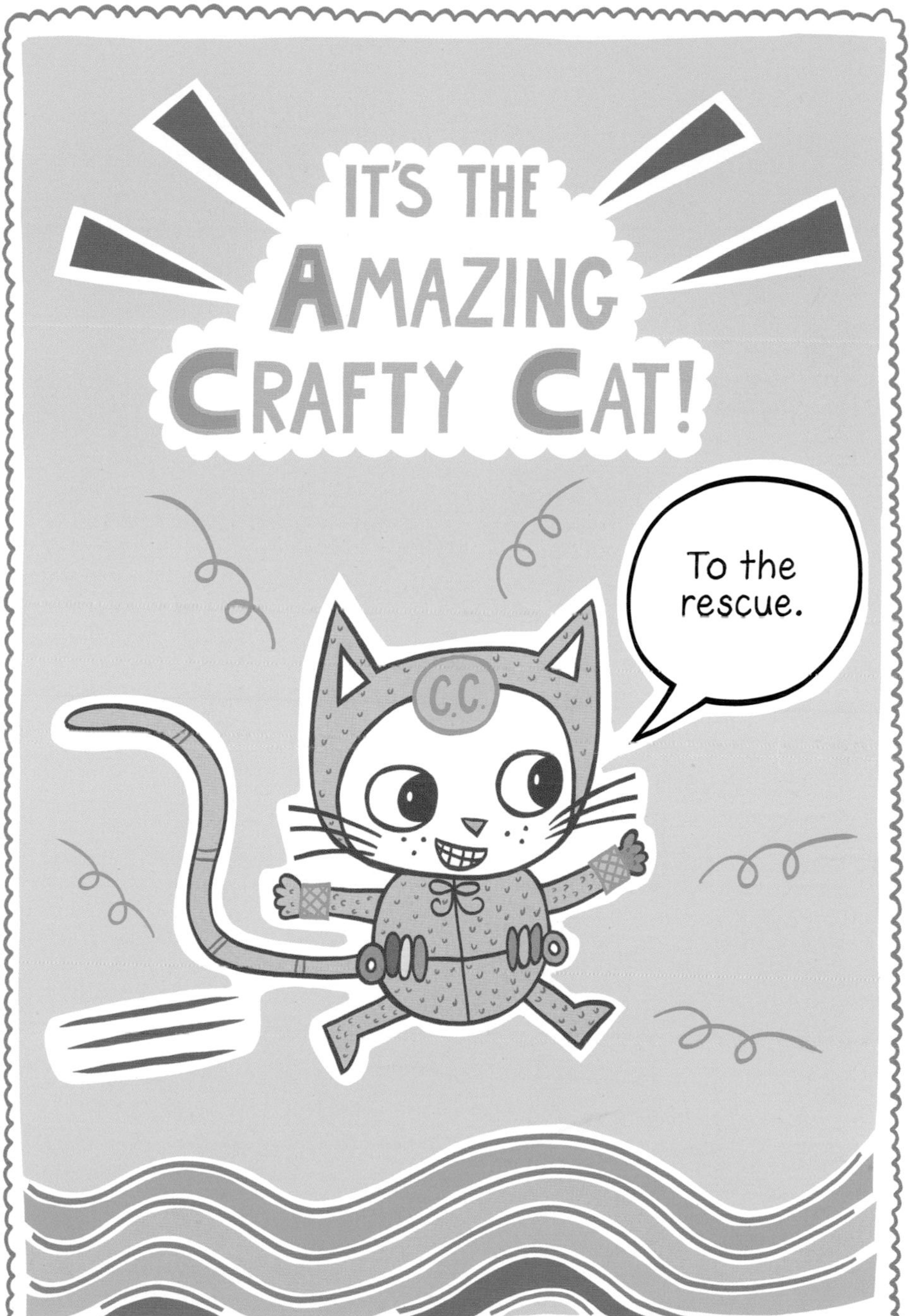
IT'S THE
AMAZING
CRAFTY CAT!
To the rescue.

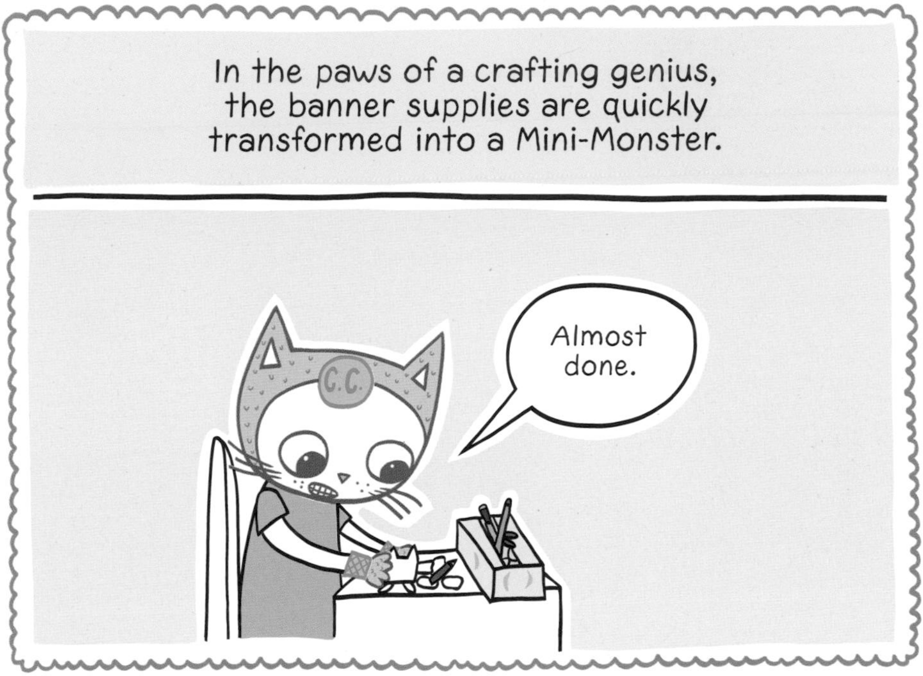
In the paws of a crafting genius, the banner supplies are quickly transformed into a Mini-Monster.
Almost done.
C.C.

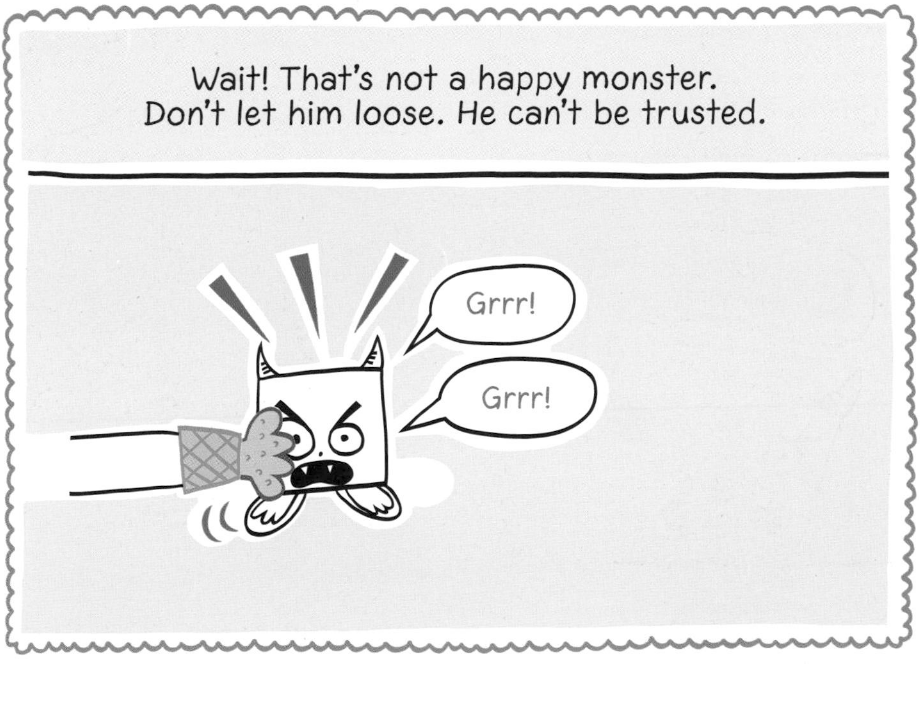
Wait! That's not a happy monster. Don't let him loose. He can't be trusted.
Grrr!
Grrr!

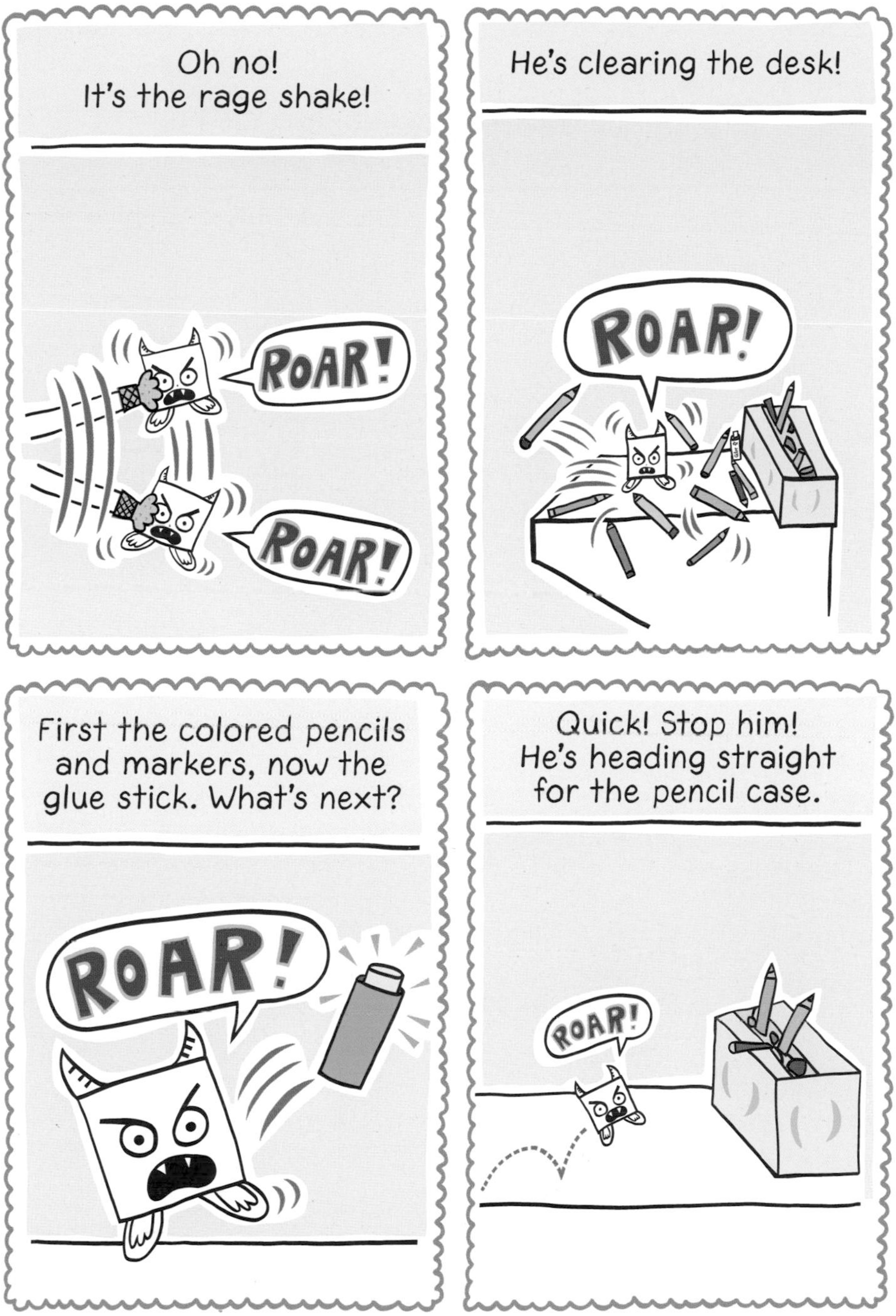
Oh no!
It's the rage shake!
ROAR!
ROAR!
He's clearing the desk!
ROAR!
First the colored pencils
and markers, now the
glue stick. What's next?
ROAR!
Quick! Stop him!
He's heading straight
for the pencil case.
ROAR!

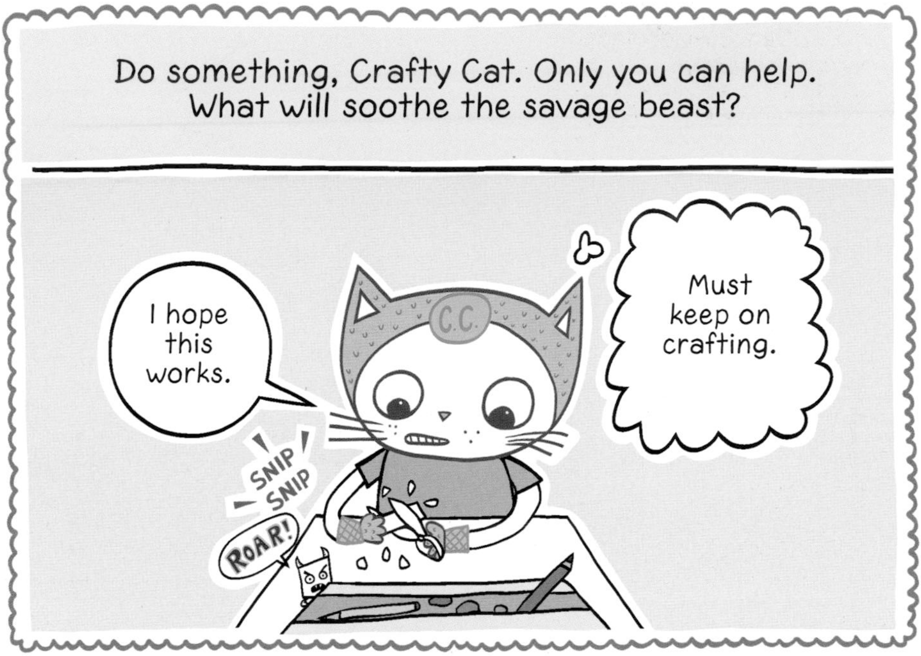
Do something, Crafty Cat. Only you can help.
What will soothe the savage beast?
I hope this works.
Must keep on crafting.
C.C.
SNIP SNIP
ROAR!

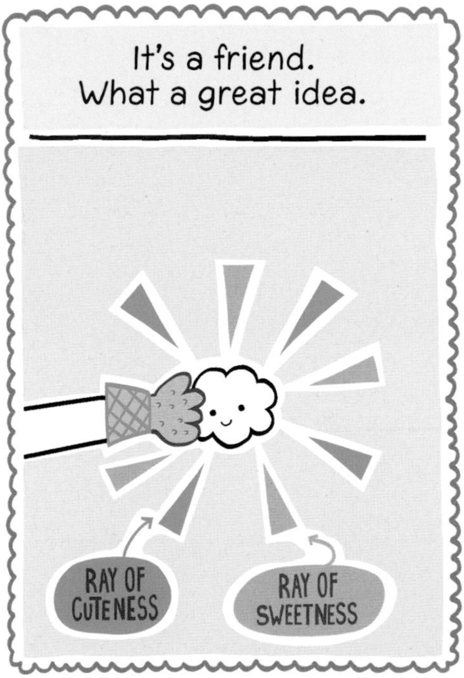
It's a friend.
What a great idea.
RAY OF CUTENESS
RAY OF SWEETNESS

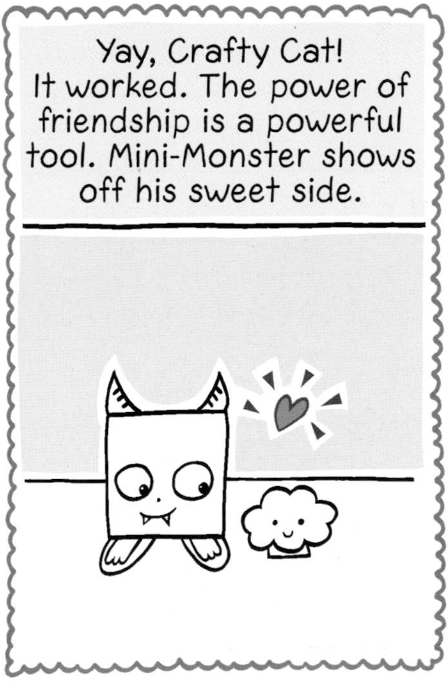
Yay, Crafty Cat!
It worked. The power of friendship is a powerful tool. Mini-Monster shows off his sweet side.

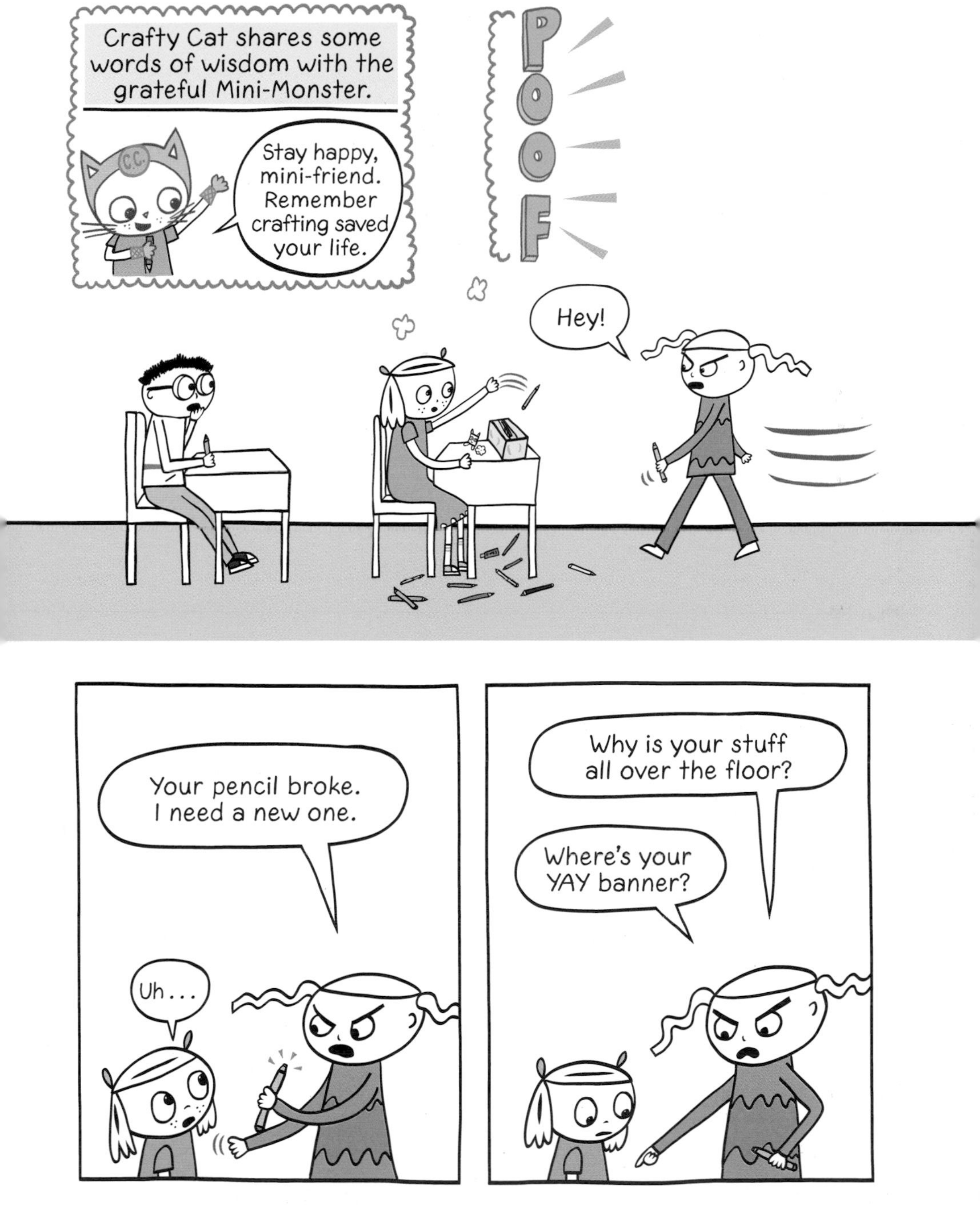
Crafty Cat shares some words of wisdom with the grateful Mini-Monster.
Stay happy, mini-friend. Remember crafting saved your life.
POOF
Hey!
Your pencil broke. I need a new one.
Uh...
Why is your stuff all over the floor?
Where's your YAY banner?

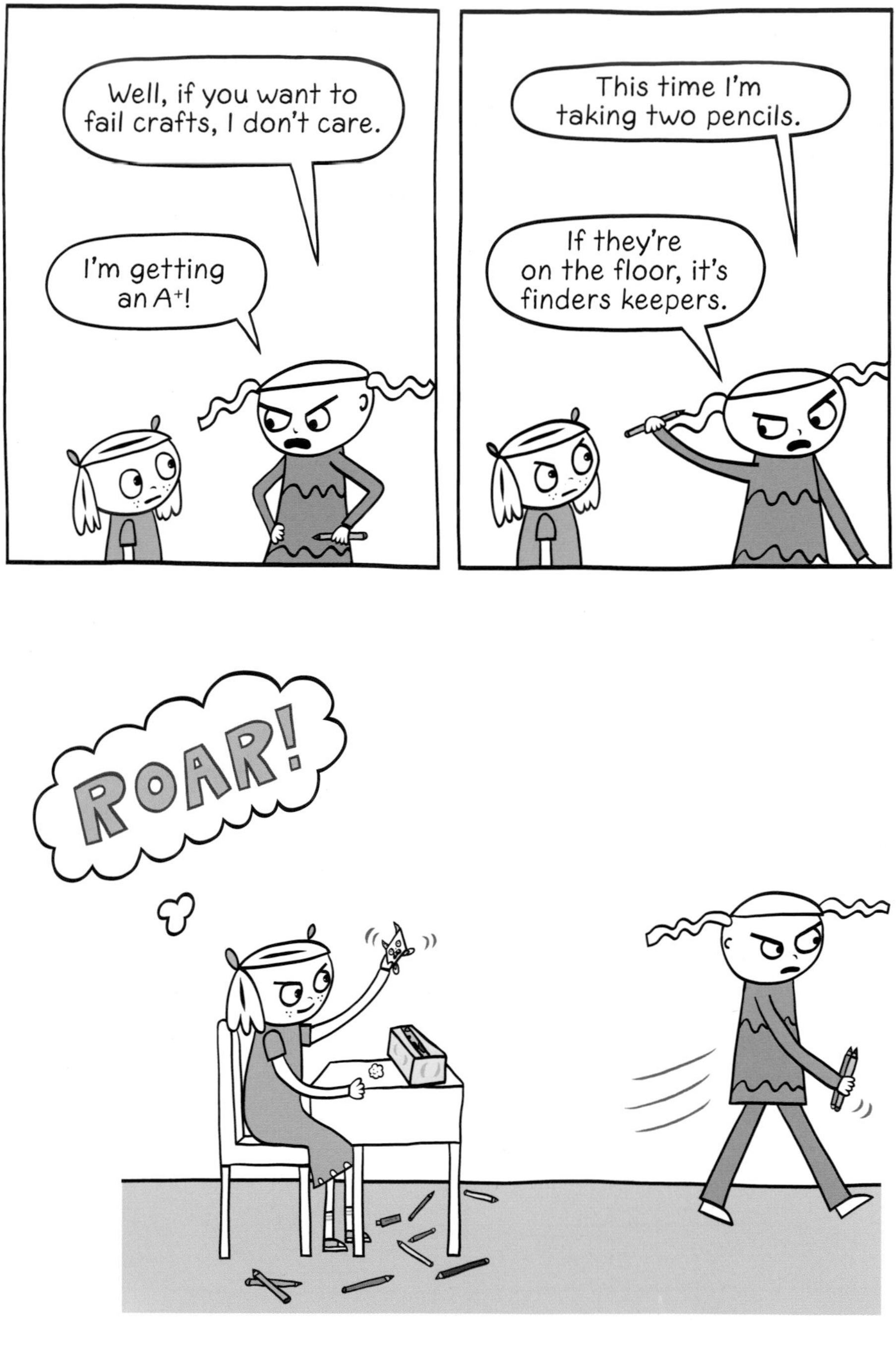
Well, if you want to fail crafts, I don't care.
I'm getting an A+!
This time I'm taking two pencils.
If they're on the floor, it's finders keepers.
ROAR!

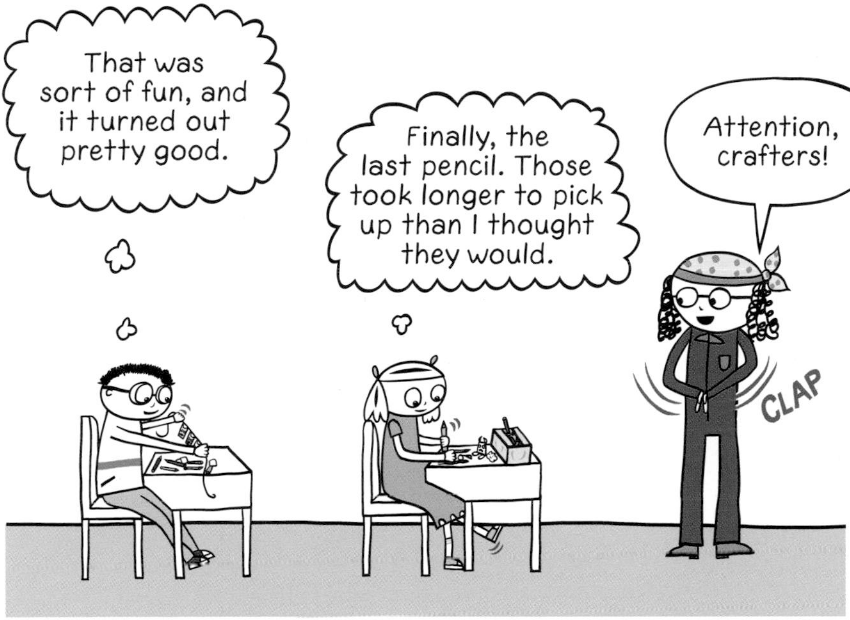
That was sort of fun, and it turned out pretty good.
Finally, the last pencil. Those took longer to pick up than I thought they would.
Attention, crafters!
CLAP

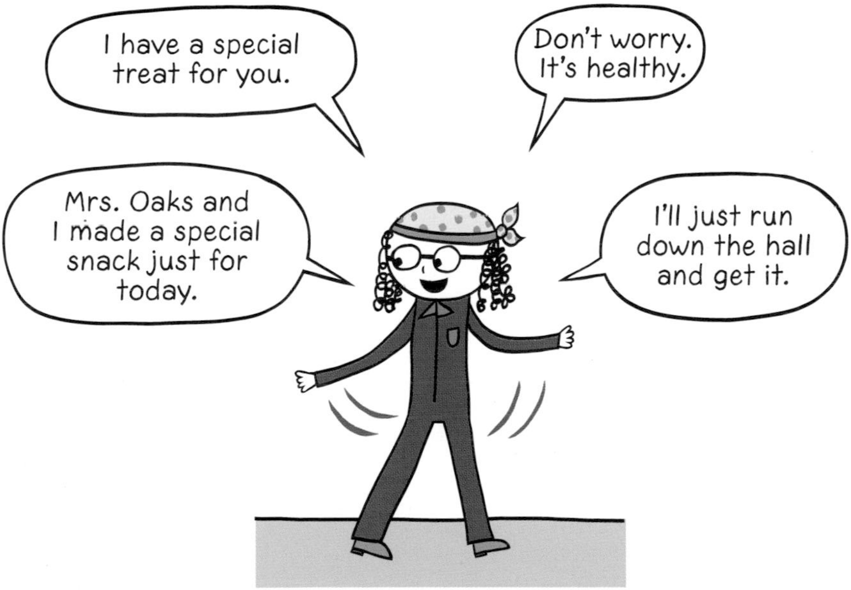
I have a special treat for you.
Don't worry. It's healthy.
Mrs. Oaks and I made a special snack just for today.
I'll just run down the hall and get it.

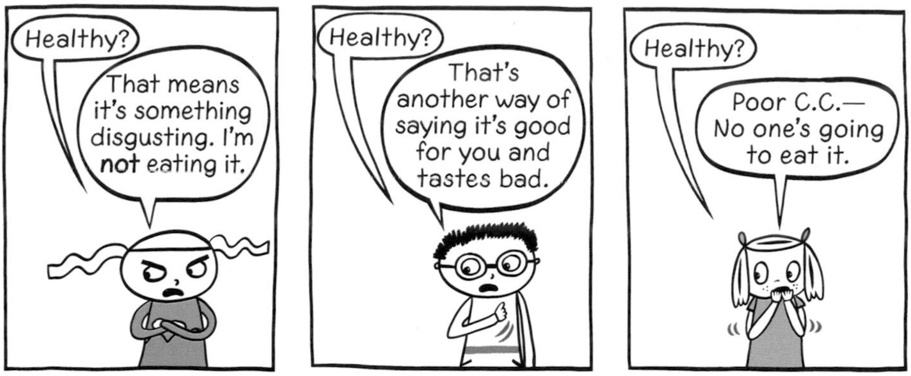
Healthy?
That means it's something disgusting. I'm **not** eating it.
Healthy?
That's another way of saying it's good for you and tastes bad.
Healthy?
Poor C.C.— No one's going to eat it.

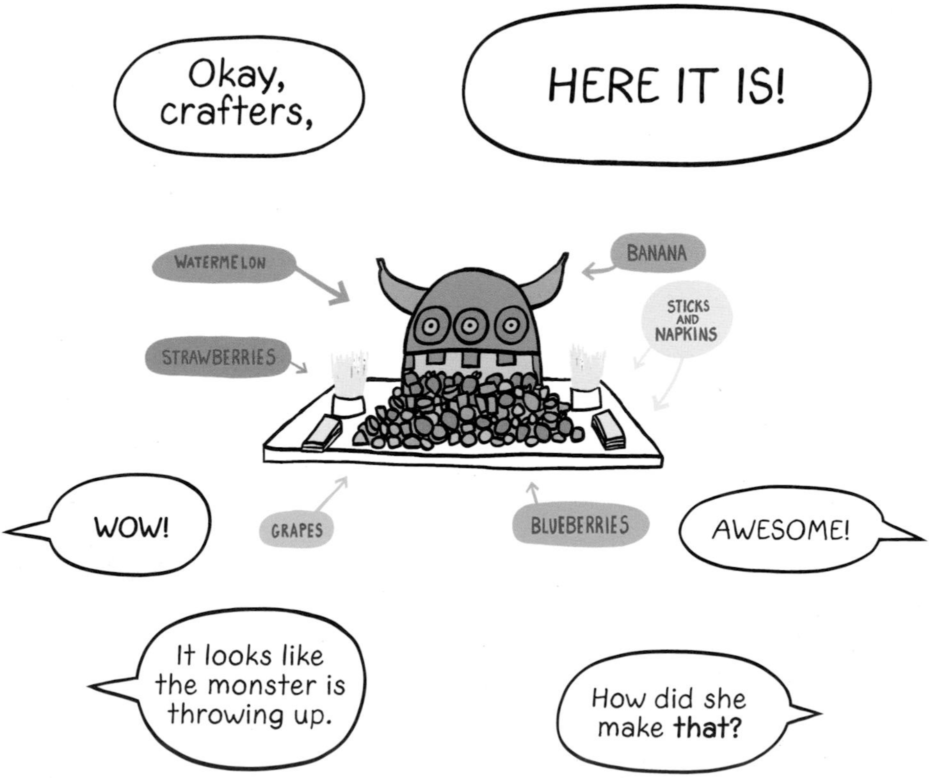
Okay, crafters,
HERE IT IS!
WATERMELON
BANANA
STICKS AND NAPKINS
STRAWBERRIES
GRAPES
BLUEBERRIES
WOW!
AWESOME!
It looks like the monster is throwing up.
How did she make **that?**

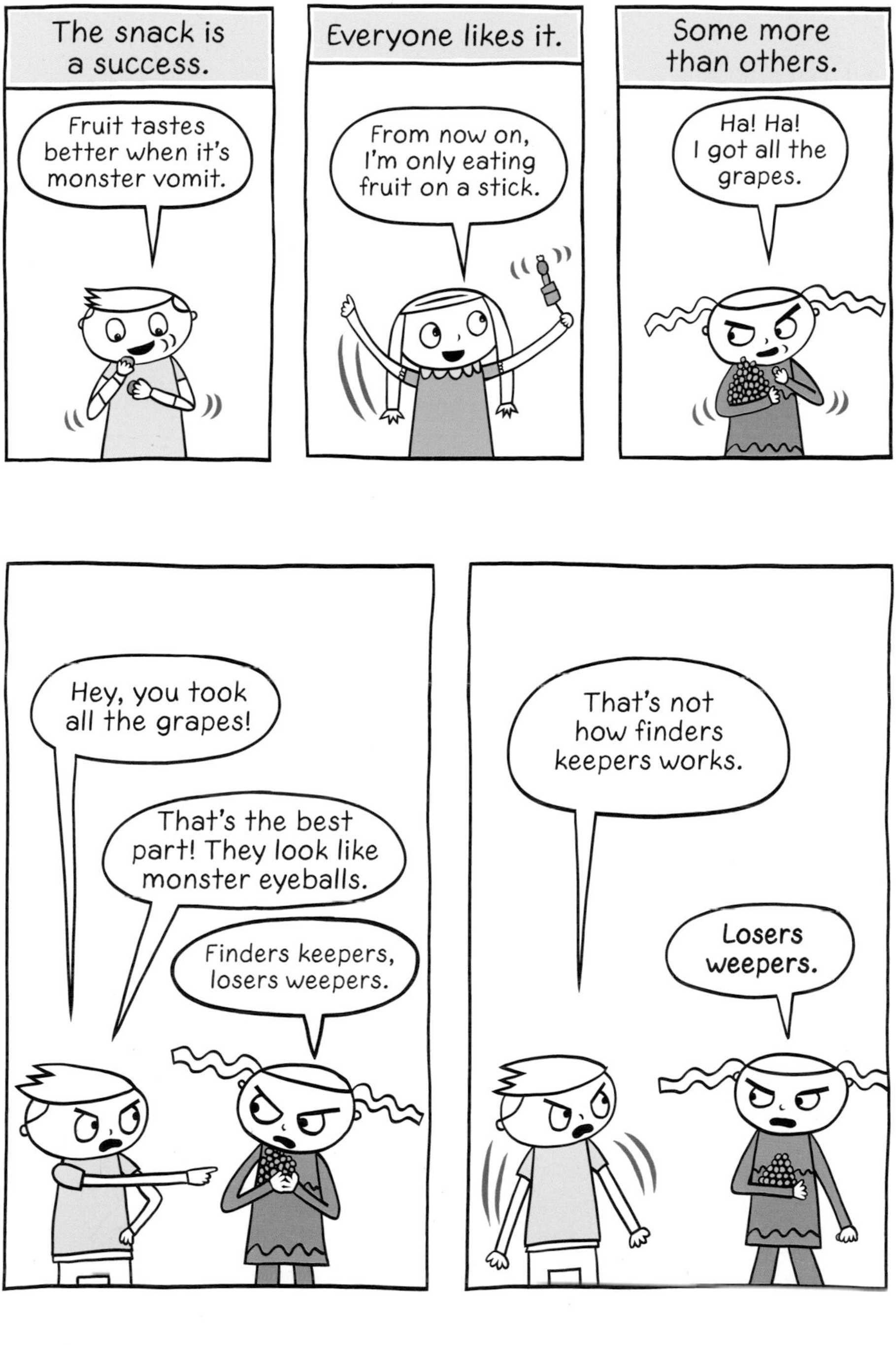
The snack is a success.
Fruit tastes better when it's monster vomit.
Everyone likes it.
From now on, I'm only eating fruit on a stick.
Some more than others.
Ha! Ha! I got all the grapes.
Hey, you took all the grapes!
That's the best part! They look like monster eyeballs.
Finders keepers, losers weepers.
That's not how finders keepers works.
Losers weepers.

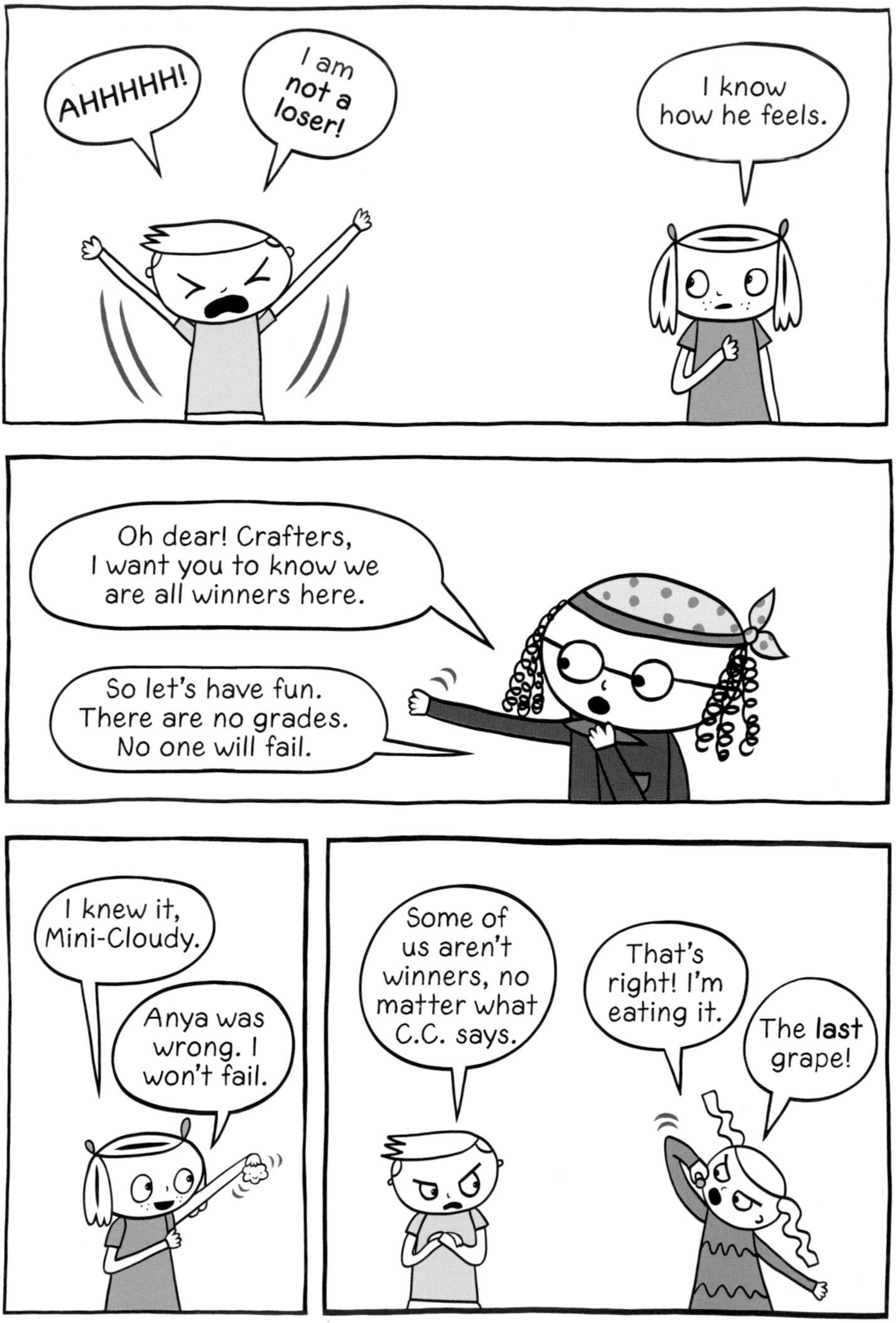
AHHHHH!
I am **not a** loser!
I know how he feels.
Oh dear! Crafters, I want you to know we are all winners here.
So let's have fun. There are no grades. No one will fail.
I knew it, Mini-Cloudy.
Anya was wrong. I won't fail.
Some of us aren't winners, no matter what C.C. says.
That's right! I'm eating it.
The **last** grape!

So, Birdie, are you ready for the next crafty challenge?

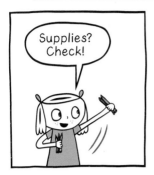

Supplies? Check!
Good spirits? Check!
I'm ready.
What are we making?

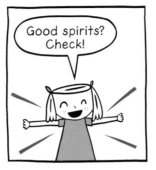

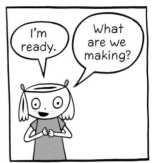

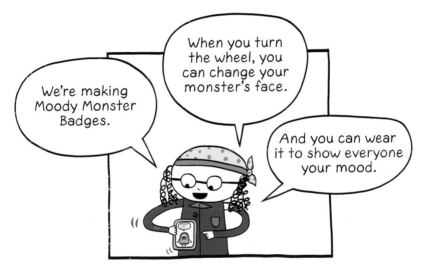

We're making Moody Monster Badges.
When you turn the wheel, you can change your monster's face.
And you can wear it to show everyone your mood.

There's room to draw four different faces.

TODAY I'M...
TODAY I'M...
TODAY I'M...
TODAY I'M...

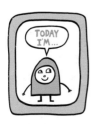

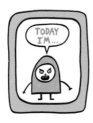

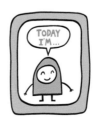

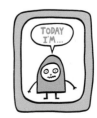

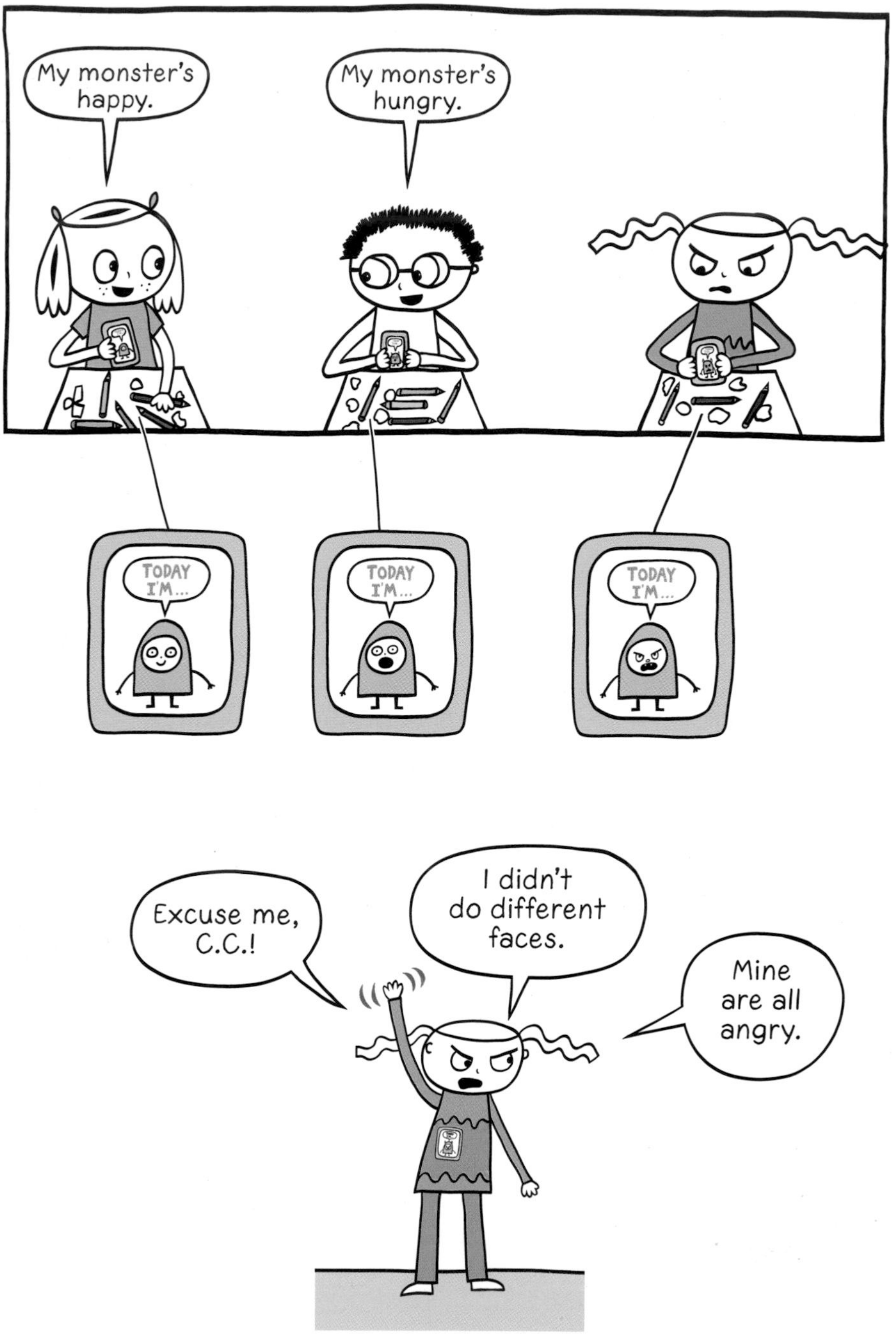
My monster's happy.
My monster's hungry.
TODAY I'M...
TODAY I'M...
TODAY I'M...
Excuse me, C.C.!
I didn't do different faces.
Mine are all angry.

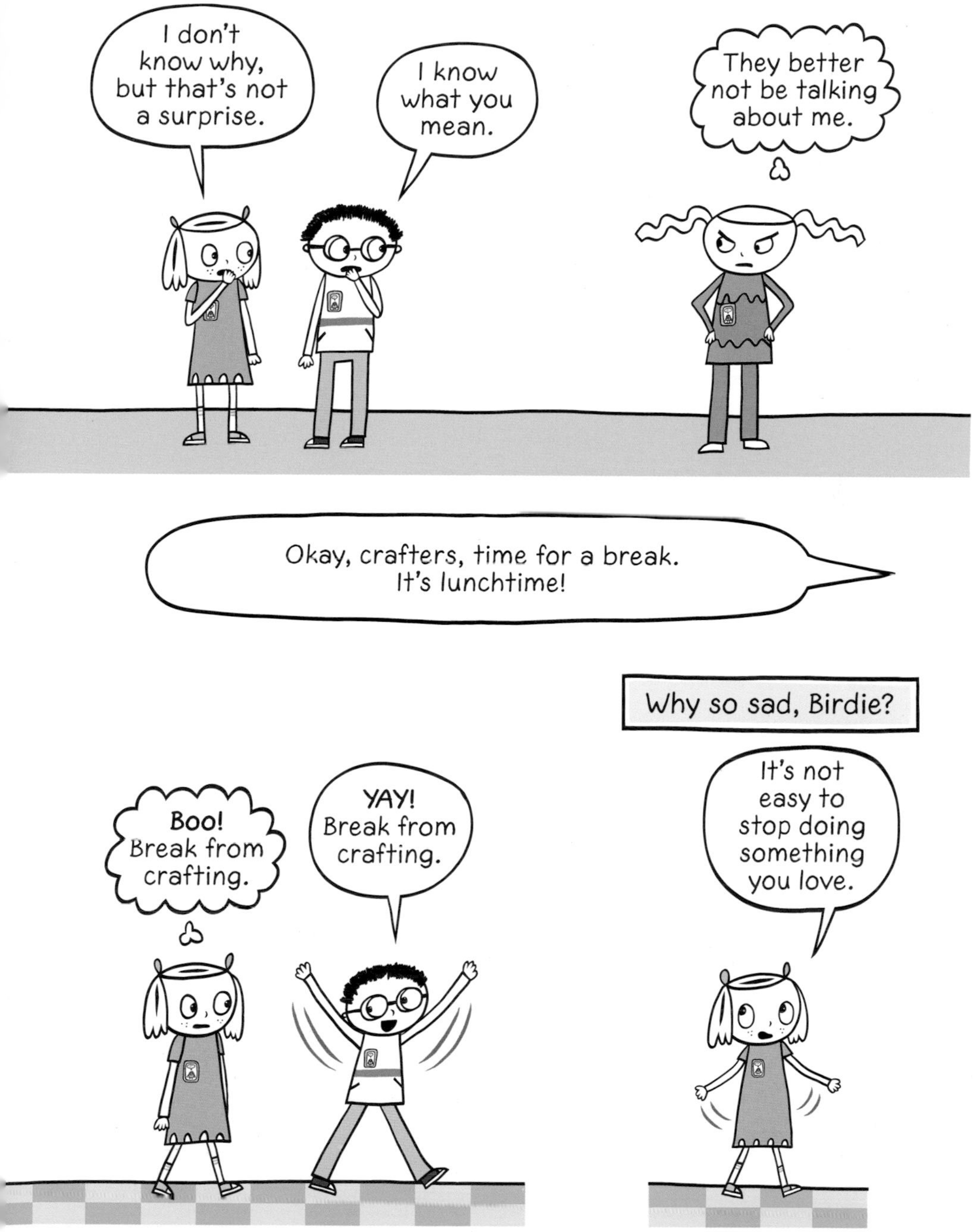
I don't know why, but that's not a surprise.
I know what you mean.
They better not be talking about me.
Okay, crafters, time for a break. It's lunchtime!
Boo! Break from crafting.
YAY! Break from crafting.
Why so sad, Birdie?
It's not easy to stop doing something you love.

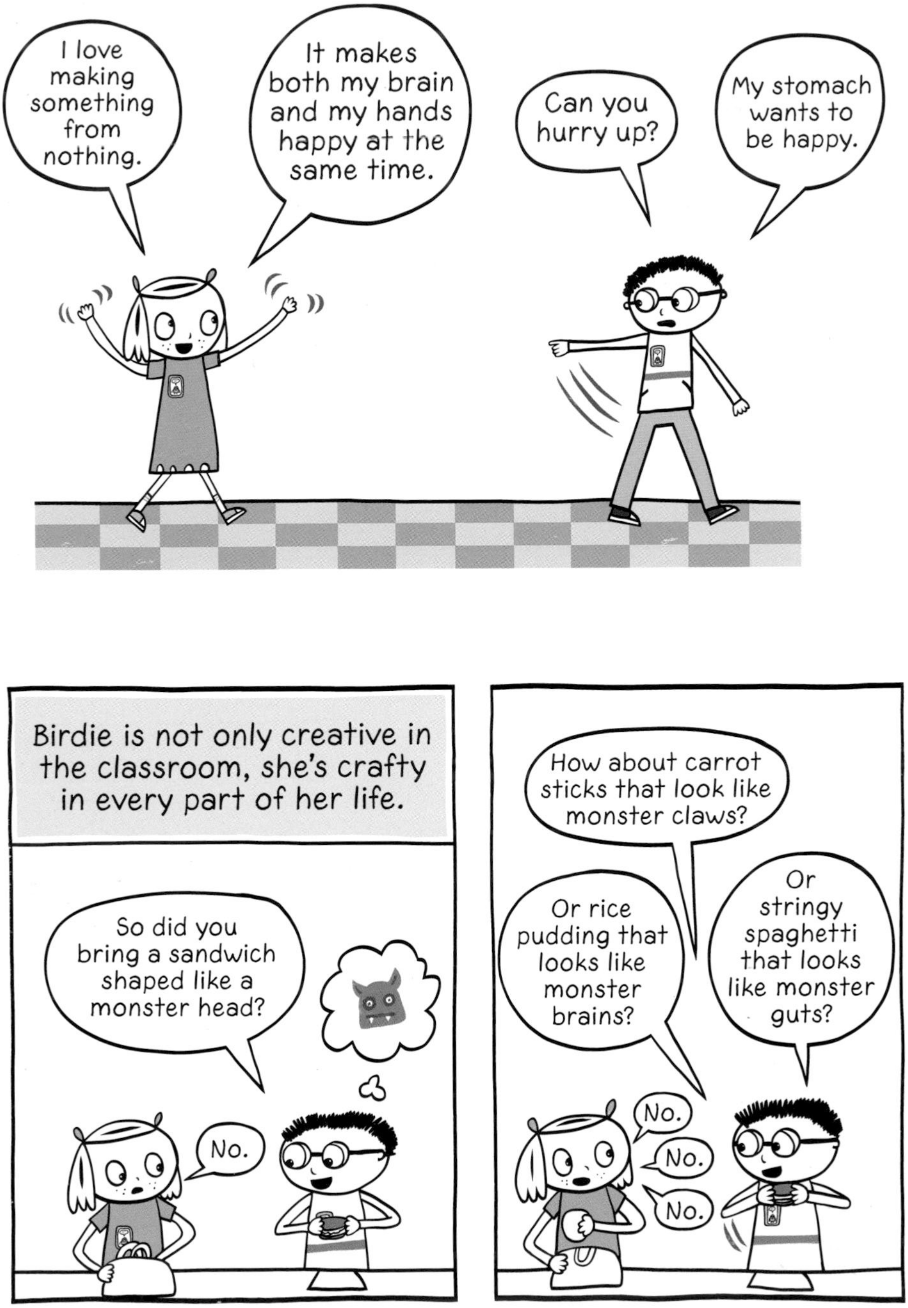
I love making something from nothing.
It makes both my brain and my hands happy at the same time.
Can you hurry up?
My stomach wants to be happy.
Birdie is not only creative in the classroom, she's crafty in every part of her life.
So did you bring a sandwich shaped like a monster head?
No.
How about carrot sticks that look like monster claws?
Or rice pudding that looks like monster brains?
Or stringy spaghetti that looks like monster guts?
No.
No.
No.

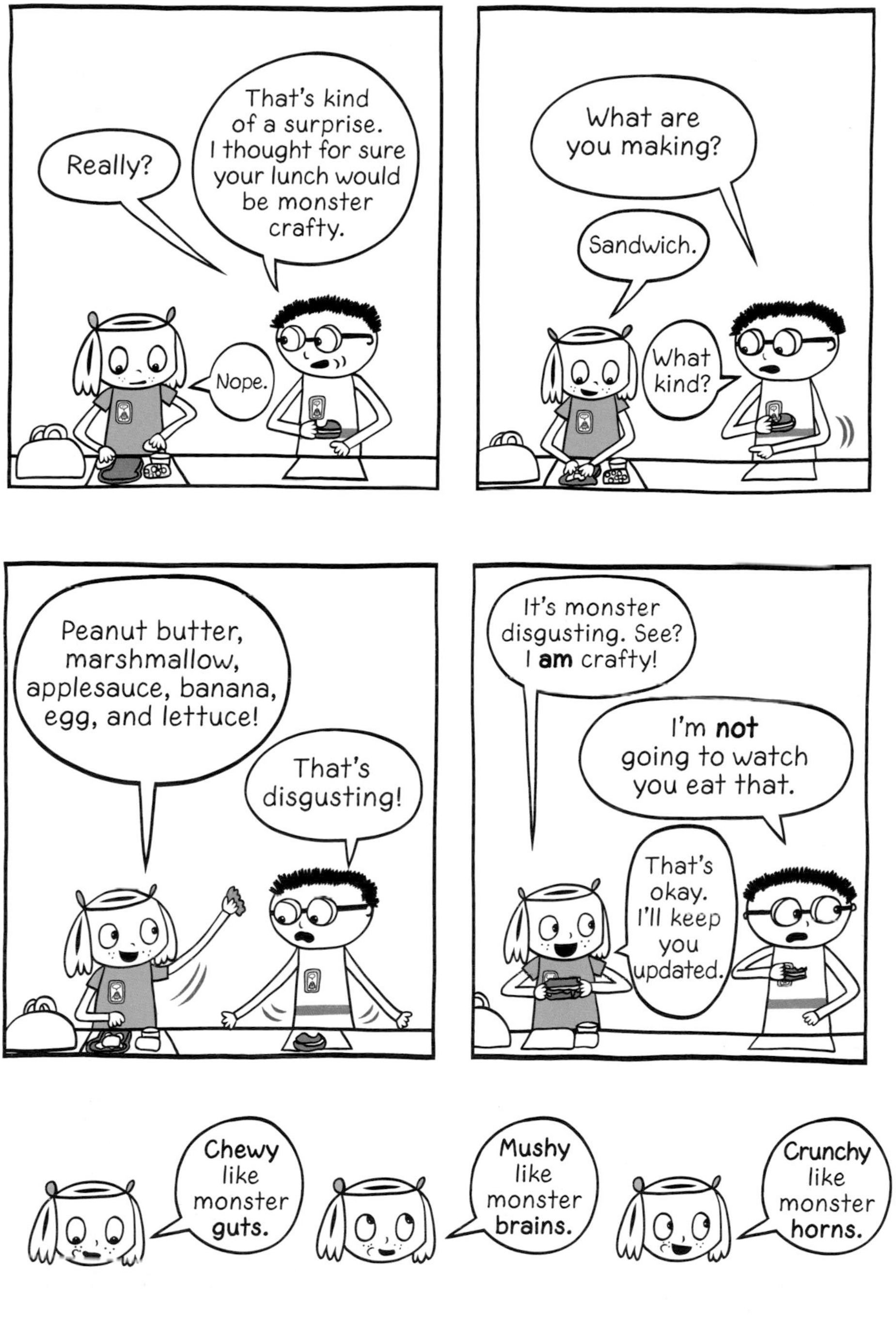
Really?
That's kind of a surprise. I thought for sure your lunch would be monster crafty.
Nope.
What are you making?
Sandwich.
What kind?
Peanut butter, marshmallow, applesauce, banana, egg, and lettuce!
That's disgusting!
It's monster disgusting. See? I **am** crafty!
I'm **not** going to watch you eat that.
That's okay. I'll keep you updated.
Chewy like monster **guts.**
Mushy like monster **brains.**
Crunchy like monster **horns.**

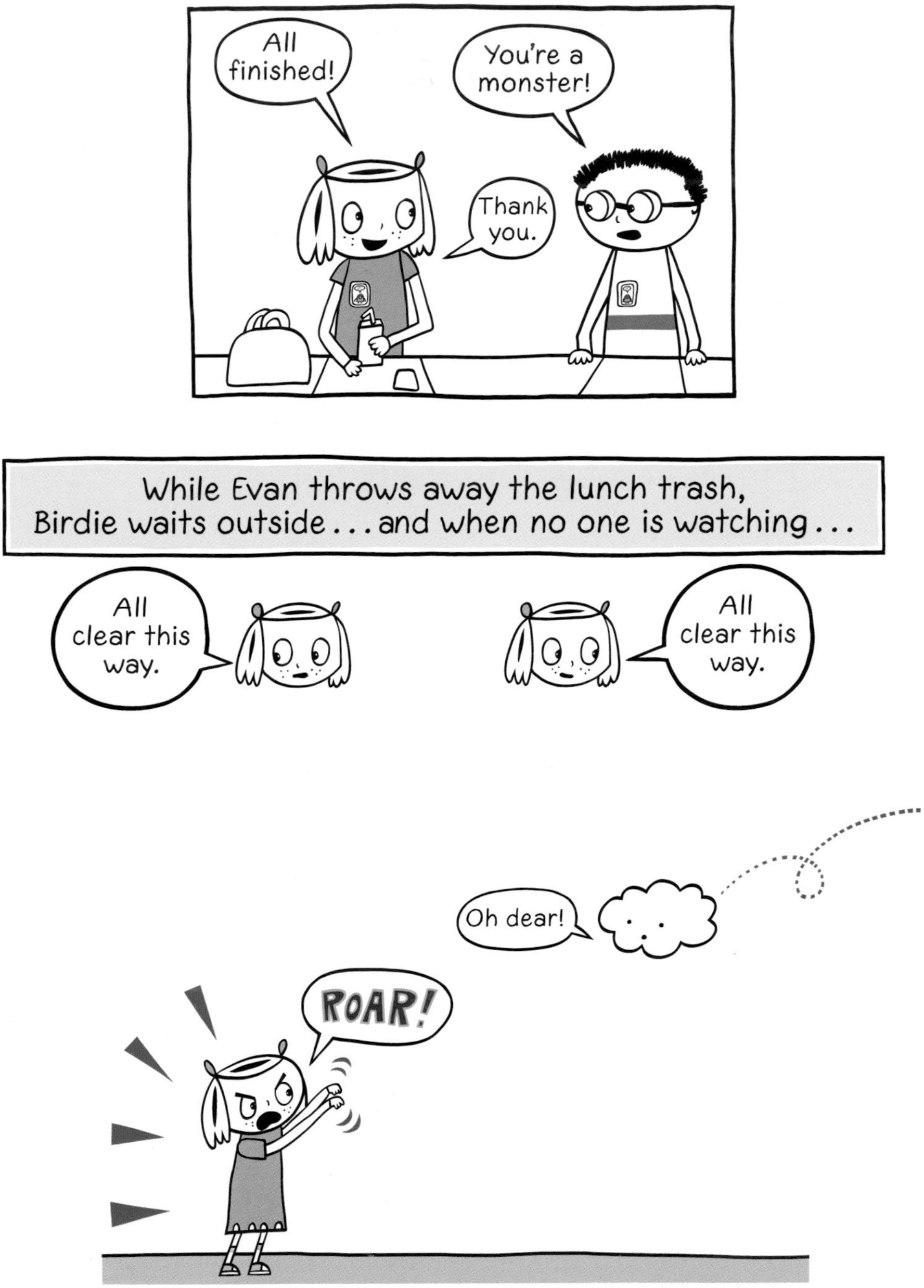
All finished!
You're a monster!
Thank you.
While Evan throws away the lunch trash, Birdie waits outside . . . and when no one is watching . . .
All clear this way.
All clear this way.
Oh dear!
ROAR!

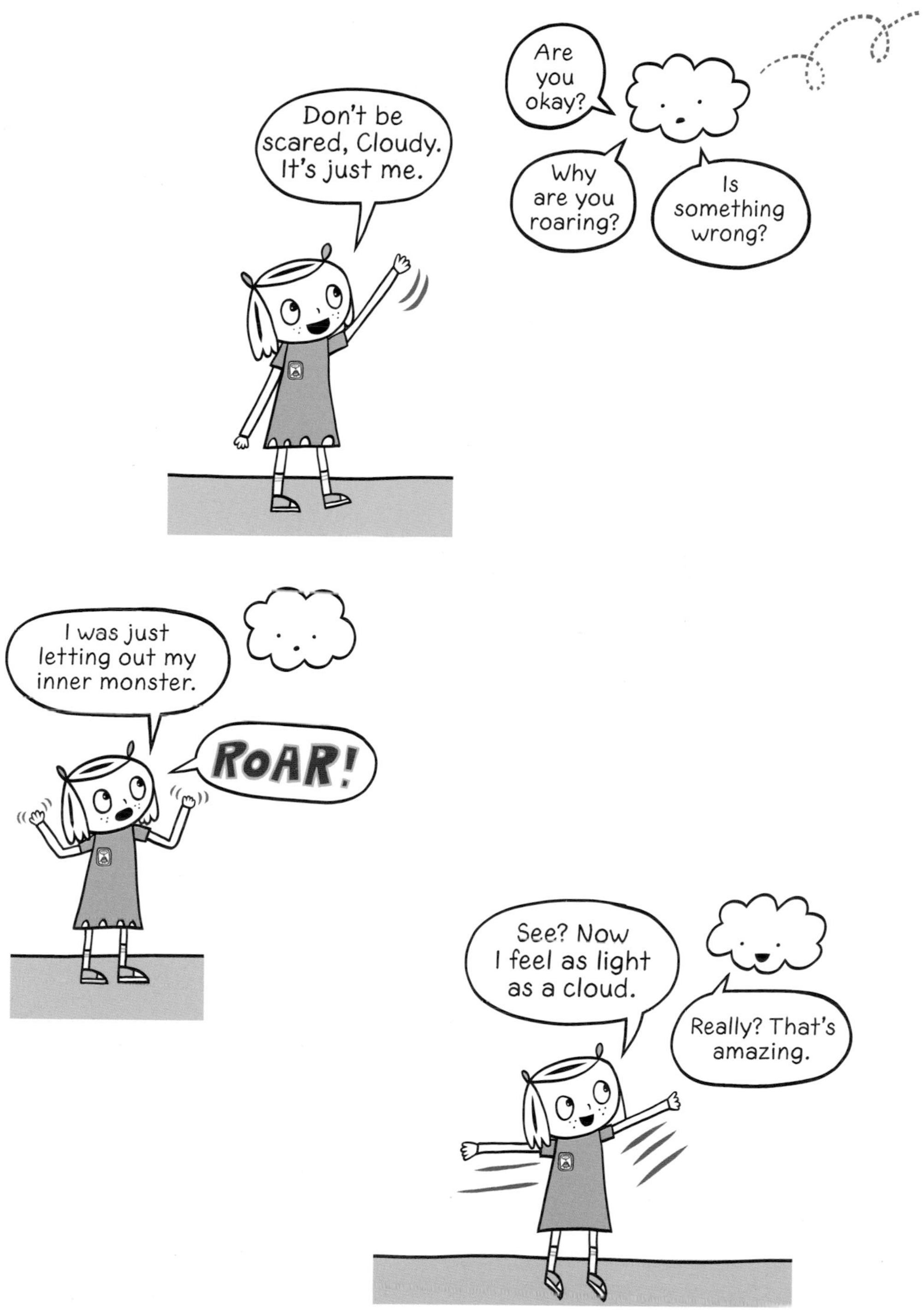
Don't be scared, Cloudy. It's just me.
Are you okay?
Why are you roaring?
Is something wrong?
I was just letting out my inner monster.
ROAR!
See? Now I feel as light as a cloud.
Really? That's amazing.

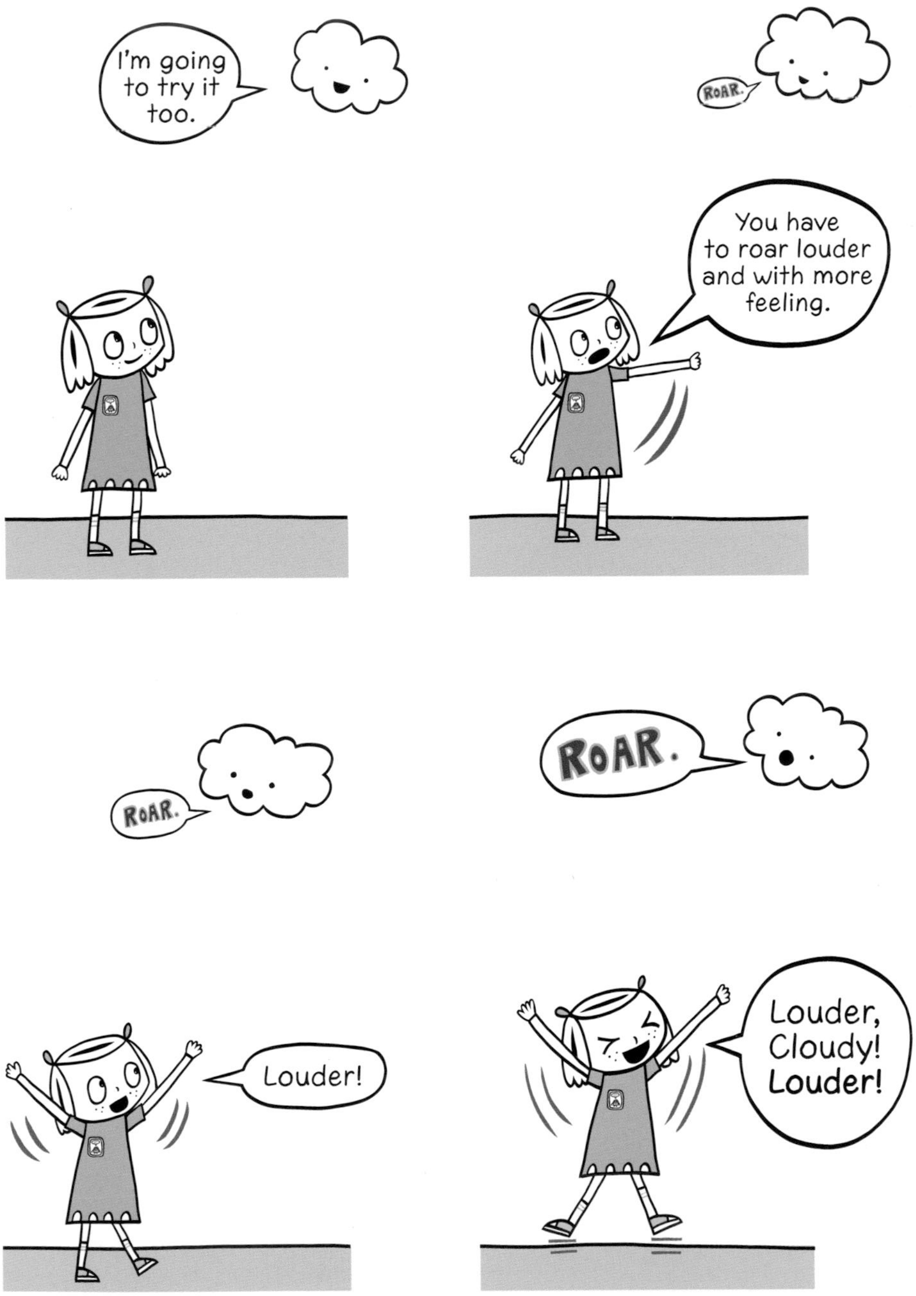
I'm going to try it too.
ROAR.
You have to roar louder and with more feeling.
ROAR.
ROAR.
Louder!
Louder, Cloudy! Louder!

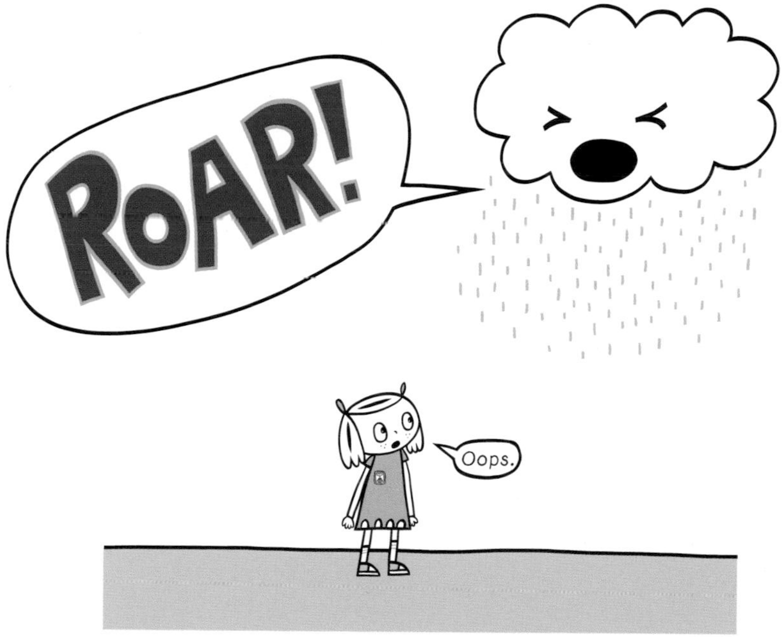
ROAR!
Oops.

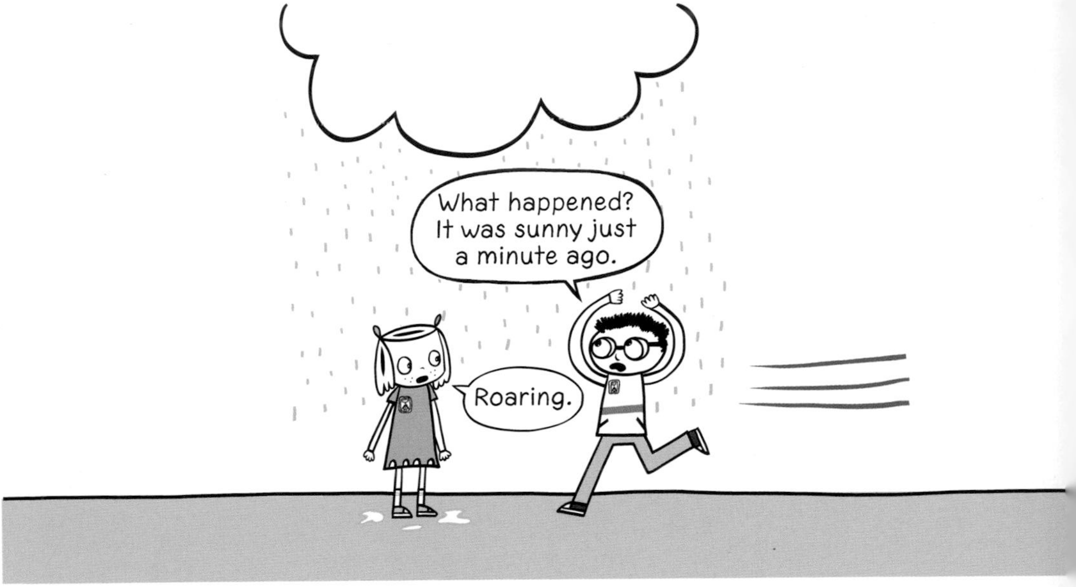
What happened? It was sunny just a minute ago.
Roaring.

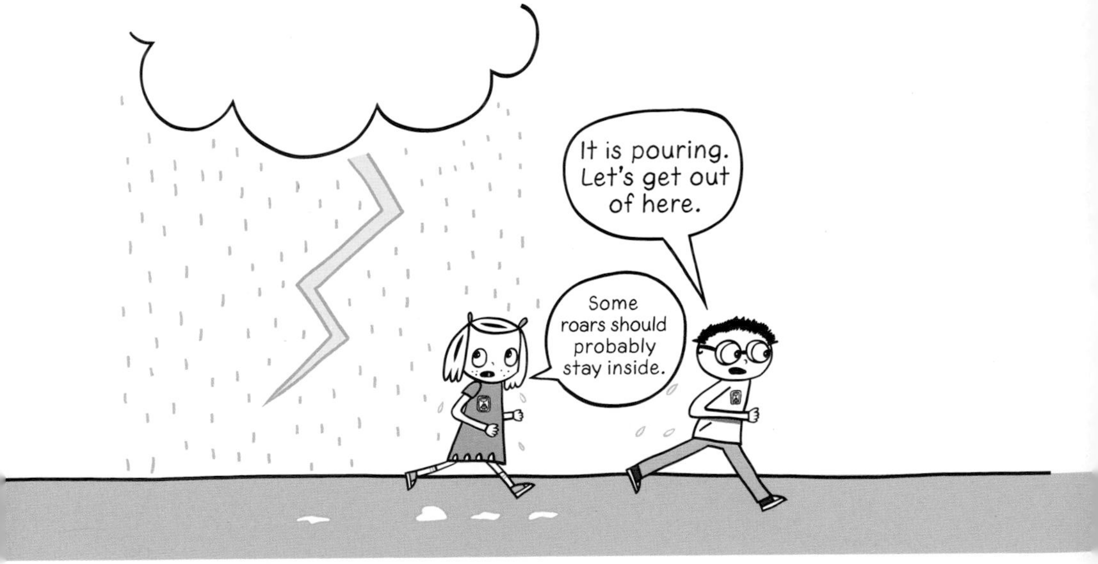
It is pouring. Let's get out of here.
Some roars should probably stay inside.

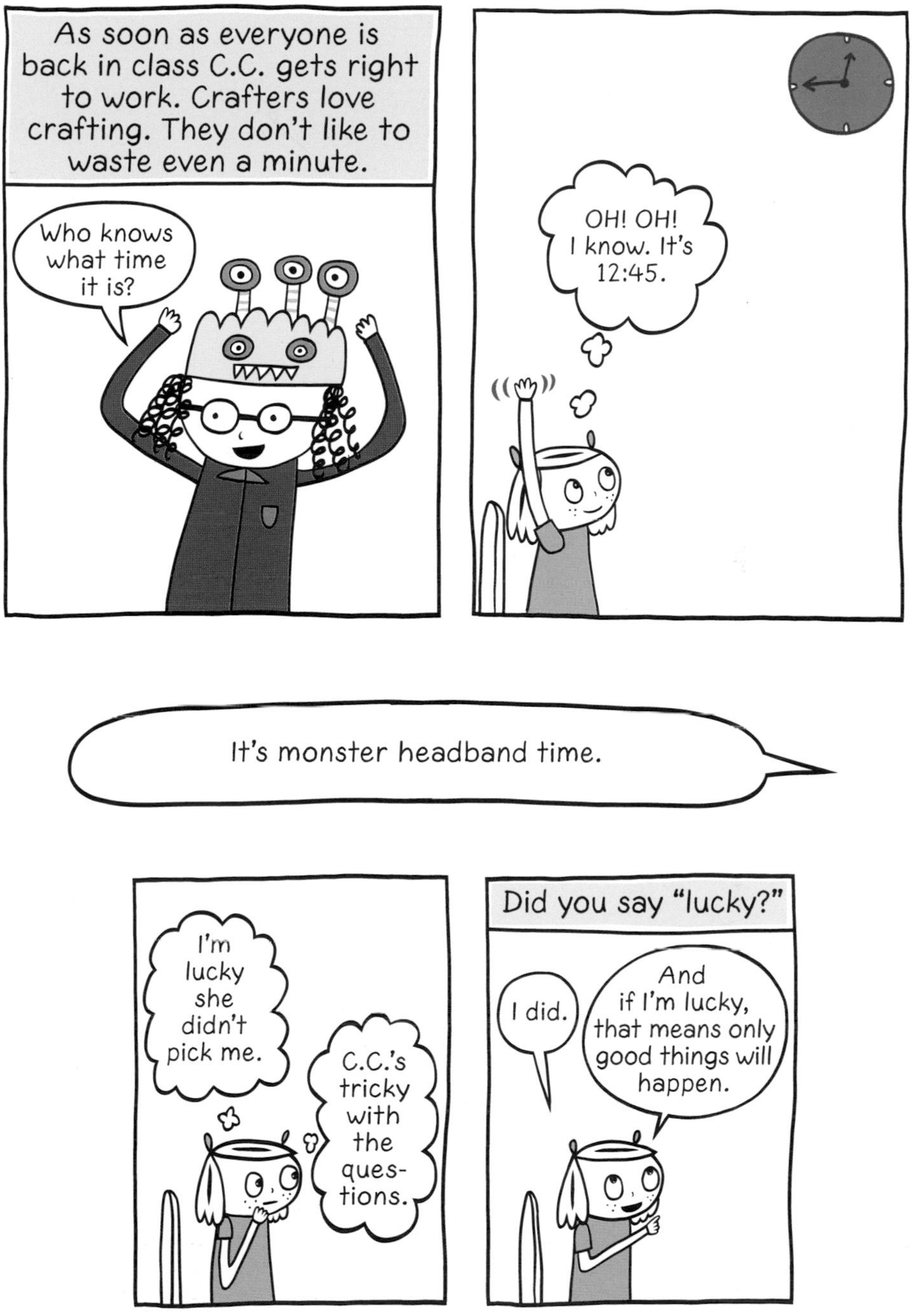
As soon as everyone is back in class C.C. gets right to work. Crafters love crafting. They don't like to waste even a minute.
Who knows what time it is?
OH! OH! I know. It's 12:45.
It's monster headband time.
I'm lucky she didn't pick me.
C.C.'s tricky with the ques-tions.
Did you say "lucky?"
I did.
And if I'm lucky, that means only good things will happen.

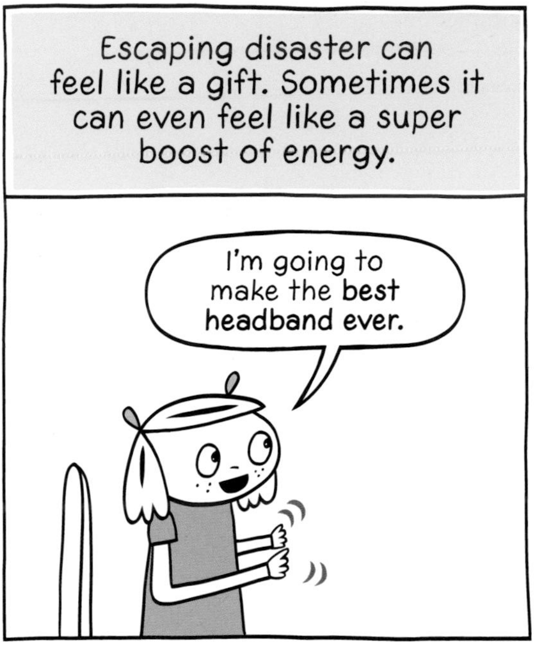
Escaping disaster can feel like a gift. Sometimes it can even feel like a super boost of energy.
I'm going to make the **best headband ever.**

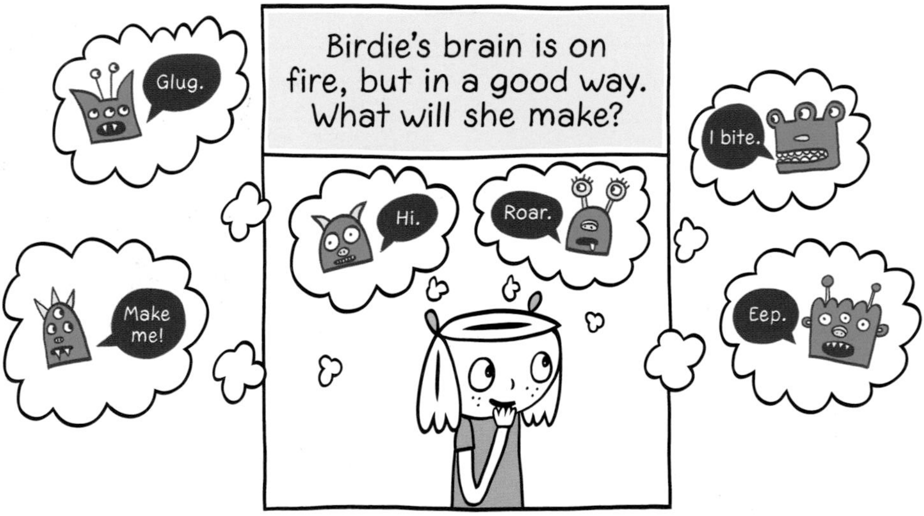
Birdie's brain is on fire, but in a good way. What will she make?
Glug.
I bite.
Hi.
Roar.
Make me!
Eep.

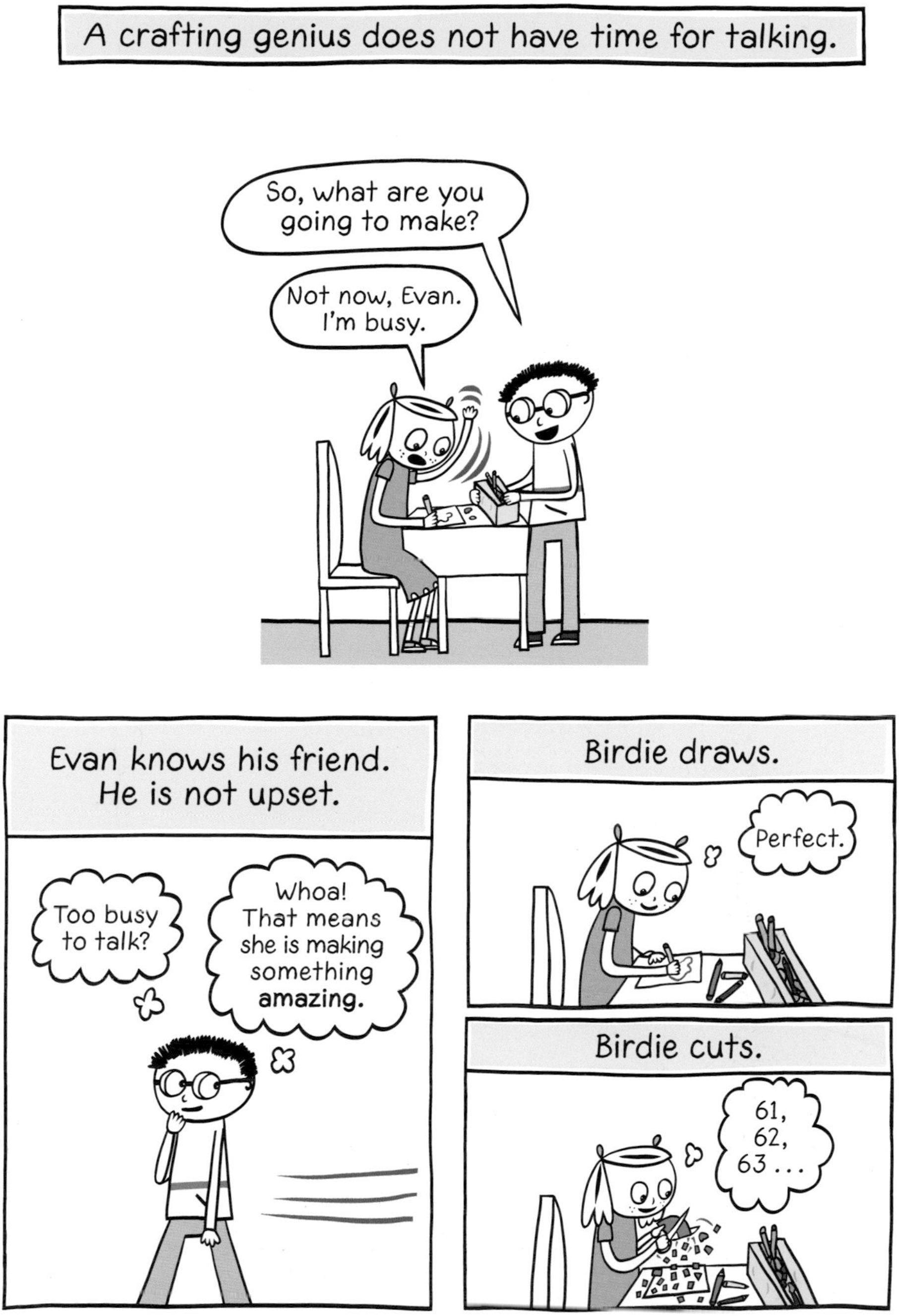
A crafting genius does not have time for talking.
So, what are you going to make?
Not now, Evan. I'm busy.
Evan knows his friend. He is not upset.
Too busy to talk?
Whoa! That means she is making something **amazing.**
Birdie draws.
Perfect.
Birdie cuts.
61, 62, 63 . . .

Birdie folds.
Not so easy.
Birdie glues.
My fingers are stuck.
Birdie colors.
Hello, monster.

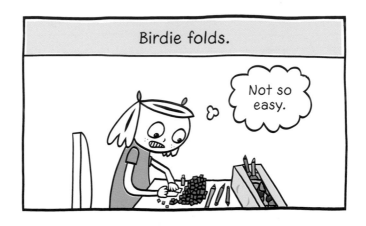

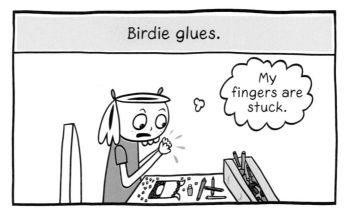

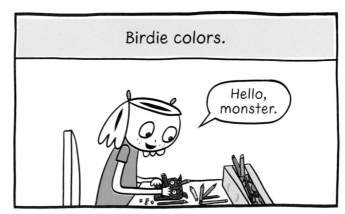

Congratulations, Birdie! The monster headband is a masterpiece.

BOING

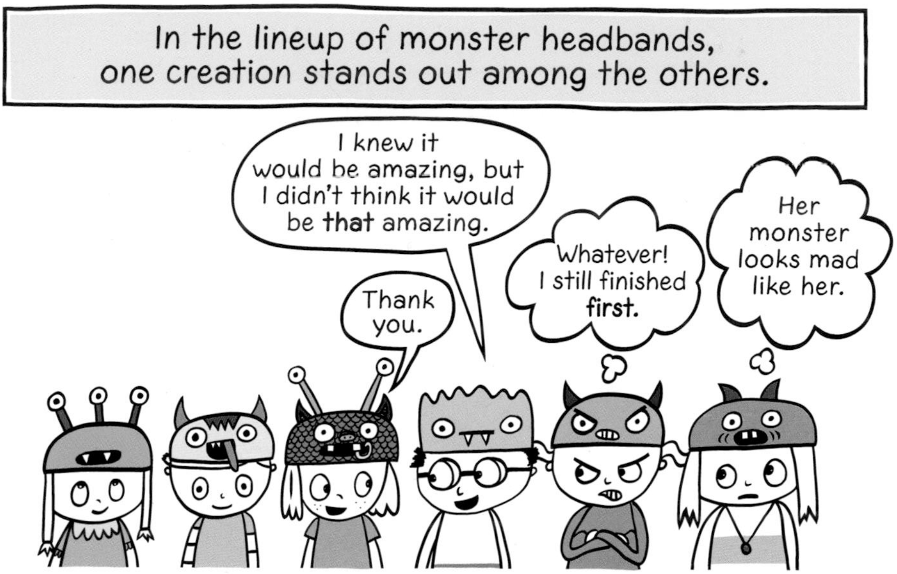
In the lineup of monster headbands, one creation stands out among the others.
I knew it would be amazing, but I didn't think it would be **that** amazing.
Thank you.
Whatever! I still finished **first.**
Her monster looks mad like her.

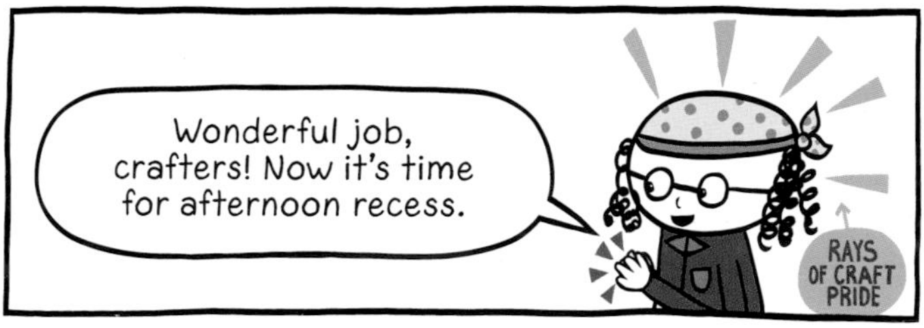
Wonderful job, crafters! Now it's time for afternoon recess.
RAYS OF CRAFT PRIDE

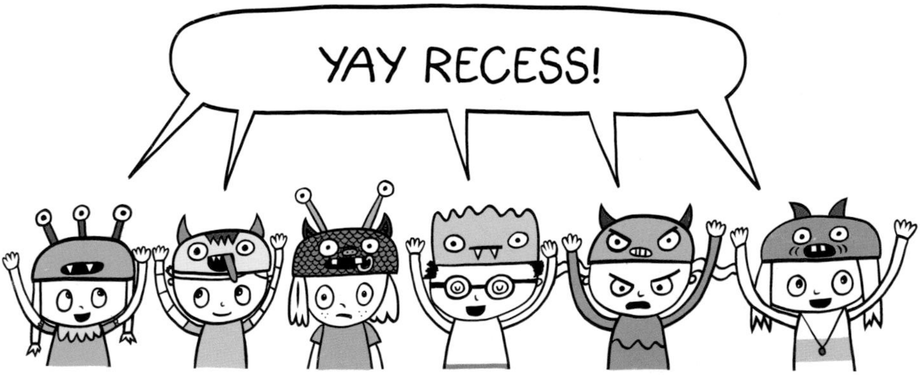
YAY RECESS!

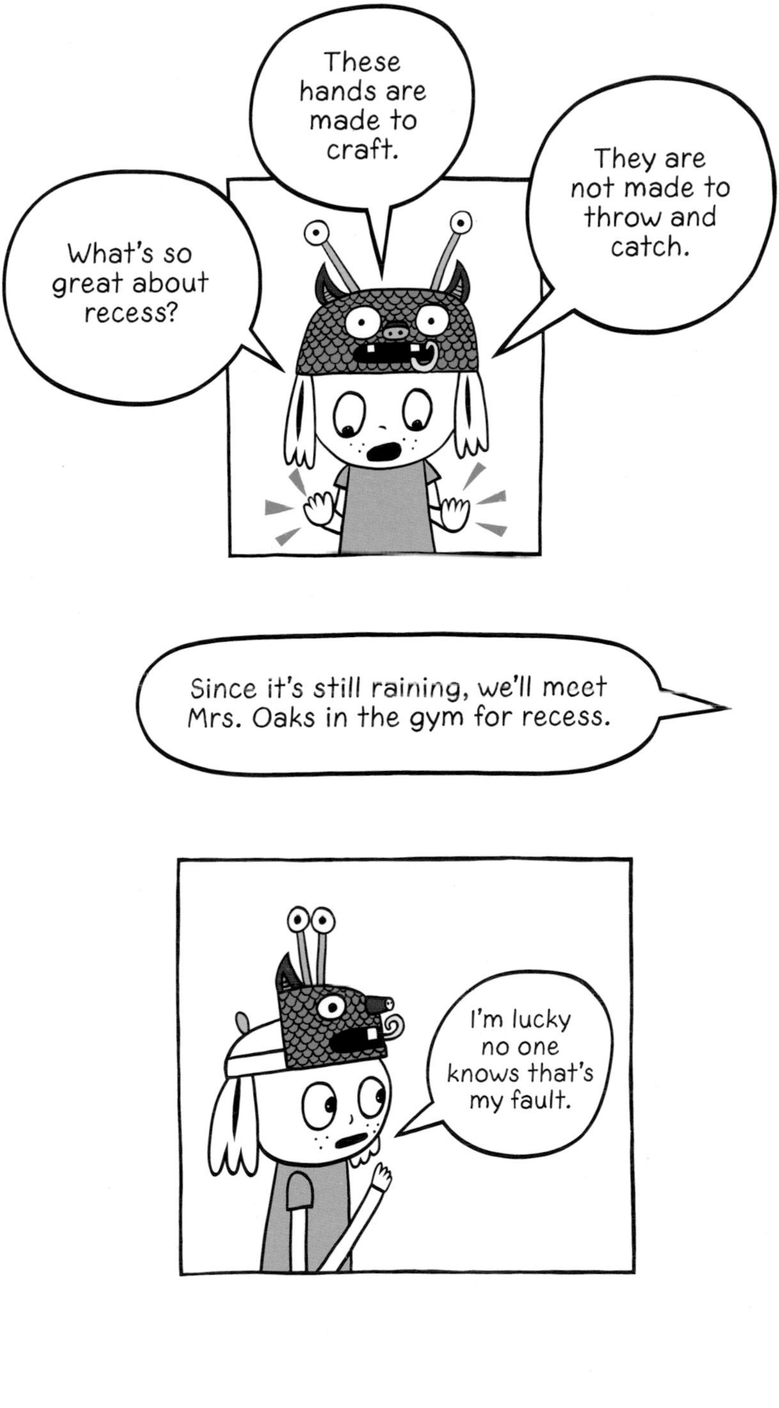
What's so great about recess?
These hands are made to craft.
They are not made to throw and catch.
Since it's still raining, we'll meet Mrs. Oaks in the gym for recess.
I'm lucky no one knows that's my fault.

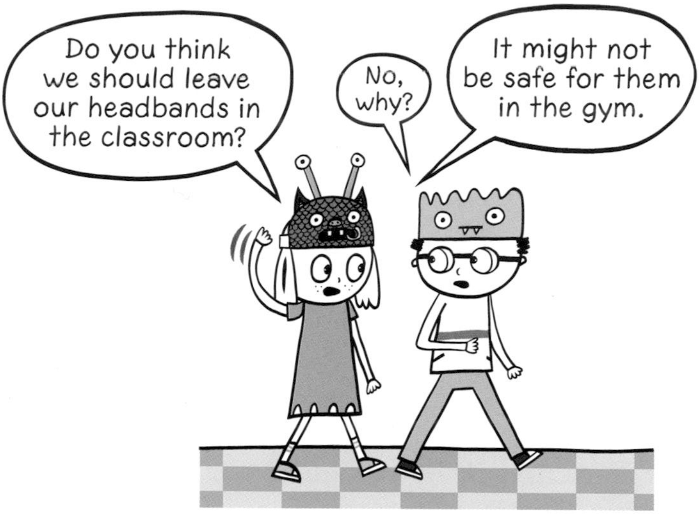
Do you think we should leave our headbands in the classroom?
No, why?
It might not be safe for them in the gym.

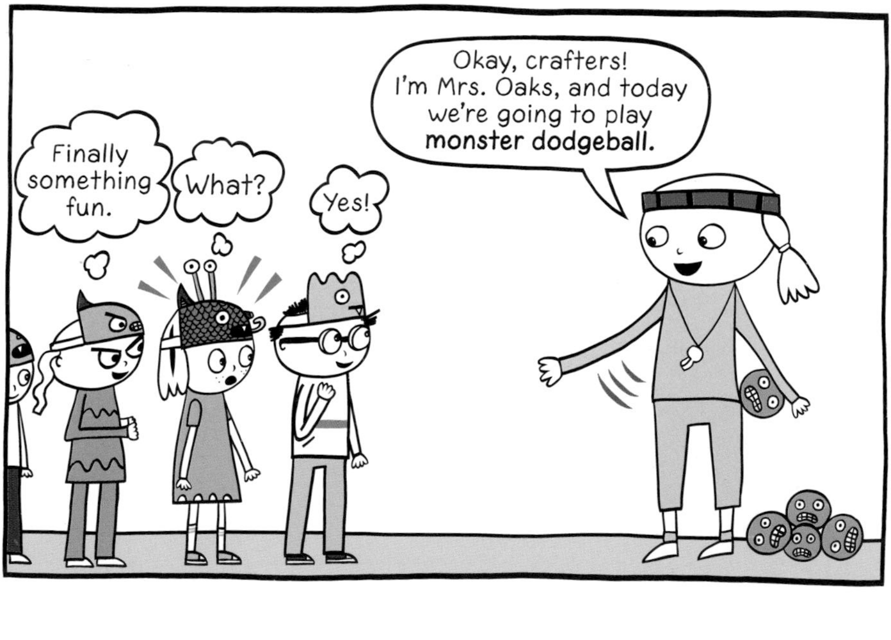
Okay, crafters! I'm Mrs. Oaks, and today we're going to play **monster dodgeball.**
Finally something fun.
What?
Yes!

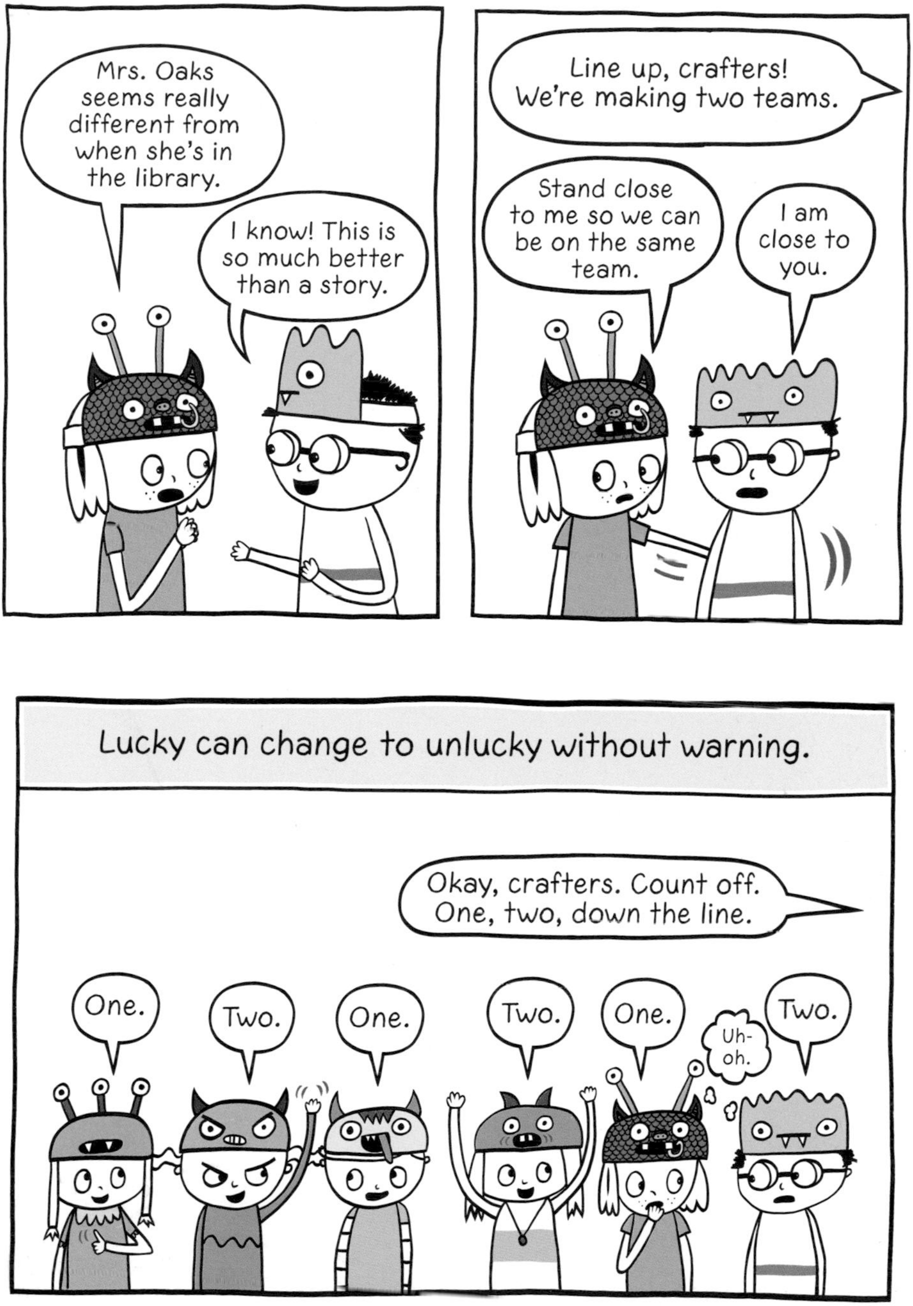
Mrs. Oaks seems really different from when she's in the library.
I know! This is so much better than a story.
Line up, crafters! We're making two teams.
Stand close to me so we can be on the same team.
I am close to you.
Lucky can change to unlucky without warning.
Okay, crafters. Count off. One, two, down the line.
One.
Two.
One.
Two.
One.
Uh-oh.
Two.

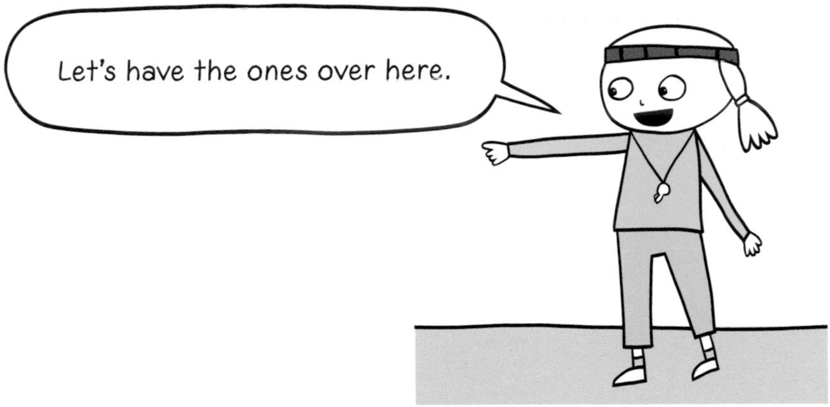
Let's have the ones over here.

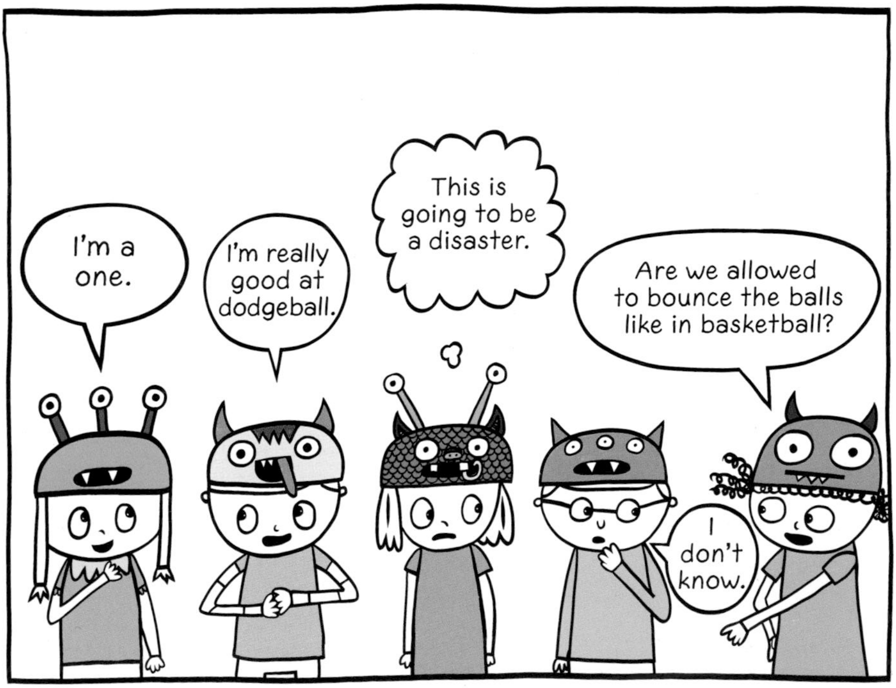
I'm a one.
I'm really good at dodgeball.
This is going to be a disaster.
Are we allowed to bounce the balls like in basketball?
I don't know.

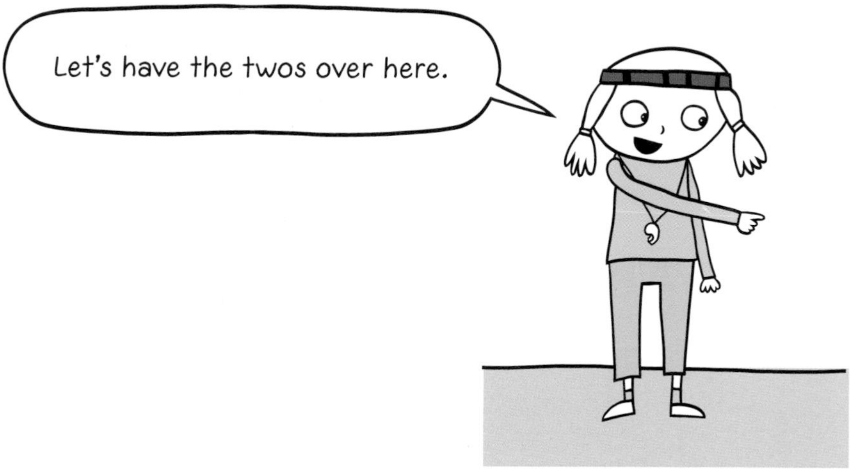
Let's have the twos over here.

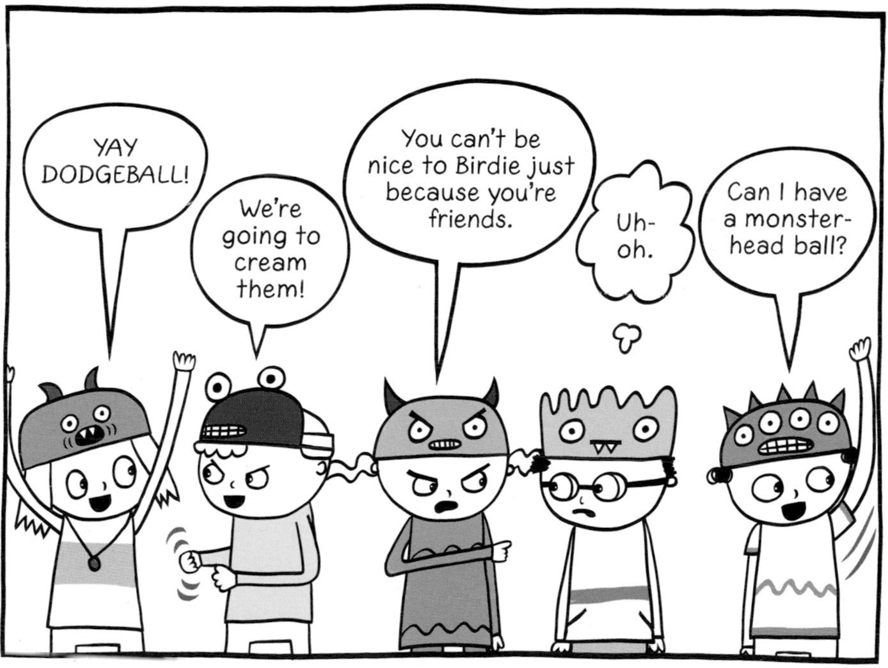
YAY DODGEBALL!
We're going to cream them!
You can't be nice to Birdie just because you're friends.
Uh-oh.
Can I have a monster-head ball?

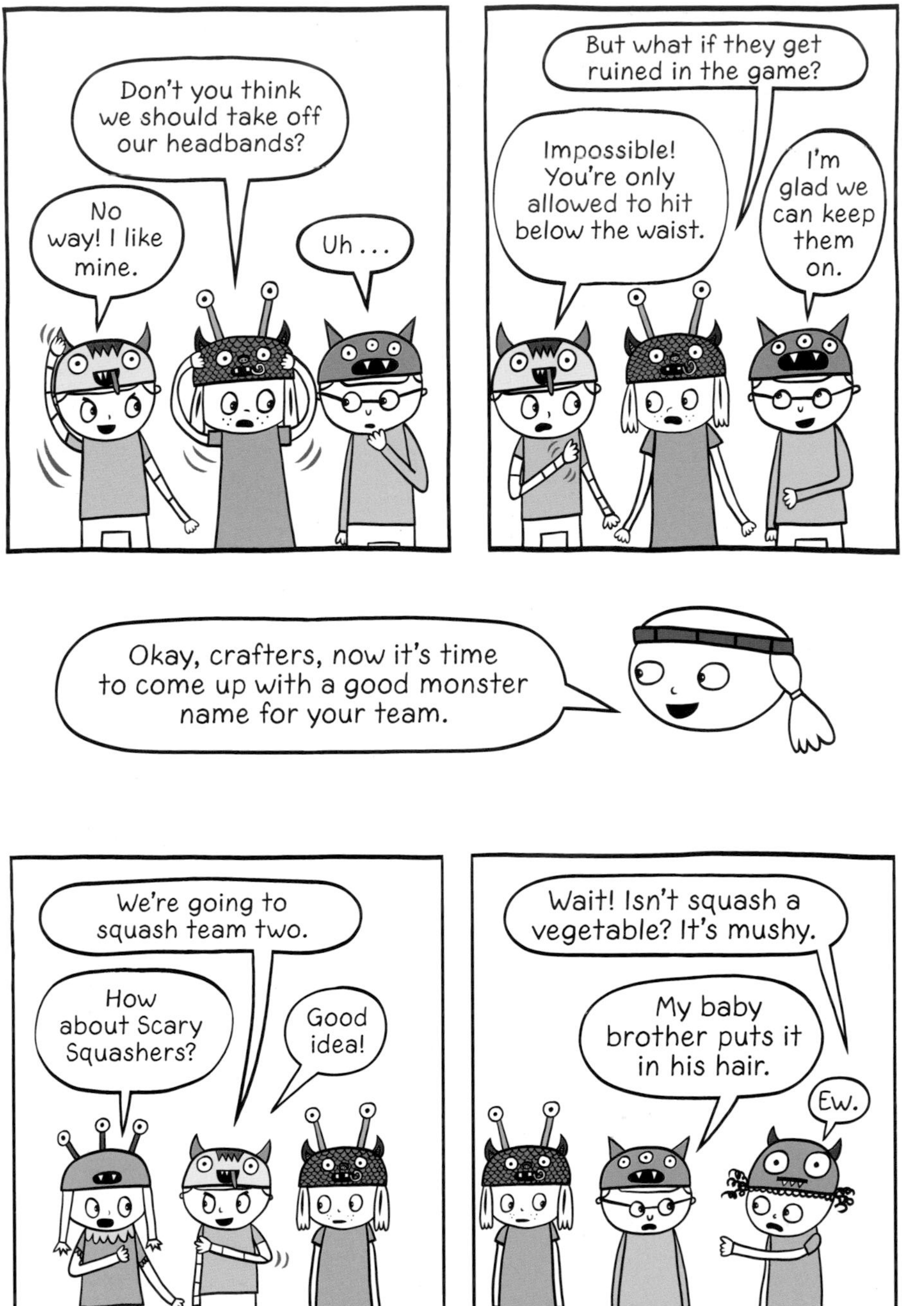
Don't you think we should take off our headbands?
No way! I like mine.
Uh . . .
But what if they get ruined in the game?
Impossible! You're only allowed to hit below the waist.
I'm glad we can keep them on.
Okay, crafters, now it's time to come up with a good monster name for your team.
We're going to squash team two.
How about Scary Squashers?
Good idea!
Wait! Isn't squash a vegetable? It's mushy.
My baby brother puts it in his hair.
Ew.

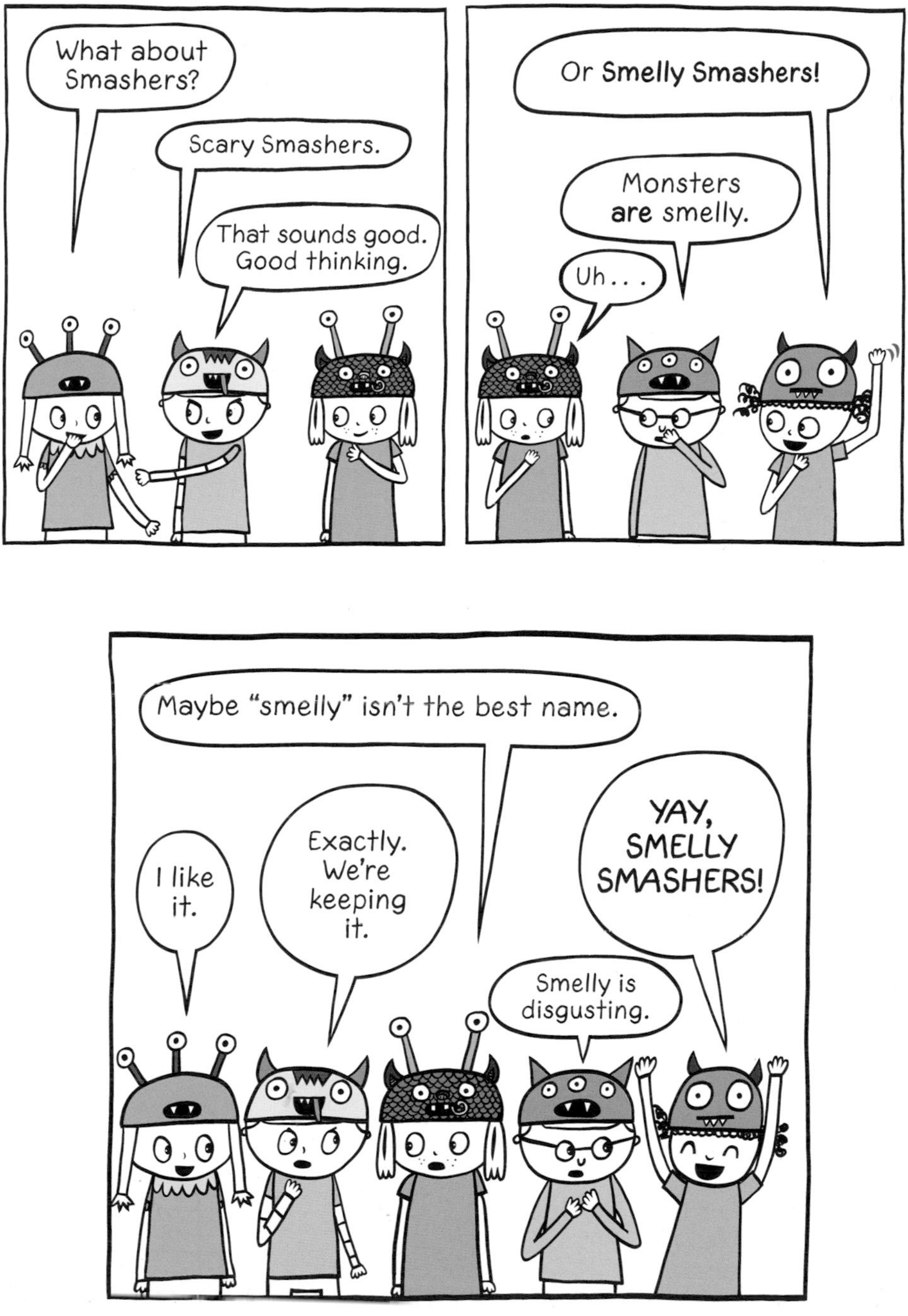
What about Smashers?
Scary Smashers.
That sounds good. Good thinking.
Or Smelly Smashers!
Monsters are smelly.
Uh . . .
Maybe "smelly" isn't the best name.
I like it.
Exactly. We're keeping it.
Smelly is disgusting.
YAY, SMELLY SMASHERS!

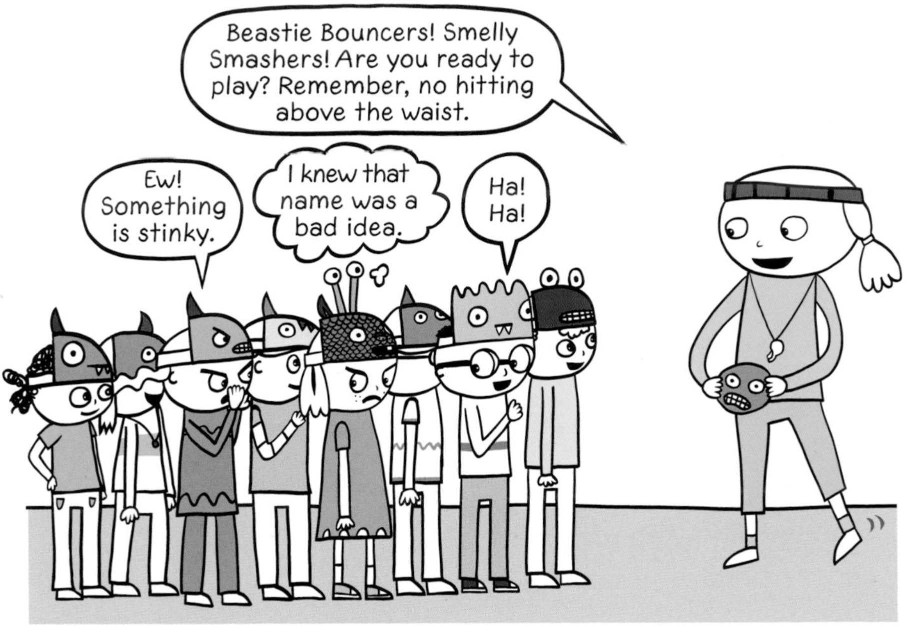
Beastie Bouncers! Smelly Smashers! Are you ready to play? Remember, no hitting above the waist.
Ew! Something is stinky.
I knew that name was a bad idea.
Ha! Ha!

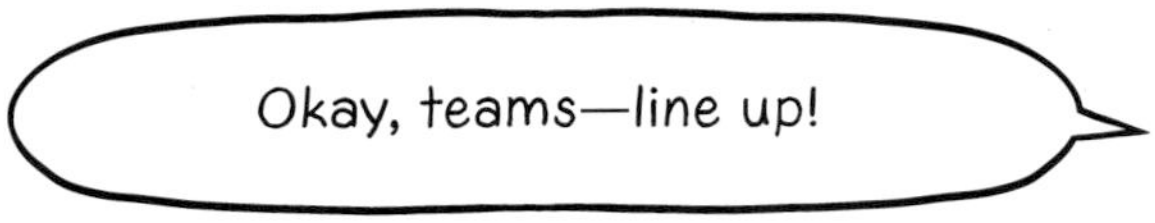
Okay, teams—line up!

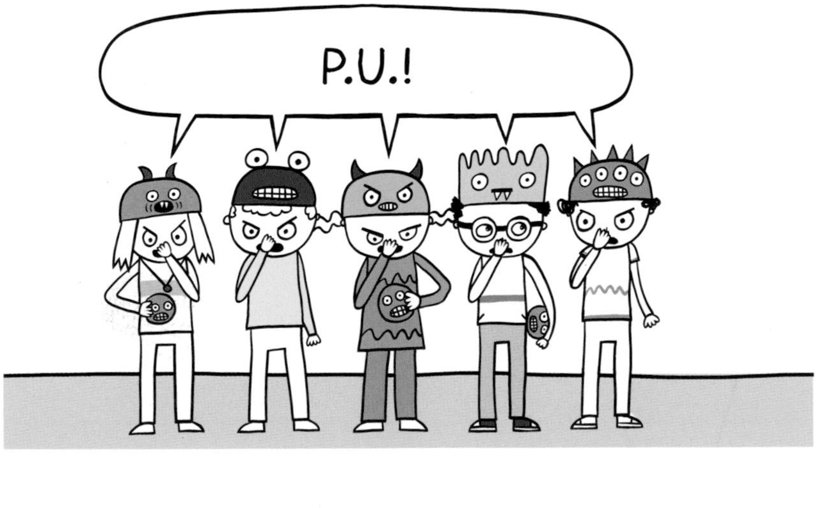
P.U.!

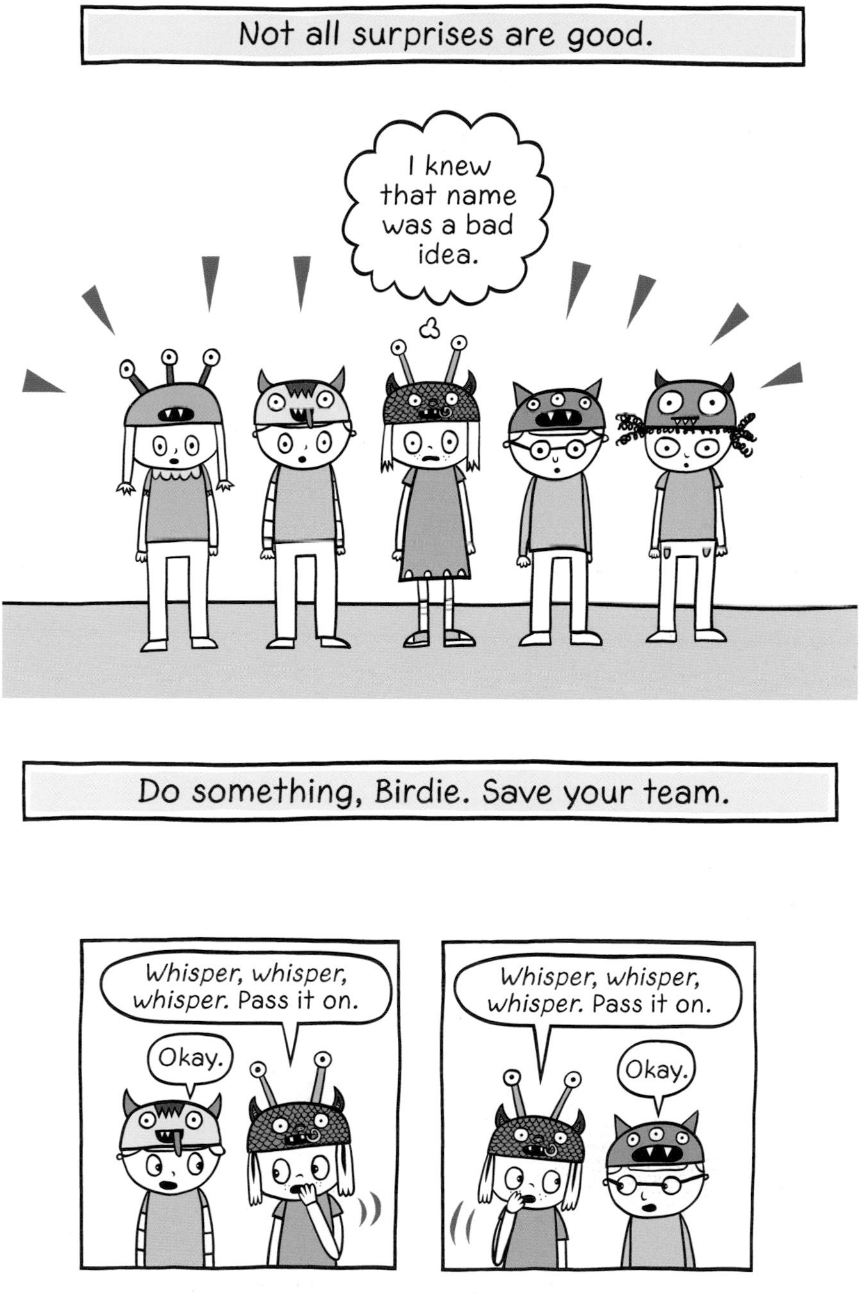
Not all surprises are good.
I knew that name was a bad idea.
Do something, Birdie. Save your team.
Whisper, whisper, whisper. Pass it on.
Okay.
Whisper, whisper, whisper. Pass it on.
Okay.

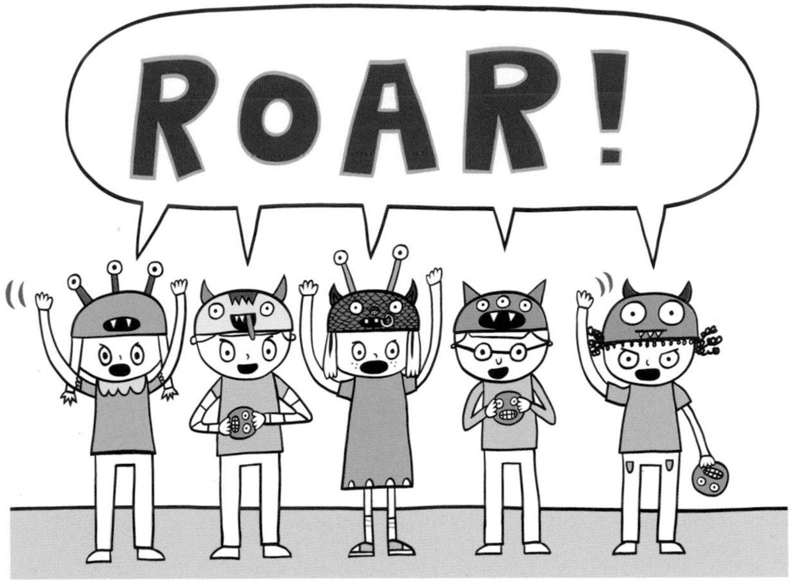
ROAR!

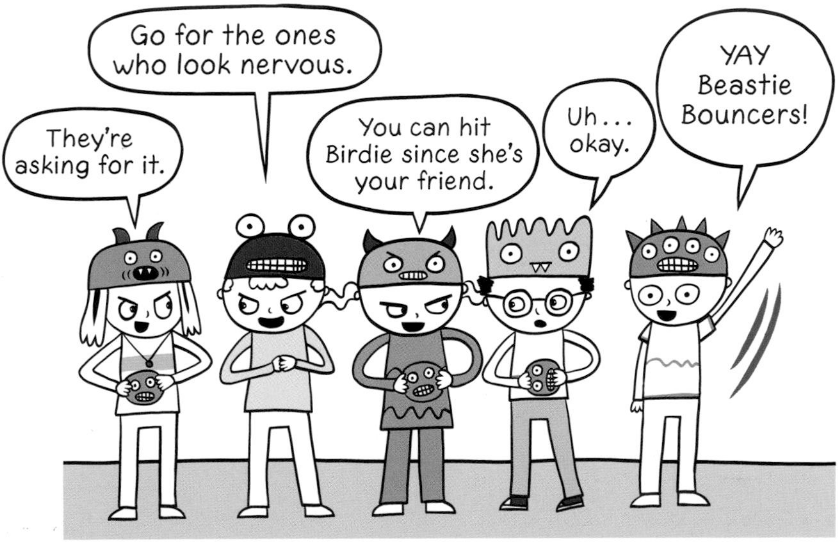
They're asking for it.
Go for the ones who look nervous.
You can hit Birdie since she's your friend.
Uh... okay.
YAY Beastie Bouncers!

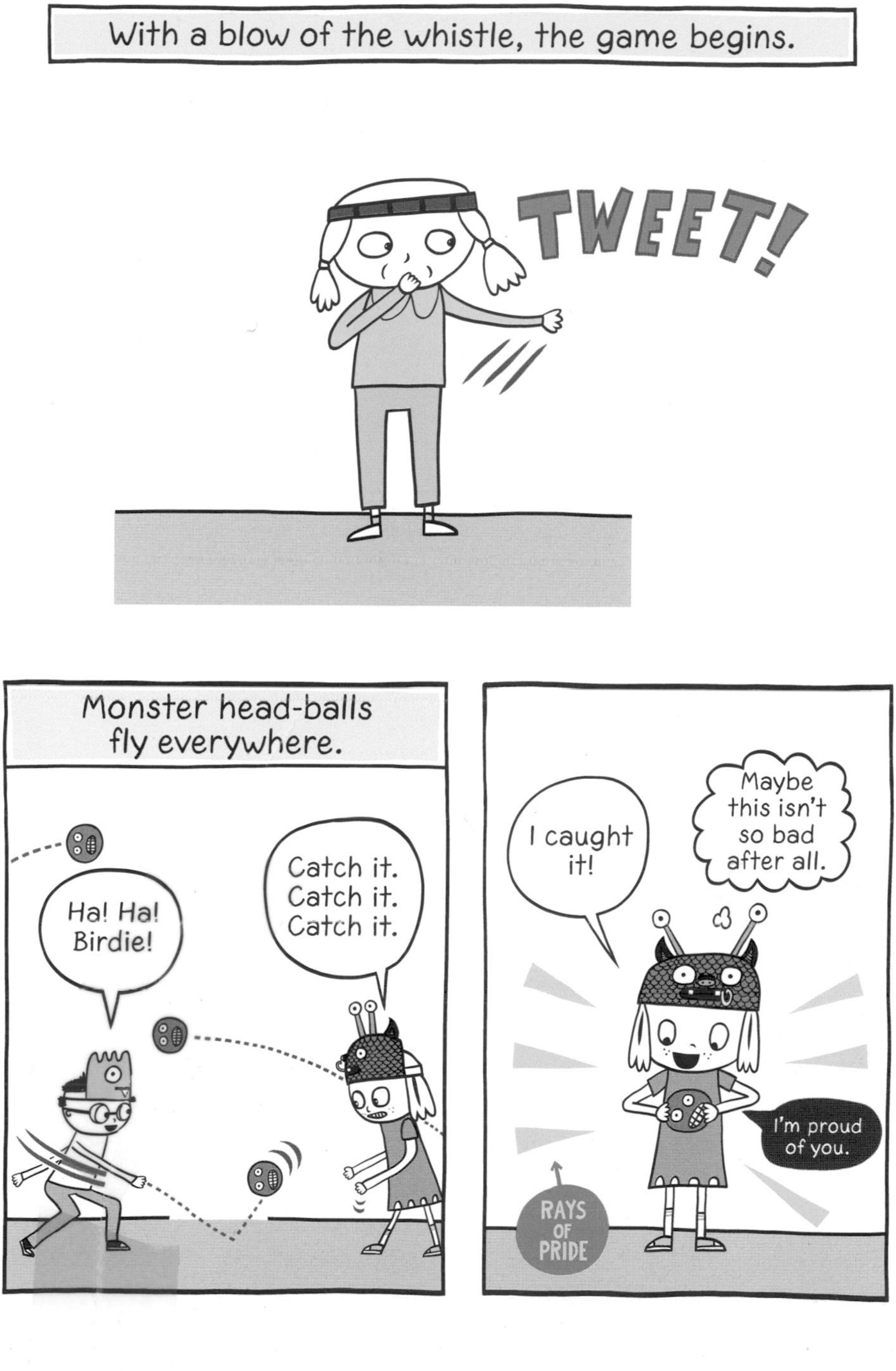
With a blow of the whistle, the game begins.
TWEET!
Monster head-balls fly everywhere.
Ha! Ha! Birdie!
Catch it. Catch it. Catch it.
I caught it!
Maybe this isn't so bad after all.
I'm proud of you.
RAYS OF PRIDE

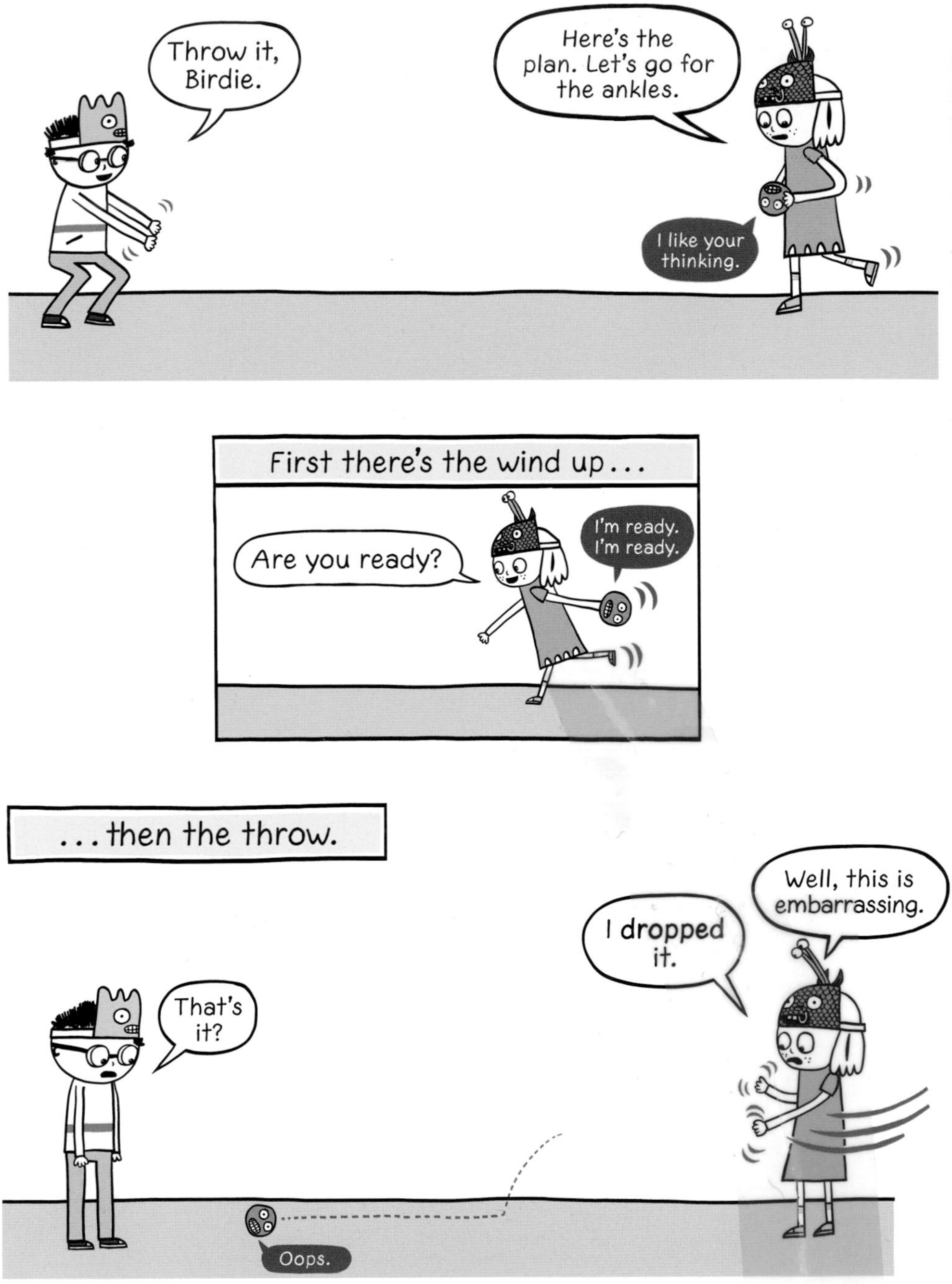
Throw it, Birdie.
Here's the plan. Let's go for the ankles.
I like your thinking.
First there's the wind up...
Are you ready?
I'm ready. I'm ready.
...then the throw.
That's it?
I dropped it.
Well, this is embarrassing.
Oops.

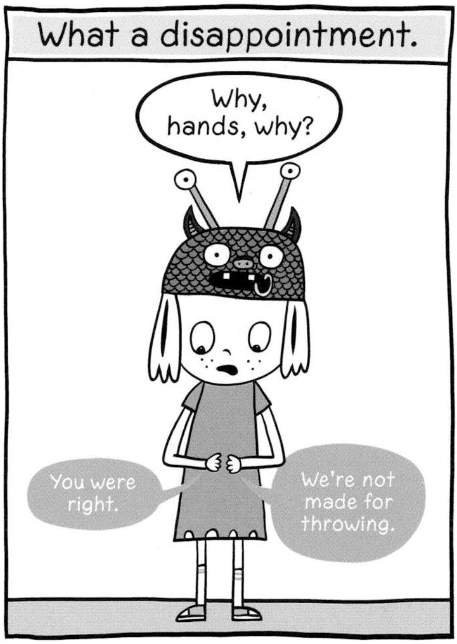
What a disappointment.
Why, hands, why?
You were right.
We're not made for throwing.

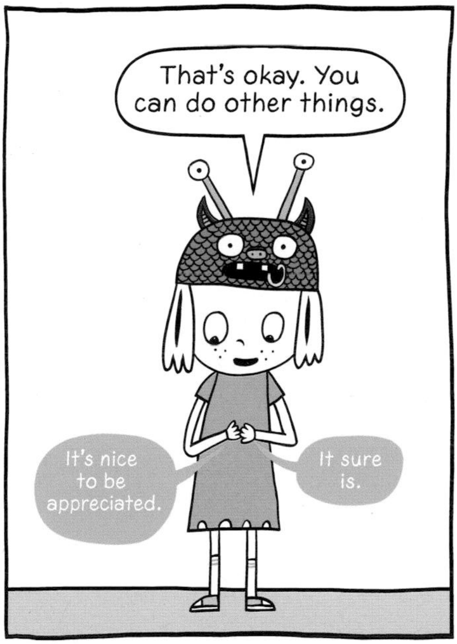
That's okay. You can do other things.
It's nice to be appreciated.
It sure is.

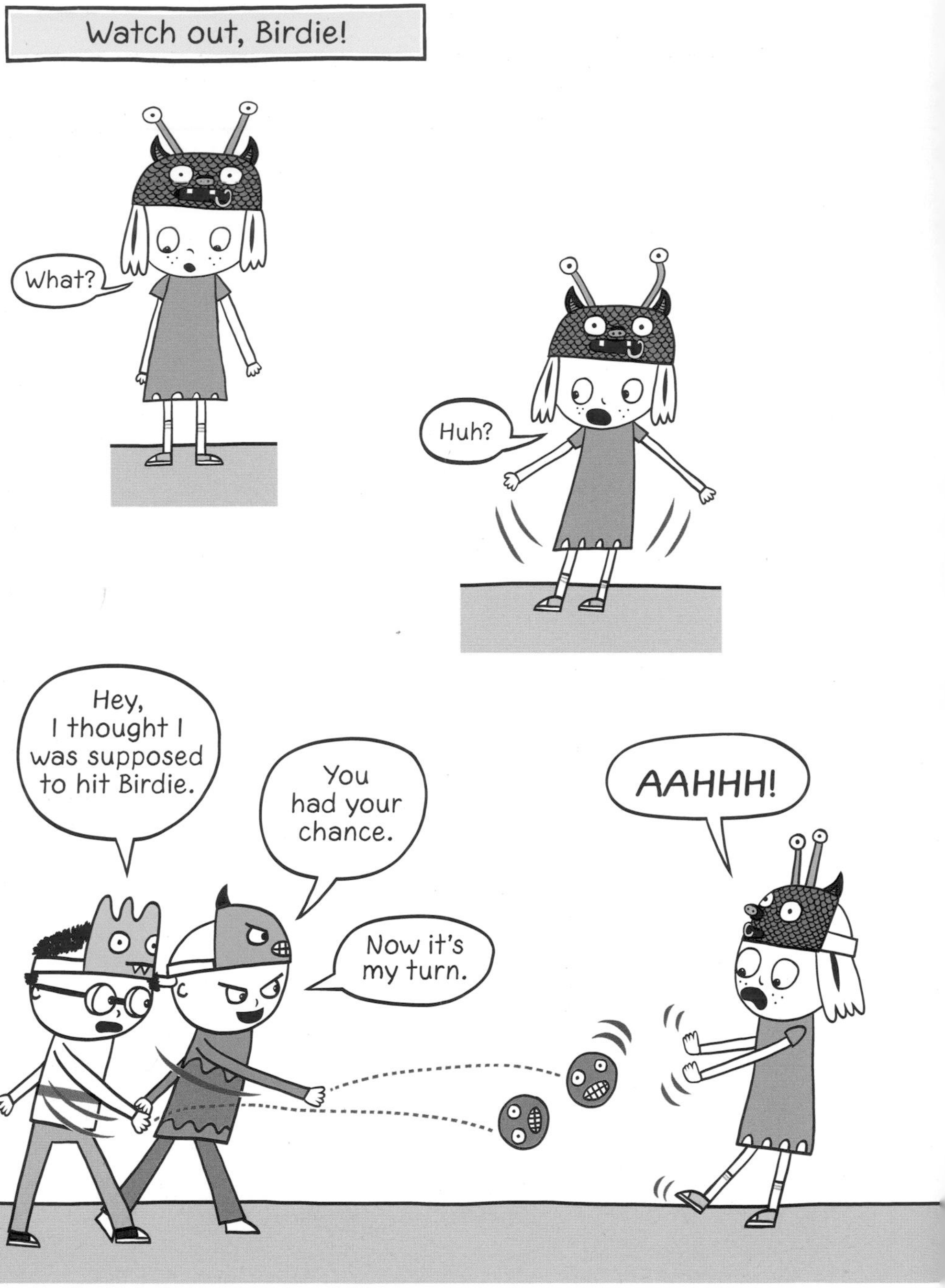

Watch out, Birdie!
What?
Huh?
Hey, I thought I was supposed to hit Birdie.
You had your chance.
Now it's my turn.
AAHHH!

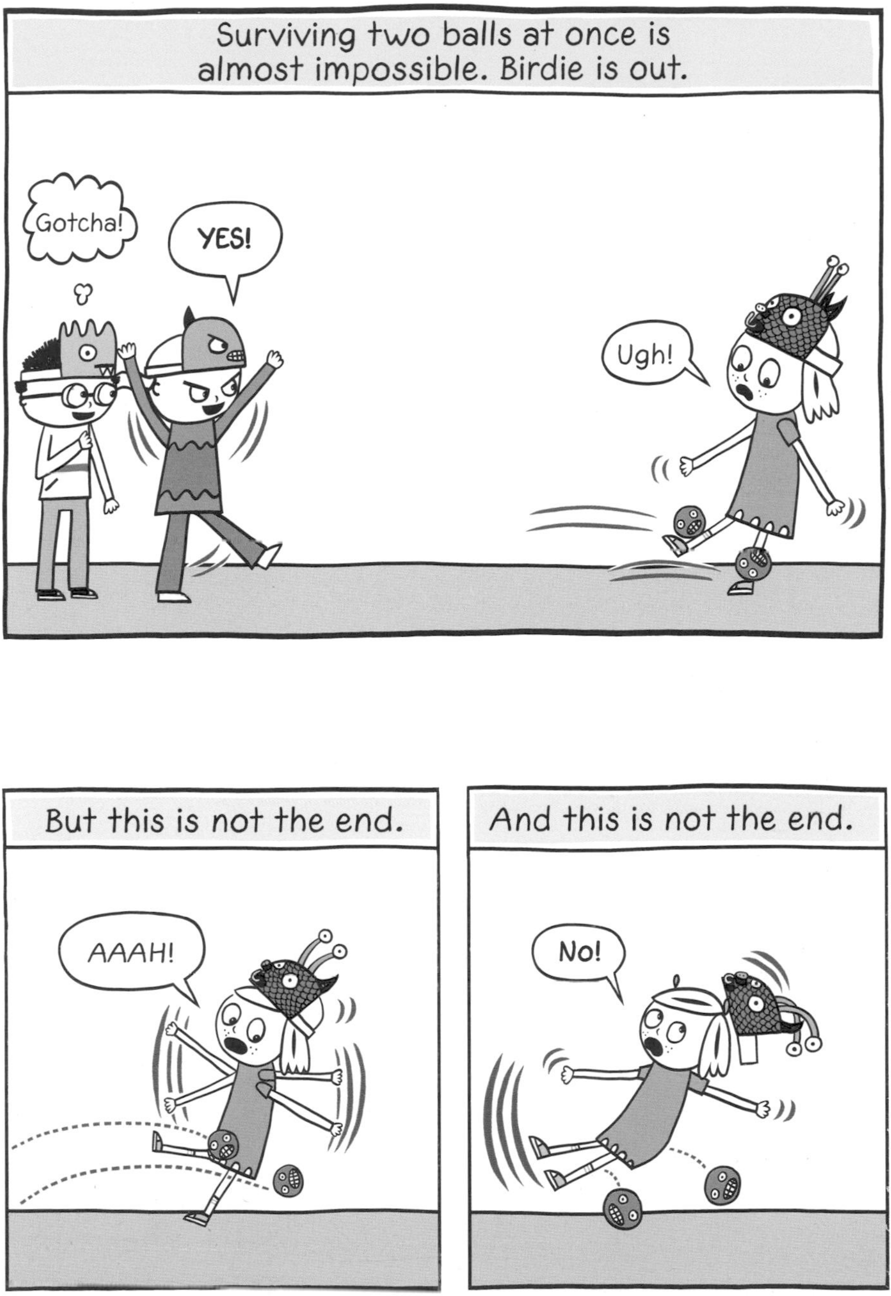
Surviving two balls at once is almost impossible. Birdie is out.
Gotcha!
YES!
Ugh!
But this is not the end.
AAAH!
And this is not the end.
No!

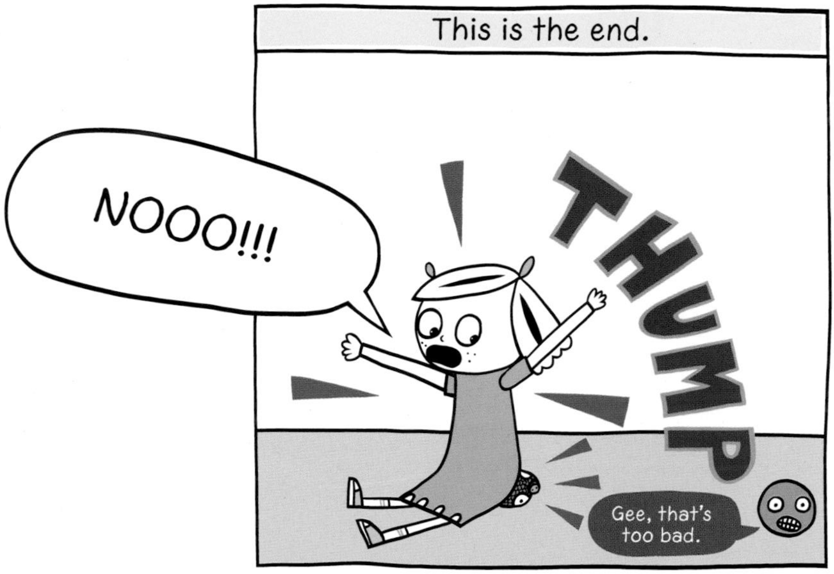
This is the end.
NOOO!!!
THUMP
Gee, that's too bad.

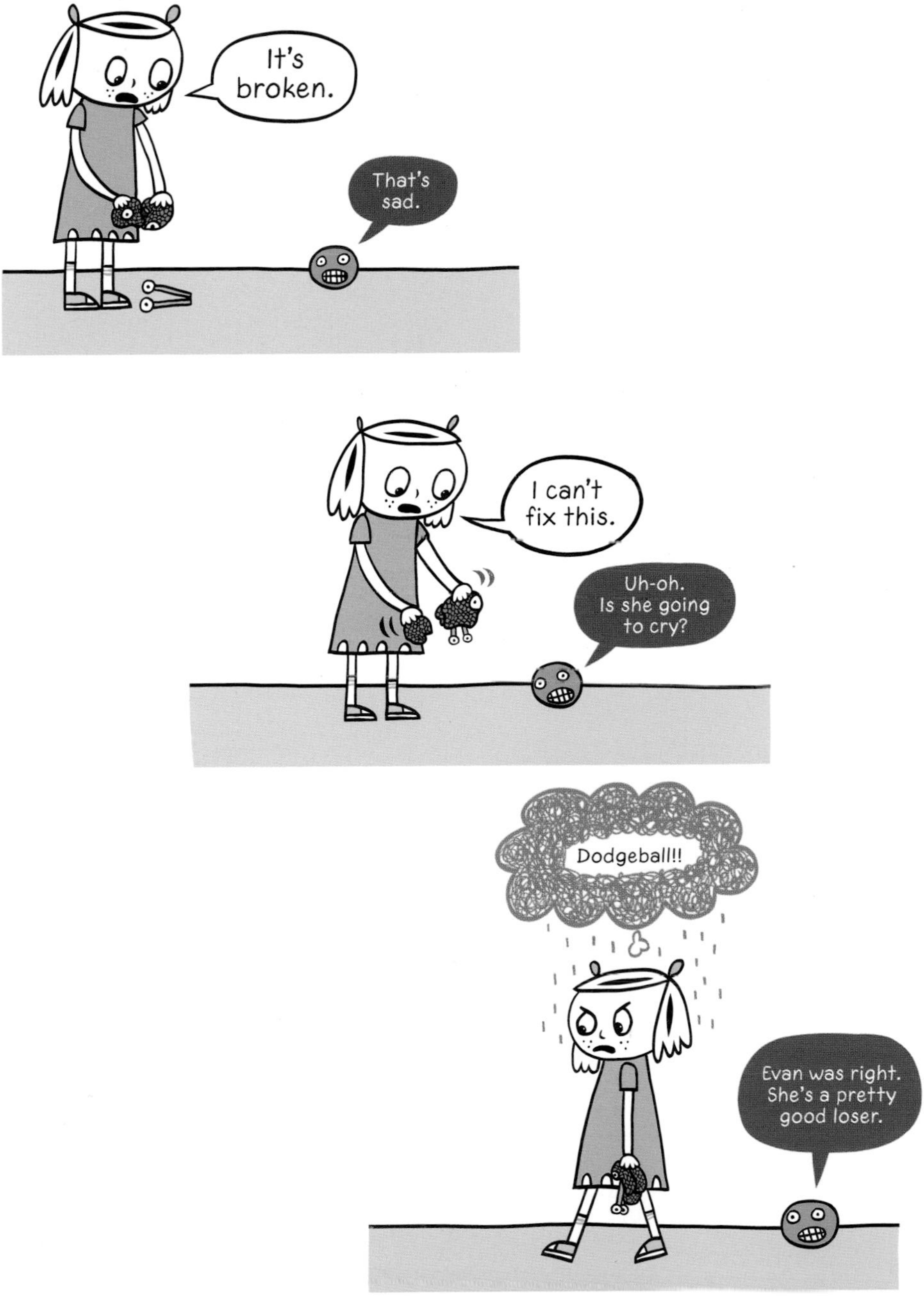
It's broken.
That's sad.
I can't fix this.
Uh-oh. Is she going to cry?
Dodgeball!!
Evan was right. She's a pretty good loser.

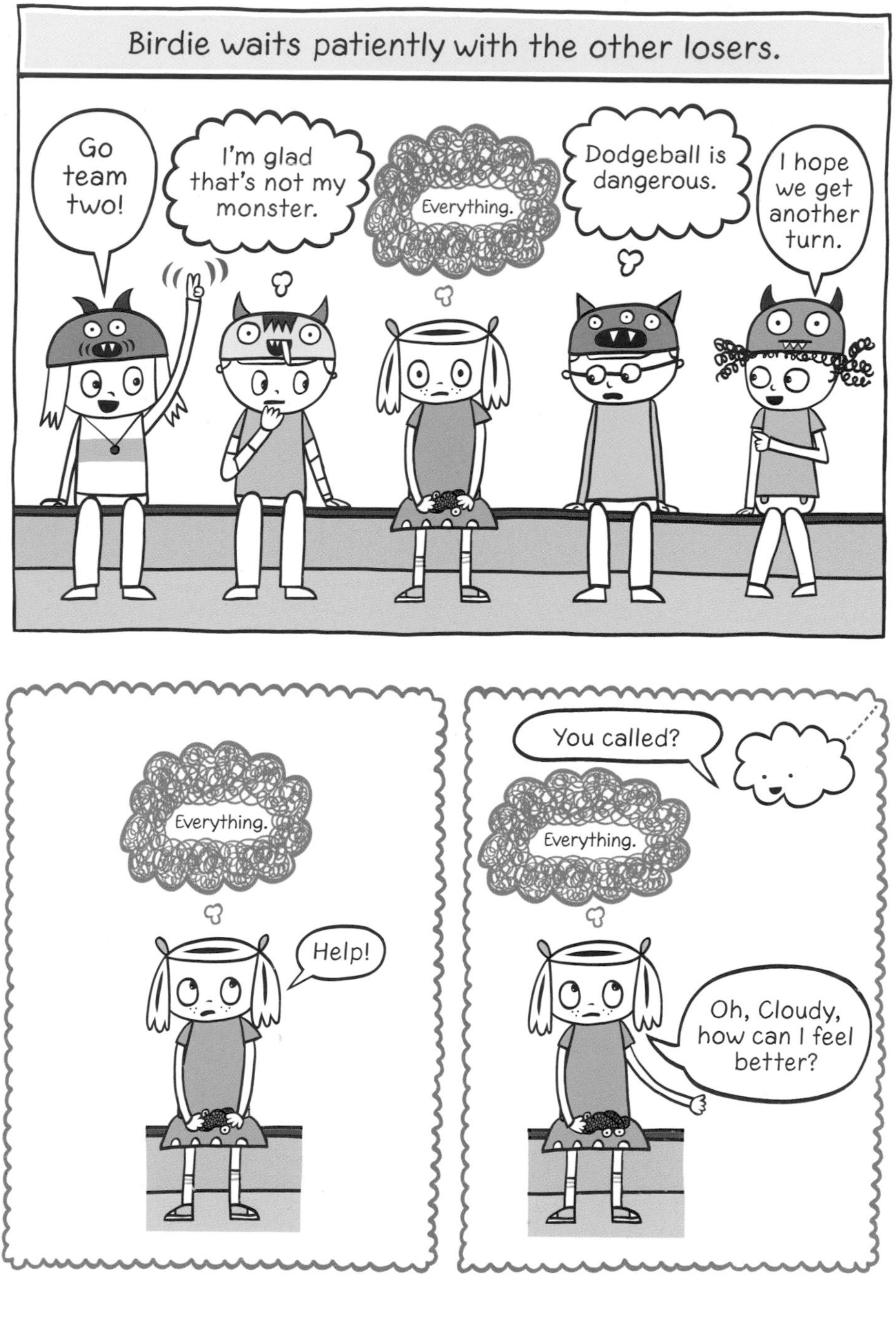
Birdie waits patiently with the other losers.
Go team two!
I'm glad that's not my monster.
Everything.
Dodgeball is dangerous.
I hope we get another turn.
Everything.
Help!
You called?
Everything.
Oh, Cloudy, how can I feel better?

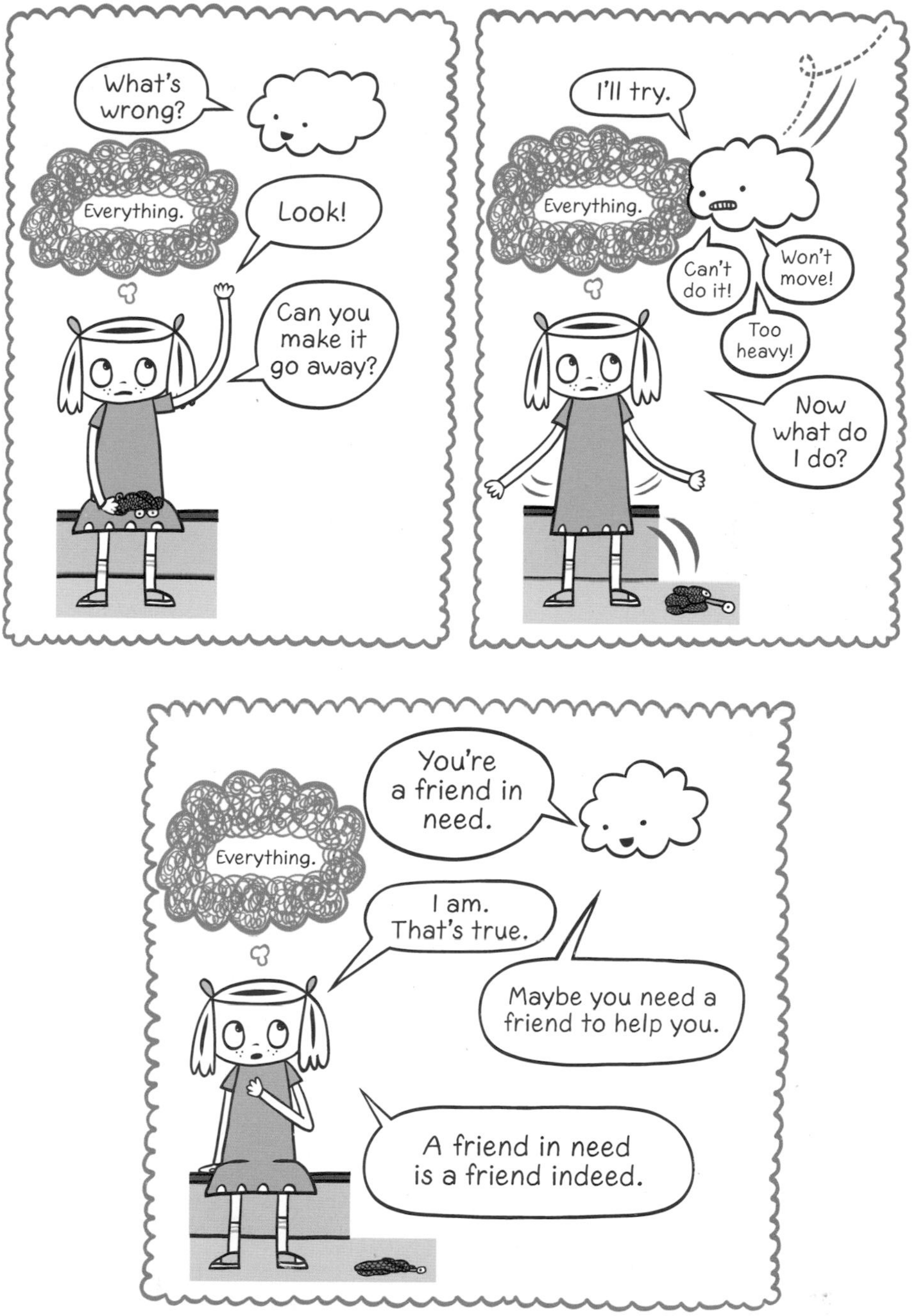
What's wrong?
Everything.
Look!
Can you make it go away?
I'll try.
Everything.
Can't do it!
Won't move!
Too heavy!
Now what do I do?
You're a friend in need.
Everything.
I am. That's true.
Maybe you need a friend to help you.
A friend in need is a friend indeed.

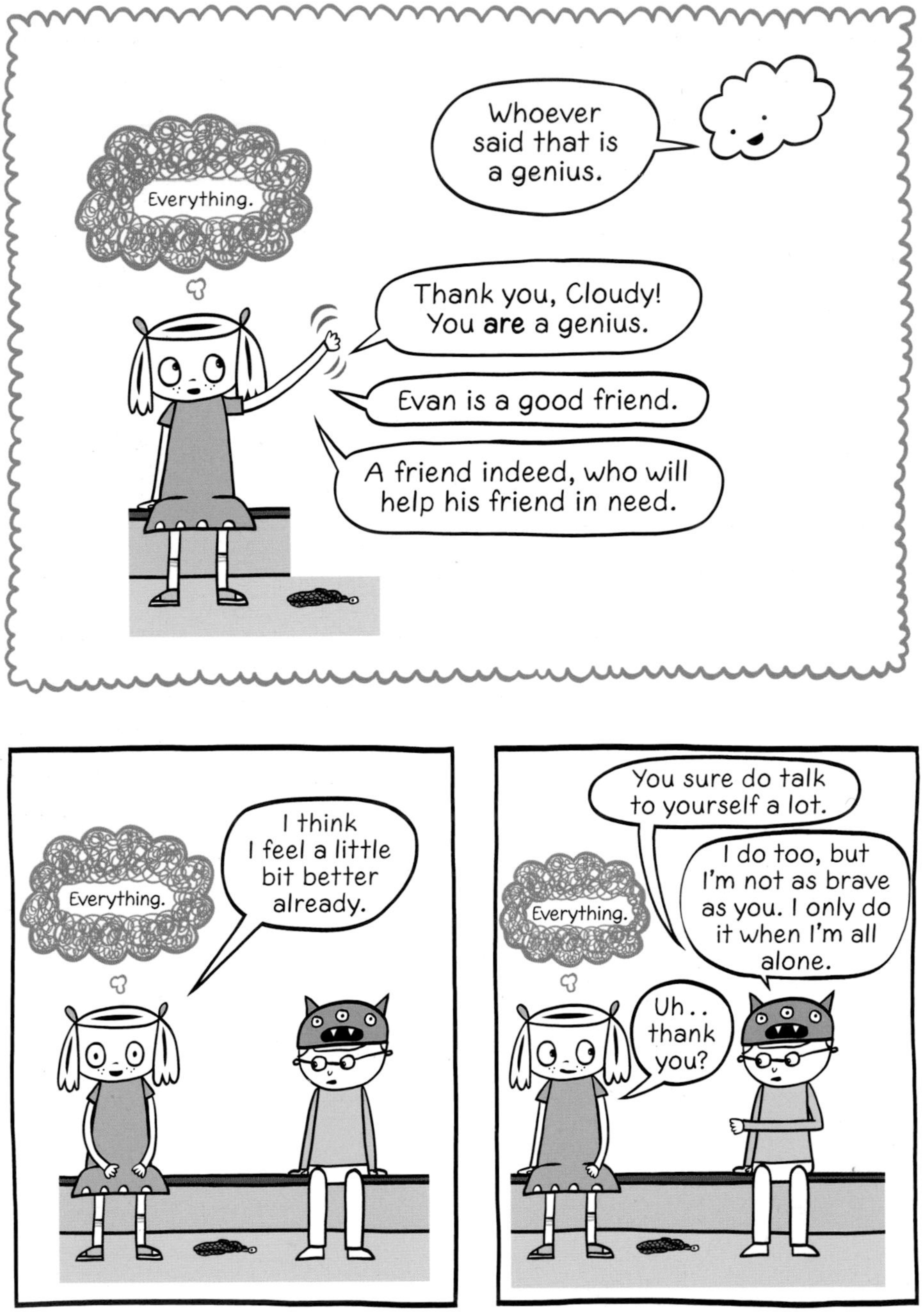

Everything.
Whoever said that is a genius.
Thank you, Cloudy! You **are** a genius.
Evan is a good friend.
A friend indeed, who will help his friend in need.
Everything.
I think I feel a little bit better already.
Everything.
You sure do talk to yourself a lot.
Uh.. thank you?
I do too, but I'm not as brave as you. I only do it when I'm all alone.

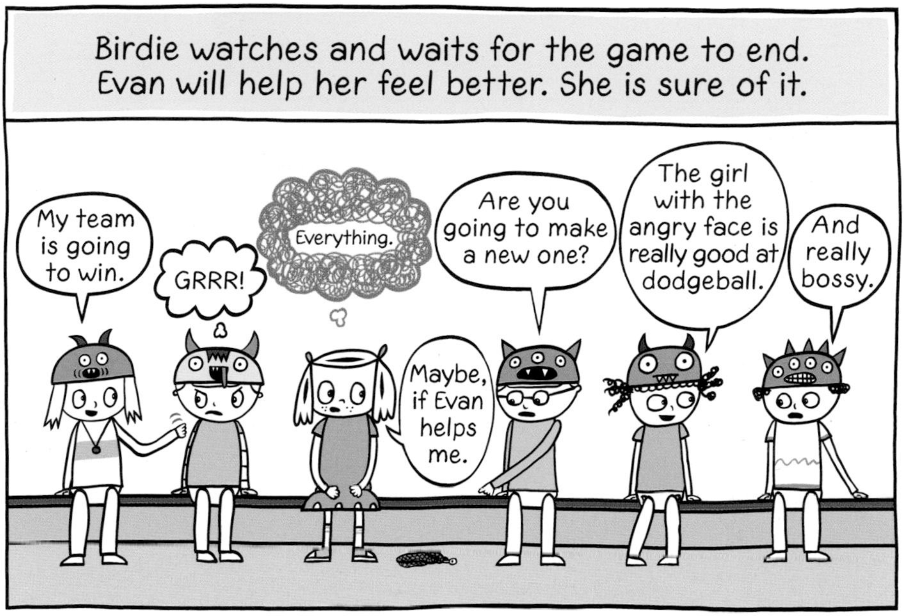
Birdie watches and waits for the game to end.
Evan will help her feel better. She is sure of it.
My team is going to win.
GRRR!
Everything.
Are you going to make a new one?
Maybe, if Evan helps me.
The girl with the angry face is really good at dodgeball.
And really bossy.

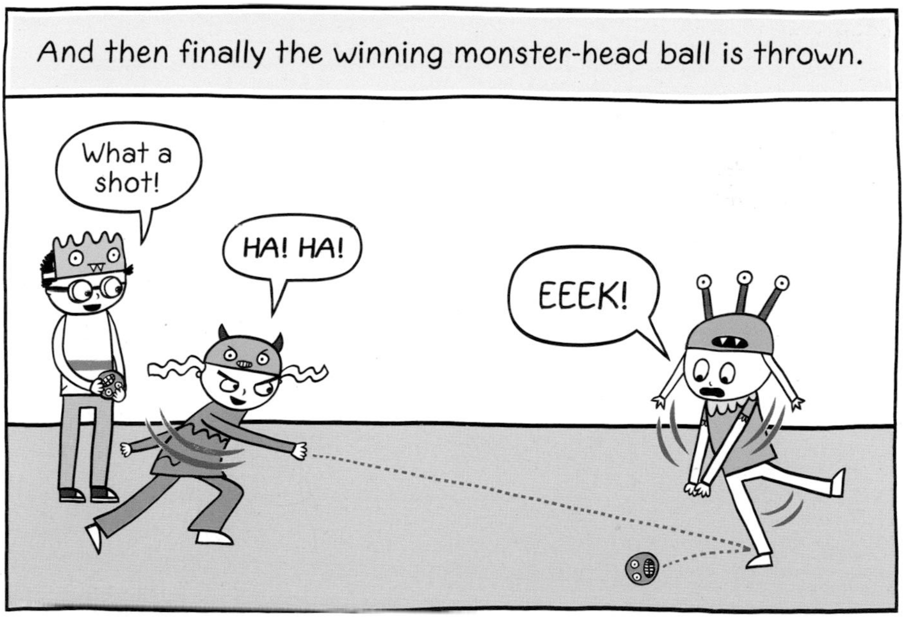
And then finally the winning monster-head ball is thrown.
What a shot!
HA! HA!
EEEK!

The gym is filed with happy exclamations.

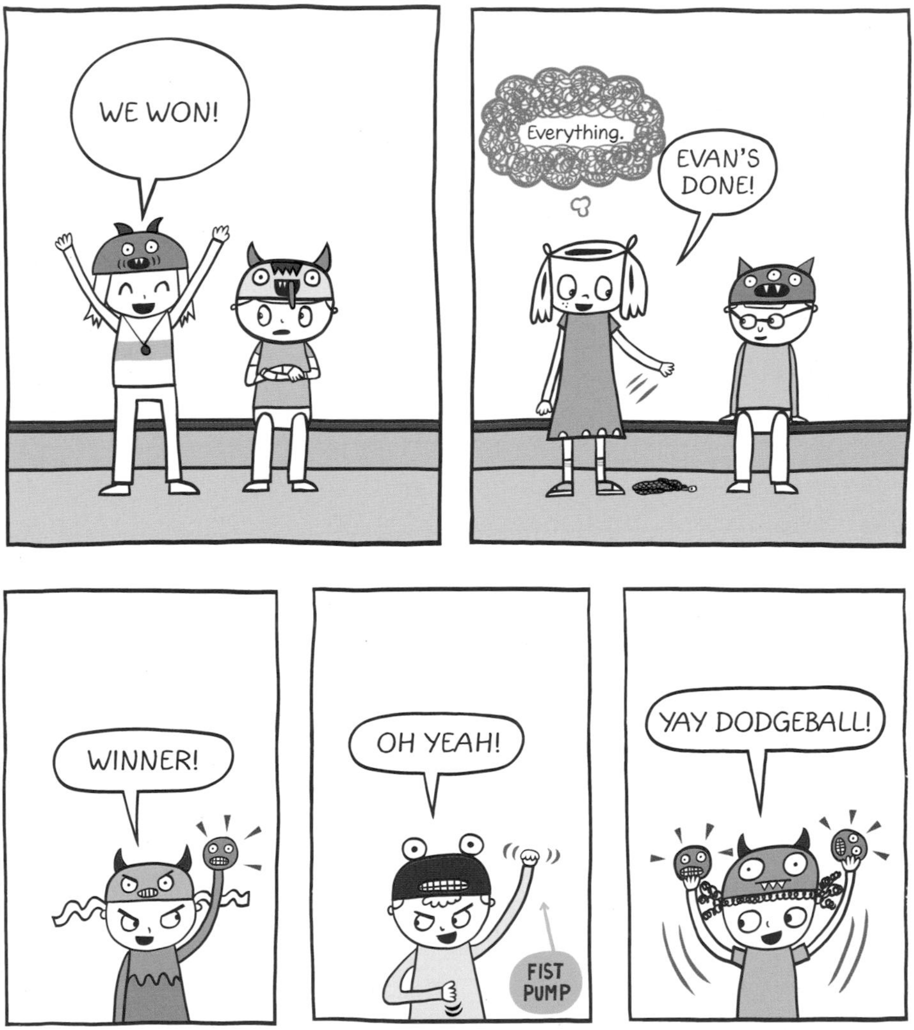
WE WON!
Everything.
EVAN'S DONE!
WINNER!
OH YEAH!
FIST PUMP
YAY DODGEBALL!

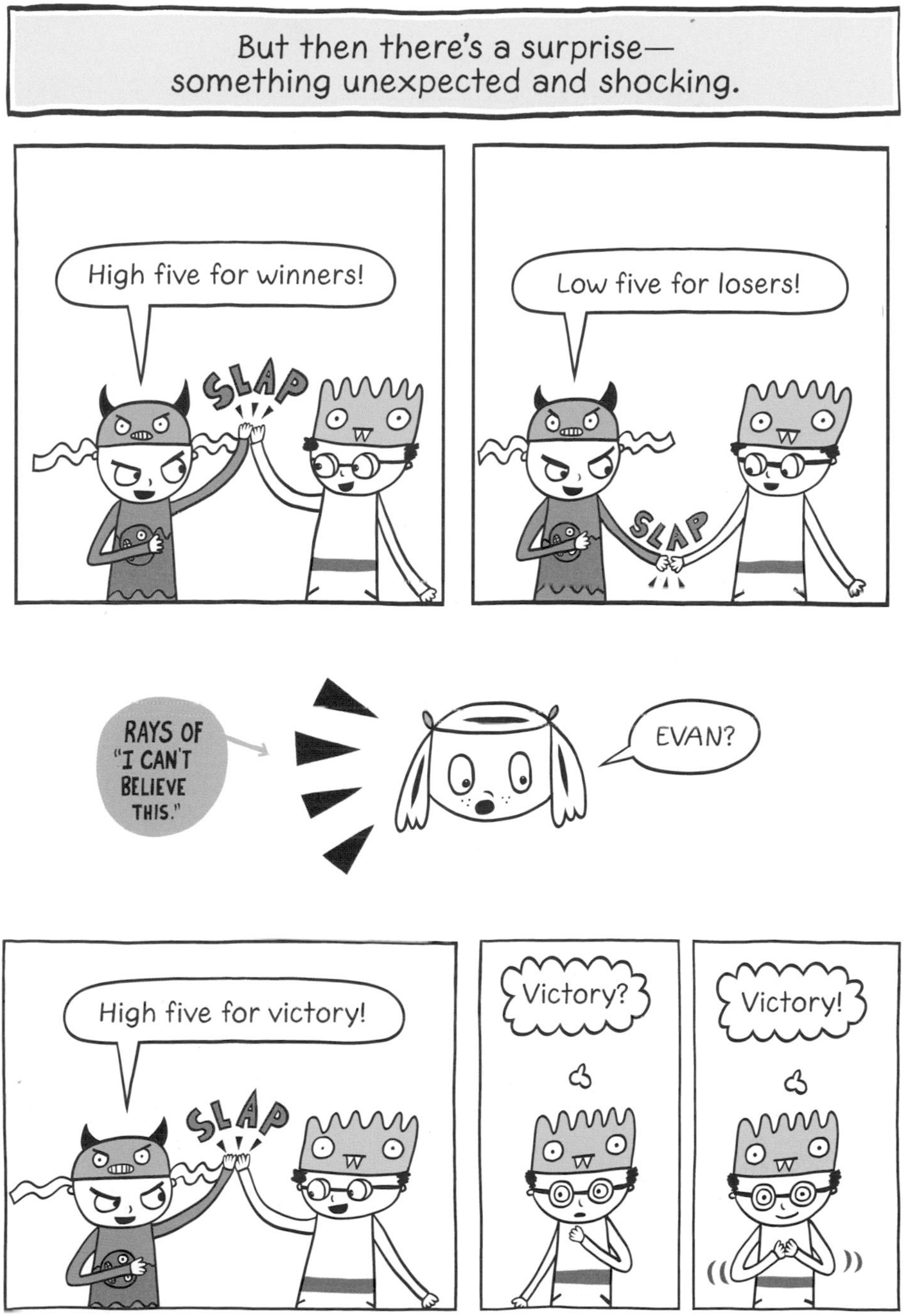
But then there's a surprise—something unexpected and shocking.
High five for winners!
SLAP
Low five for losers!
SLAP
RAYS OF "I CAN'T BELIEVE THIS."
EVAN?
High five for victory!
SLAP
Victory?
Victory!

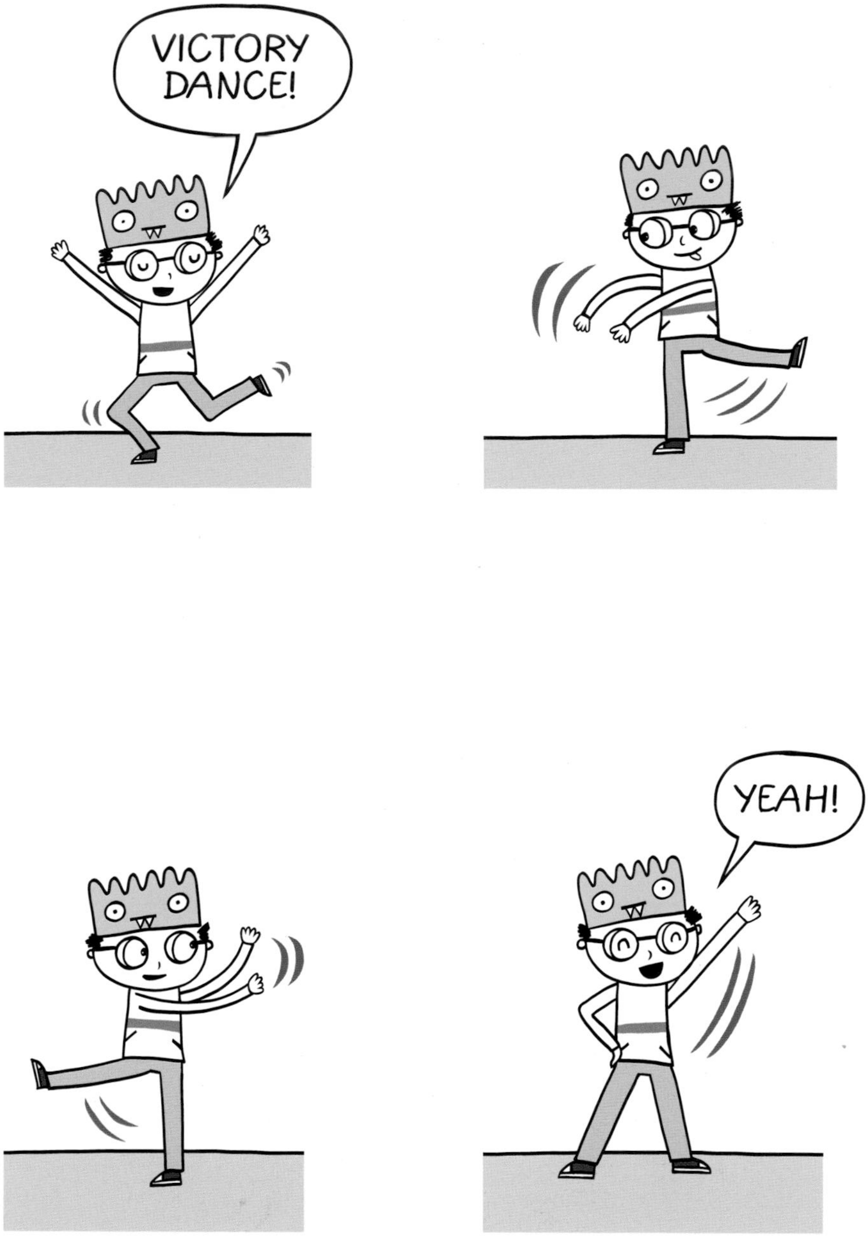
VICTORY DANCE!
YEAH!

Birdie can't believe what is happening.
My headband is broken.
I am sad.
Evan is doing a Victory Dance.
And then the pieces fit together.
Evan doesn't care about me!
BOO HOO
BOO HOO

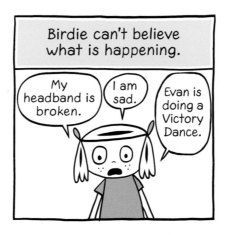

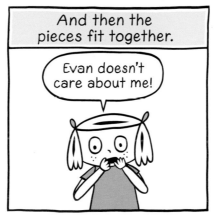

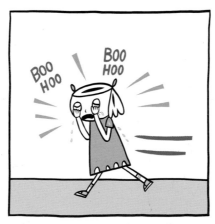

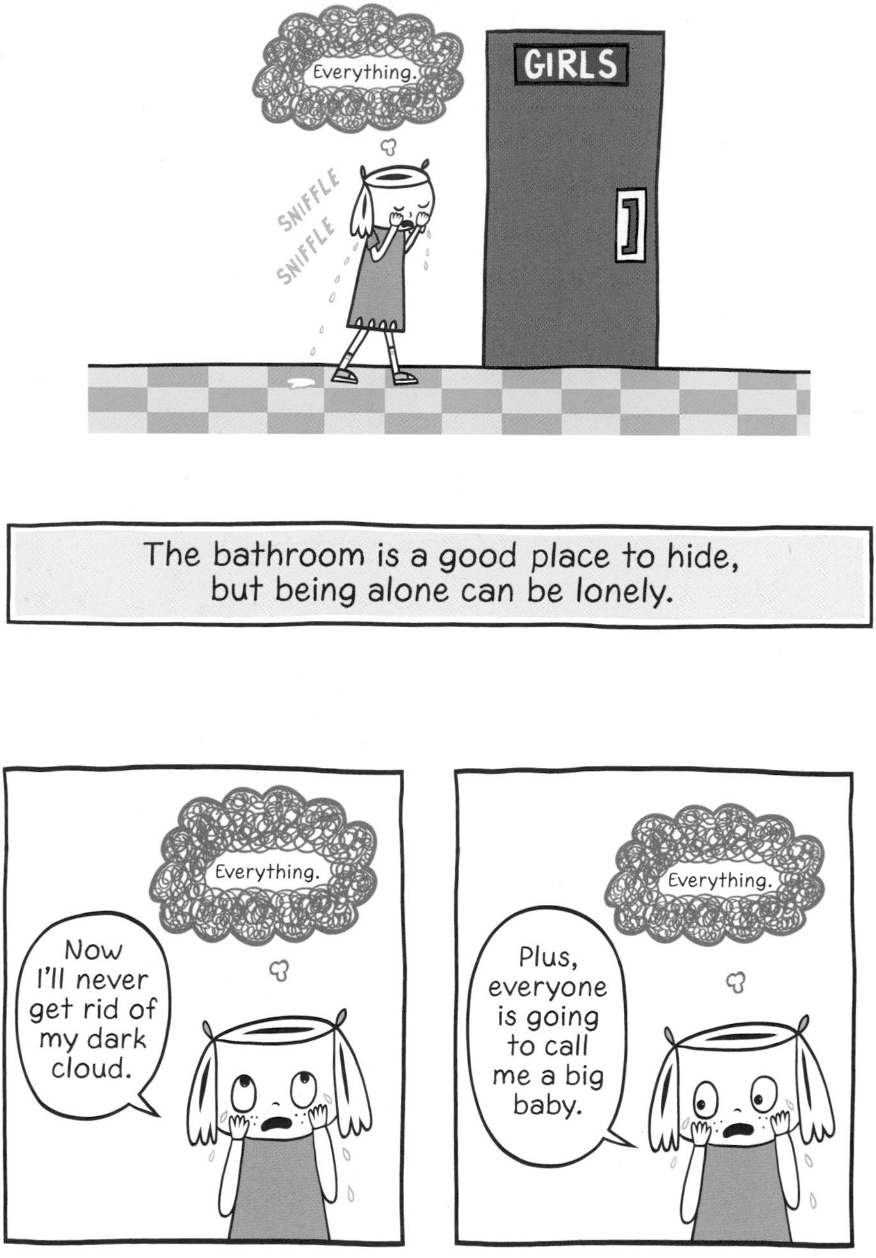
Everything.
GIRLS
SNIFFLE
SNIFFLE
The bathroom is a good place to hide, but being alone can be lonely.
Everything.
Now I'll never get rid of my dark cloud.
Everything.
Plus, everyone is going to call me a big baby.

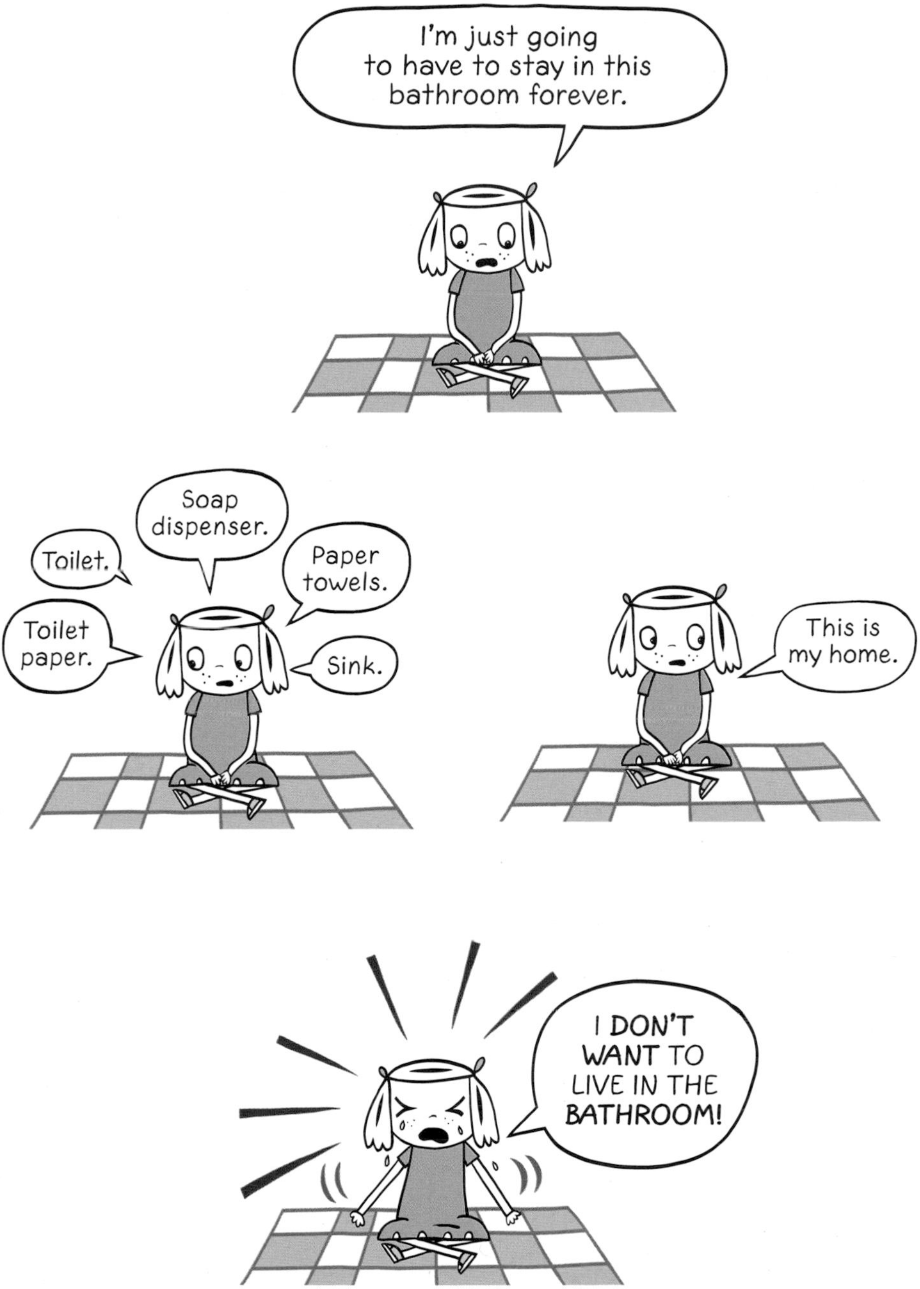
I'm just going to have to stay in this bathroom forever.
Toilet paper.
Toilet.
Soap dispenser.
Paper towels.
Sink.
This is my home.
I DON'T WANT TO LIVE IN THE BATHROOM!

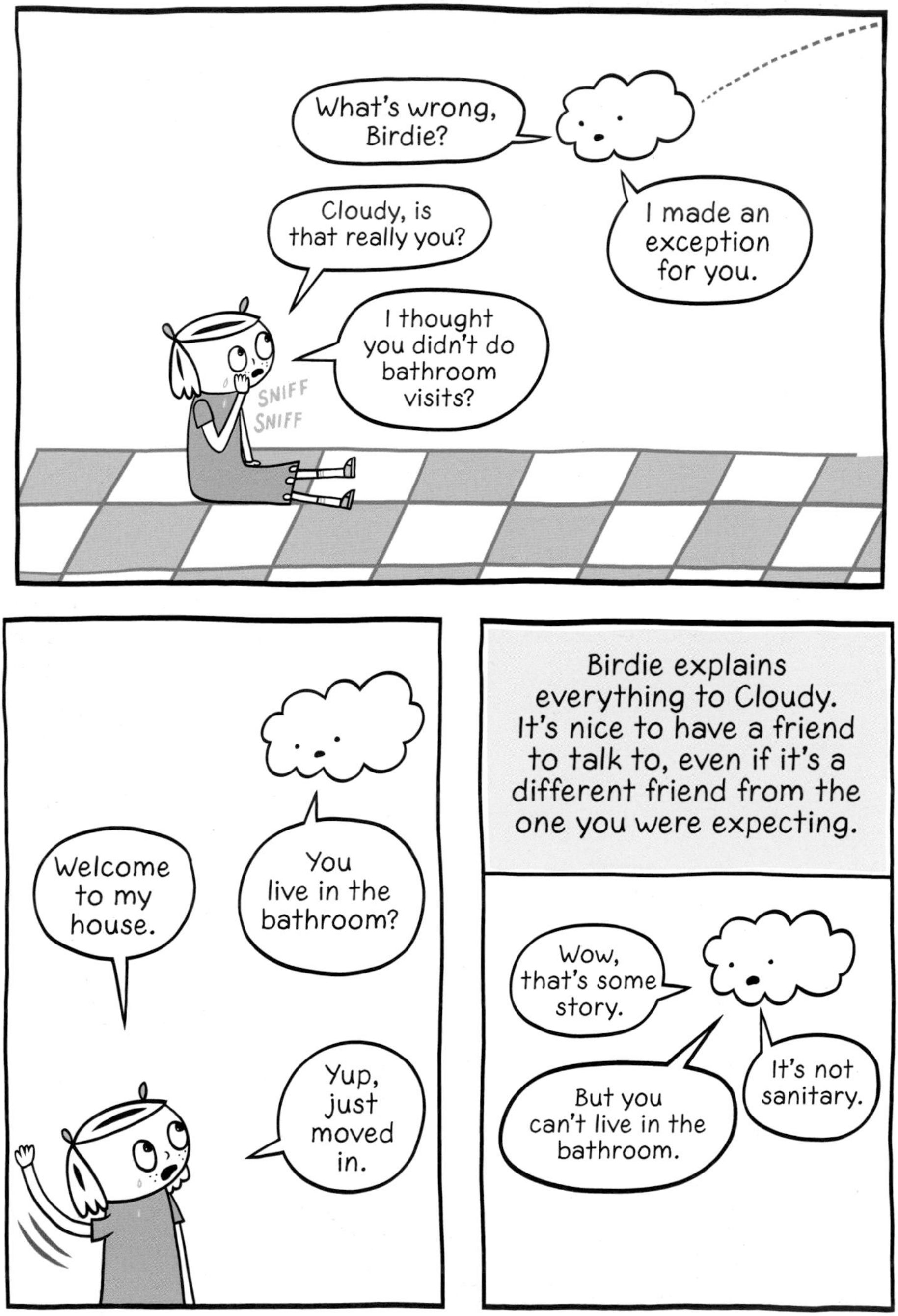
What's wrong, Birdie?
I made an exception for you.
Cloudy, is that really you?
I thought you didn't do bathroom visits?
SNIFF SNIFF
Welcome to my house.
You live in the bathroom?
Yup, just moved in.
Birdie explains everything to Cloudy. It's nice to have a friend to talk to, even if it's a different friend from the one you were expecting.
Wow, that's some story.
But you can't live in the bathroom.
It's not sanitary.

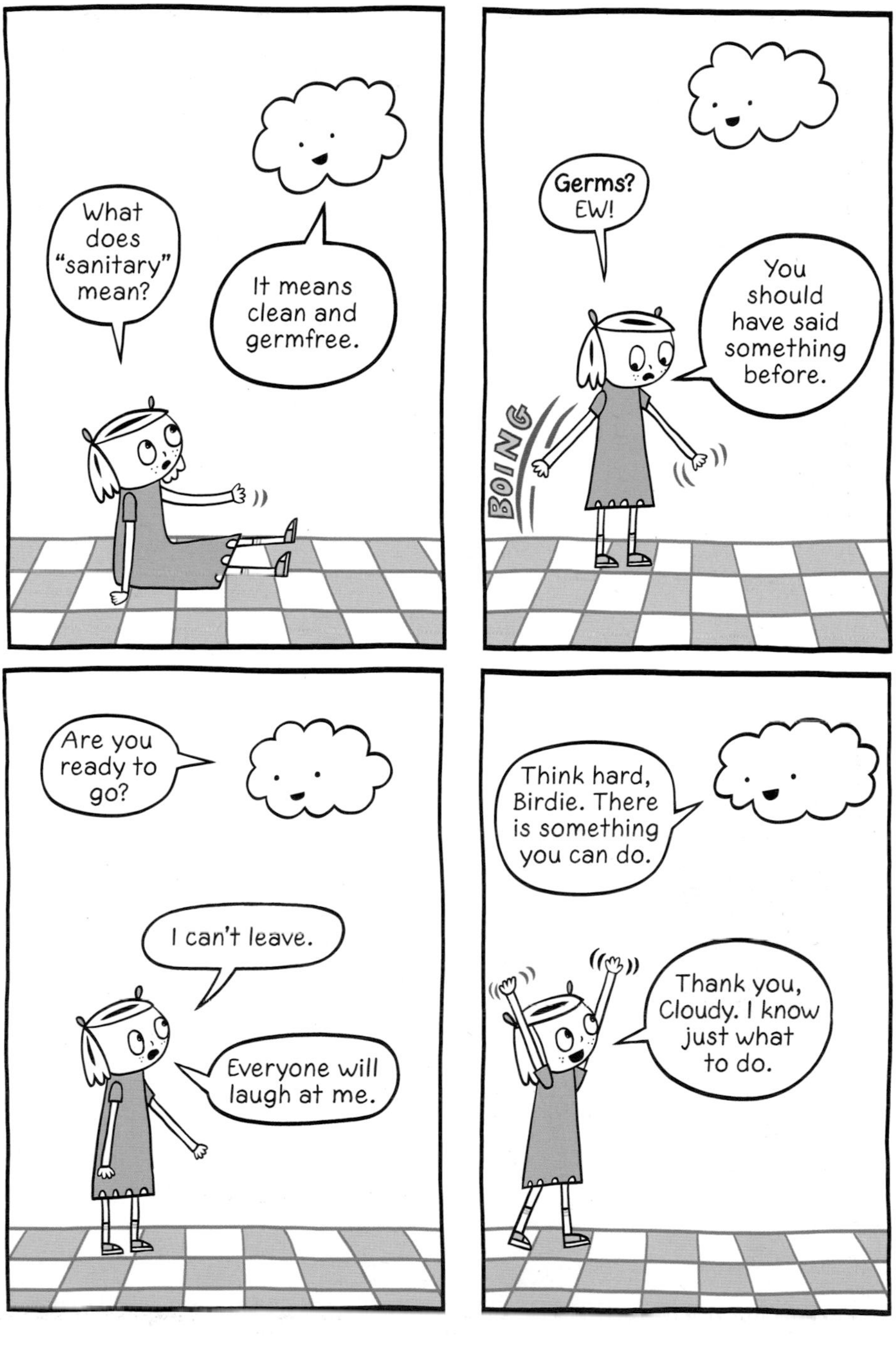
What does "sanitary" mean?
It means clean and germfree.
Germs? EW!
BOING
You should have said something before.
Are you ready to go?
I can't leave.
Everyone will laugh at me.
Think hard, Birdie. There is something you can do.
Thank you, Cloudy. I know just what to do.

POINTY PINS

BEAUTIFUL BUTTONS

COLORFUL CARDBOARD

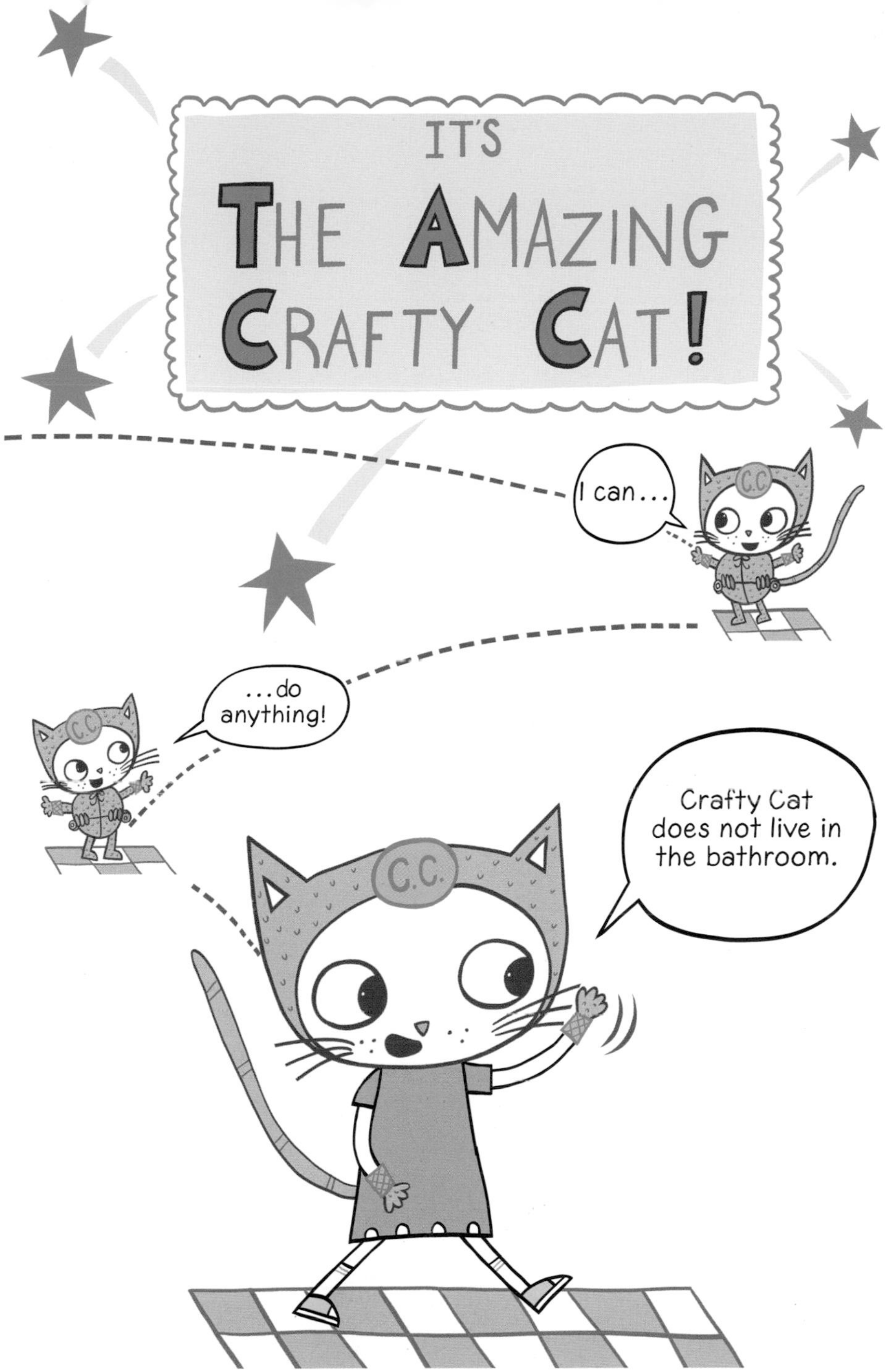
IT'S
THE AMAZING
CRAFTY CAT!
I can...
...do anything!
Crafty Cat does not live in the bathroom.

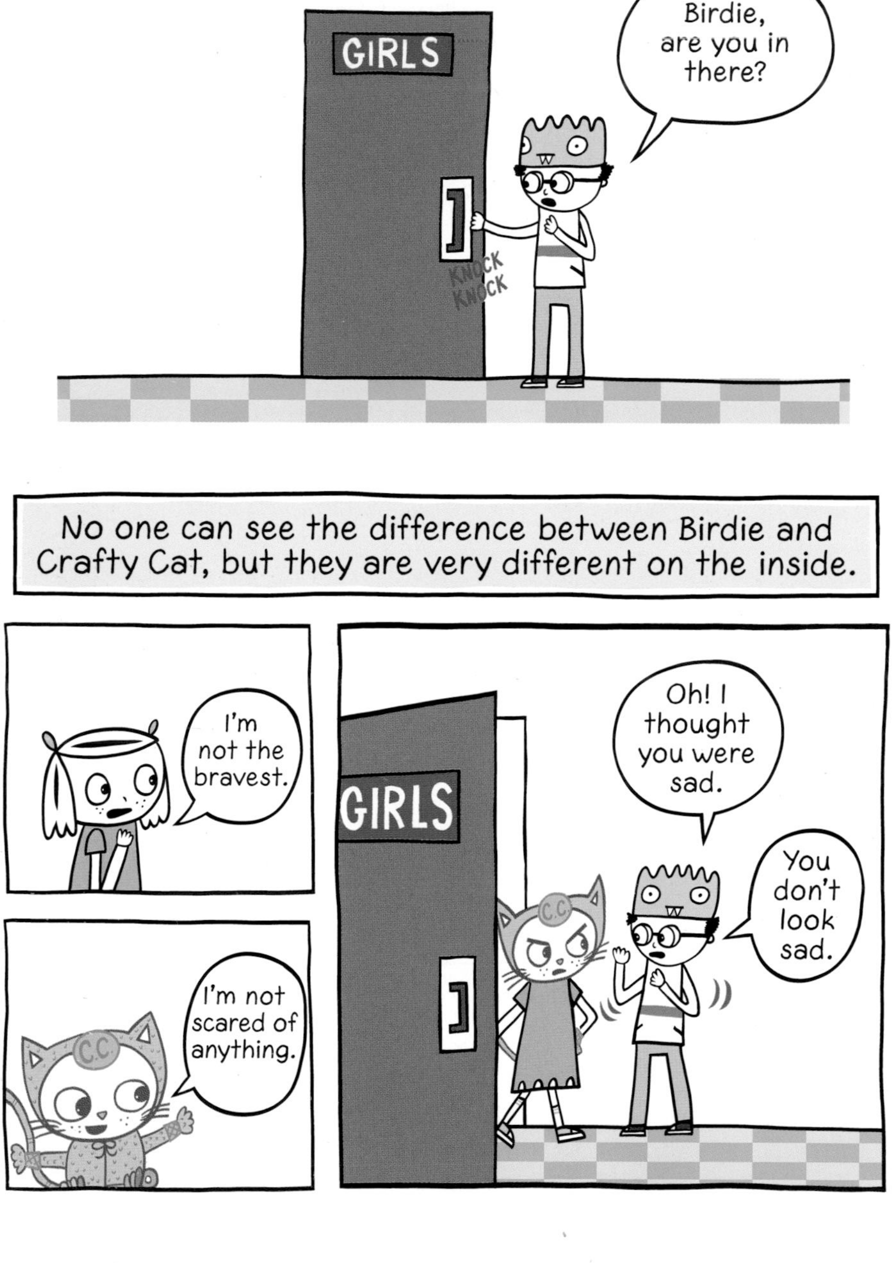
GIRLS
Birdie, are you in there?
KNOCK KNOCK
No one can see the difference between Birdie and Crafty Cat, but they are very different on the inside.
I'm not the bravest.
I'm not scared of anything.
GIRLS
Oh! I thought you were sad.
You don't look sad.

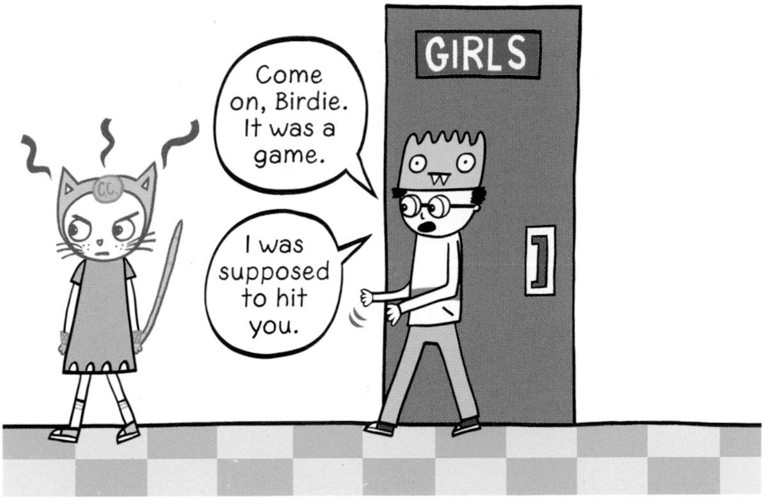
GIRLS
Come on, Birdie. It was a game.
I was supposed to hit you.

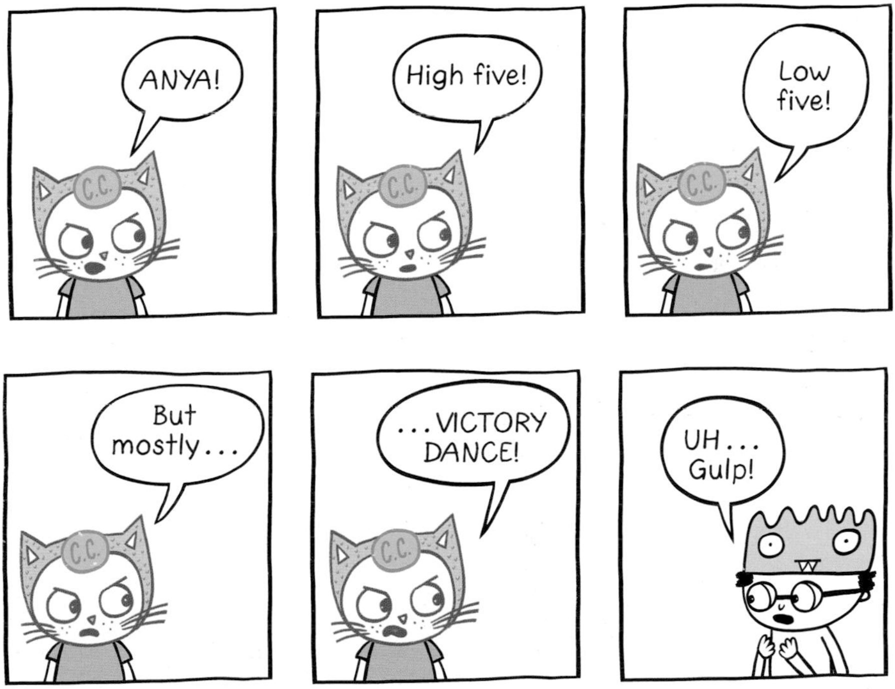
ANYA!
High five!
Low five!
But mostly...
...VICTORY DANCE!
UH... Gulp!

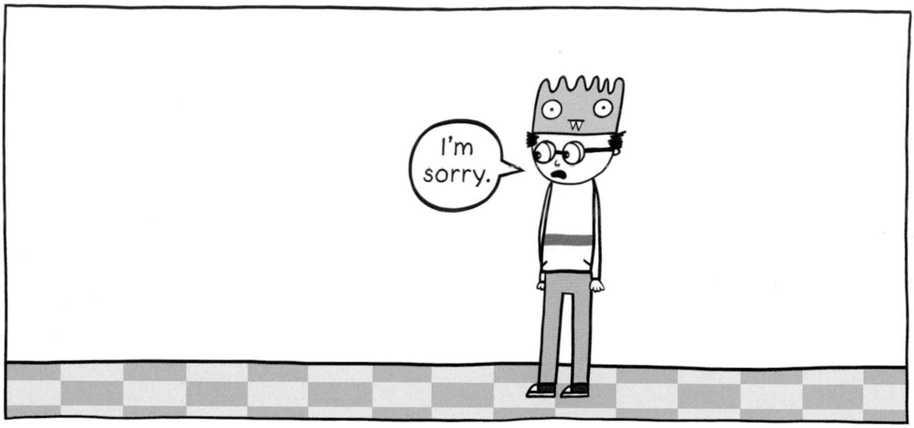
I'm sorry.

Back in the classroom, Crafty Cat gets right to work. Her sleepy monster is special.

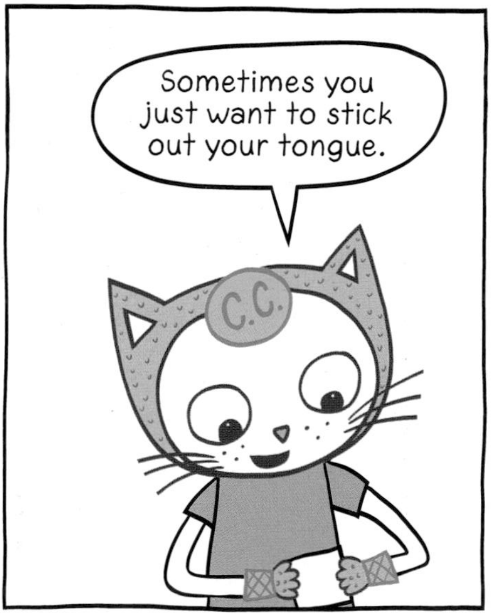
Sometimes you just want to stick out your tongue.
C.C.

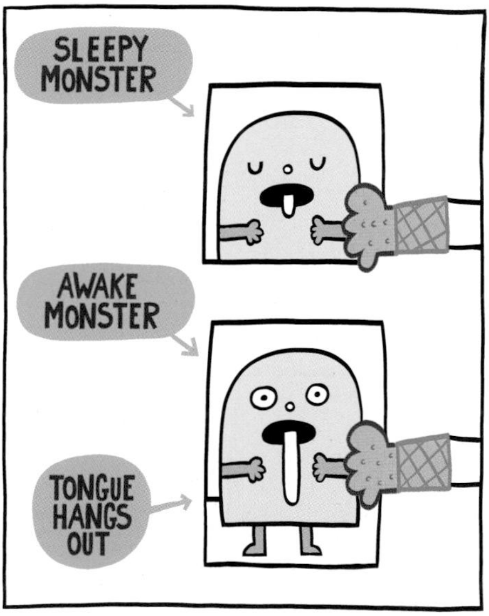
SLEEPY MONSTER
AWAKE MONSTER
TONGUE HANGS OUT

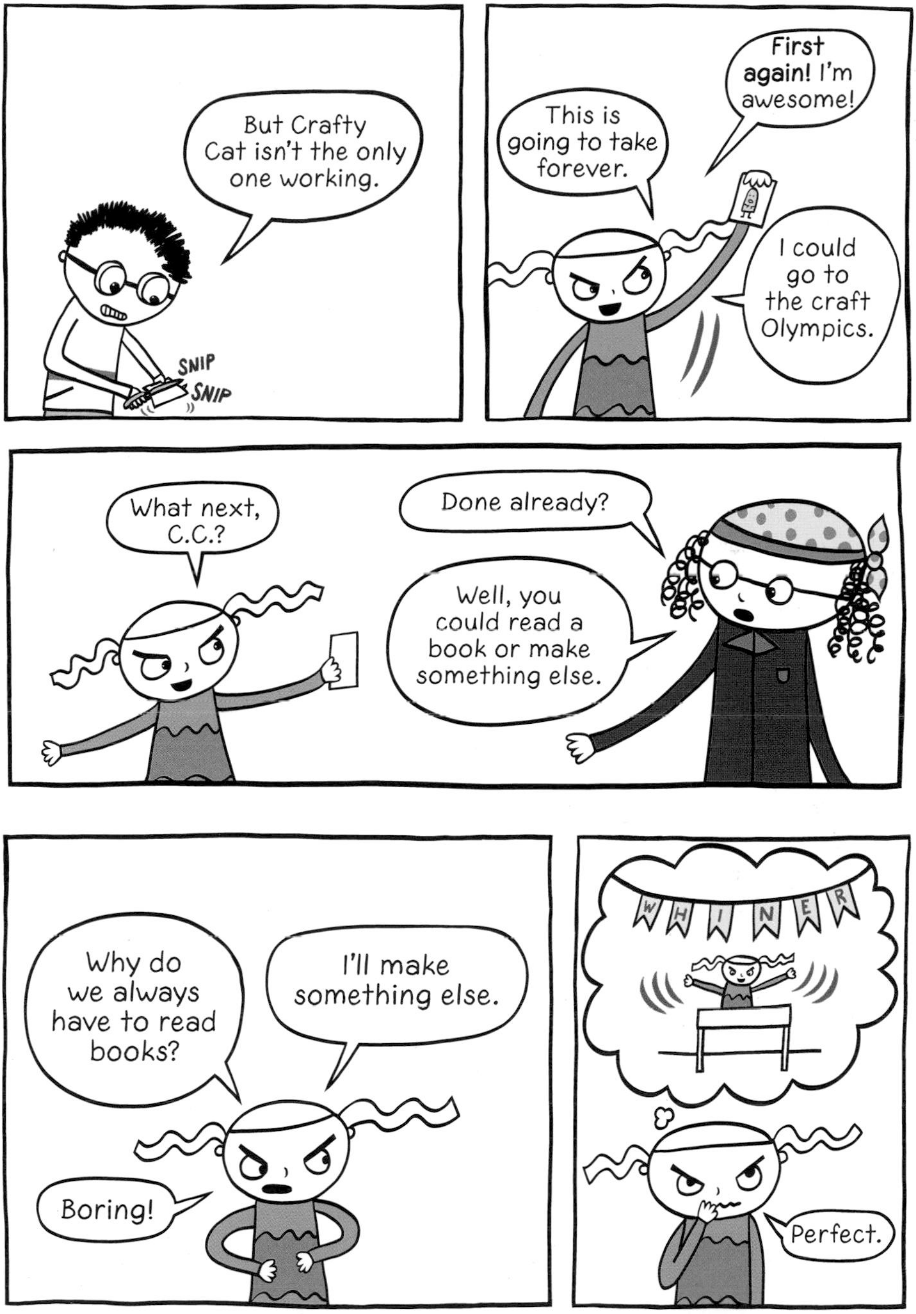
But Crafty Cat isn't the only one working.
SNIP
SNIP
This is going to take forever.
First again! I'm awesome!
I could go to the craft Olympics.
What next, C.C.?
Done already?
Well, you could read a book or make something else.
Why do we always have to read books?
I'll make something else.
Boring!
WHINER
Perfect.

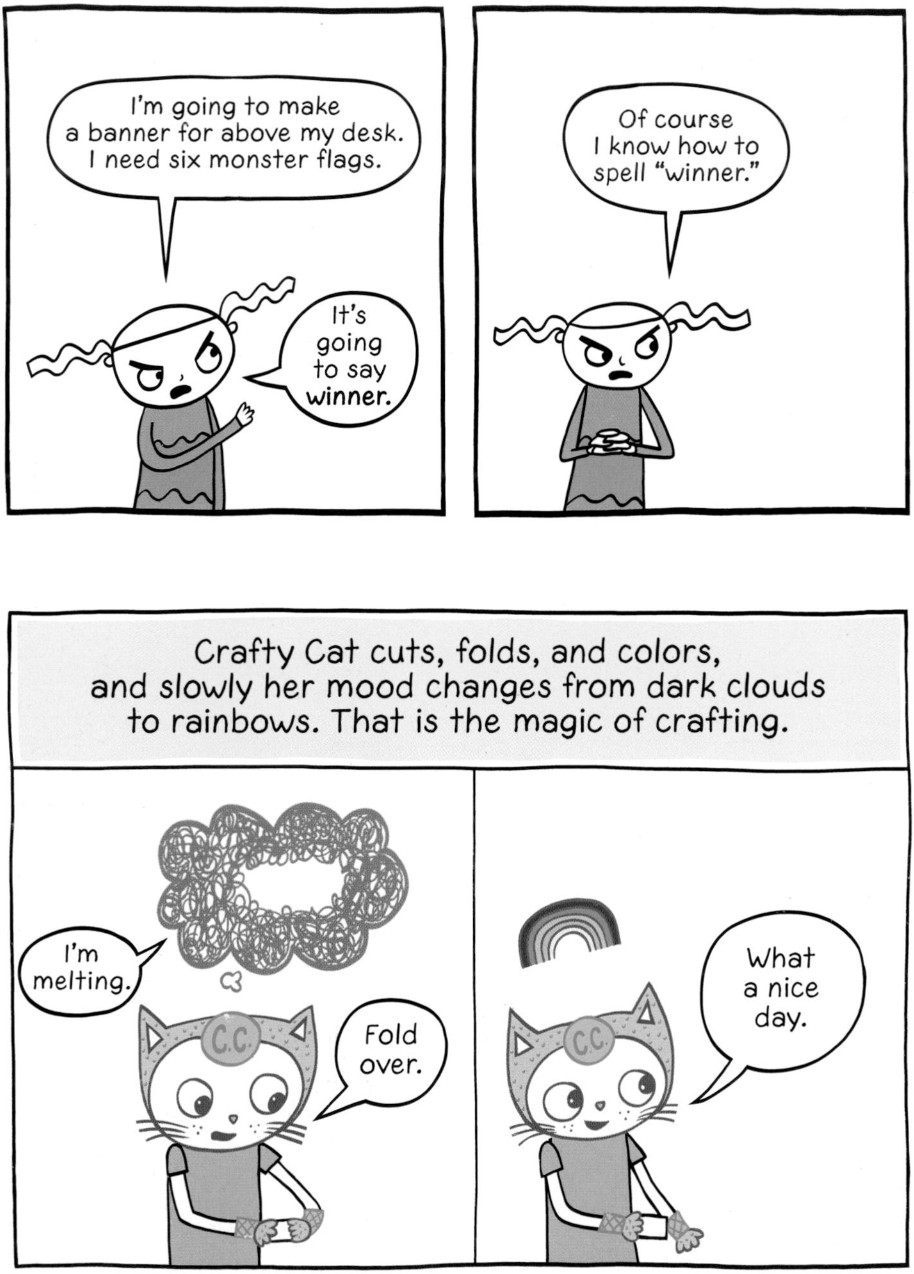
I'm going to make a banner for above my desk. I need six monster flags.
It's going to say **winner.**
Of course I know how to spell "winner."
Crafty Cat cuts, folds, and colors, and slowly her mood changes from dark clouds to rainbows. That is the magic of crafting.
I'm melting.
Fold over.
C.C.
What a nice day.
C.C.

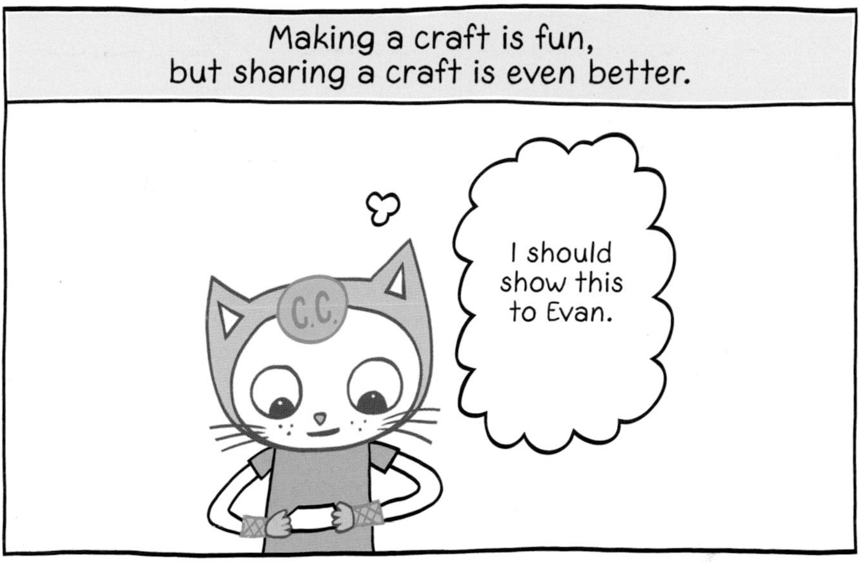
Making a craft is fun,
but sharing a craft is even better.
C.C.
I should show this to Evan.

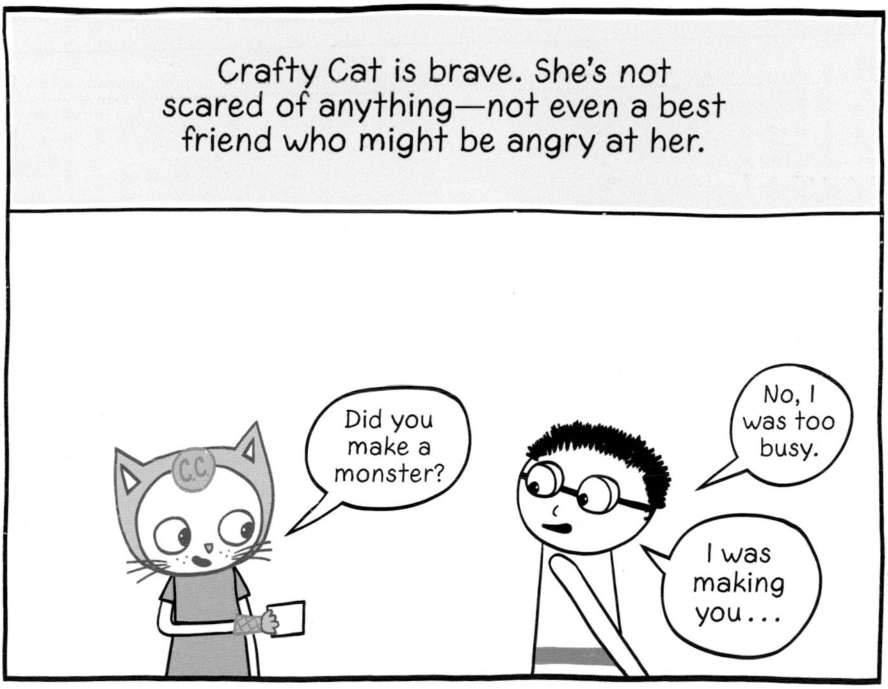
Crafty Cat is brave. She's not scared of anything—not even a best friend who might be angry at her.
C.C.
Did you make a monster?
No, I was too busy.
I was making you . . .

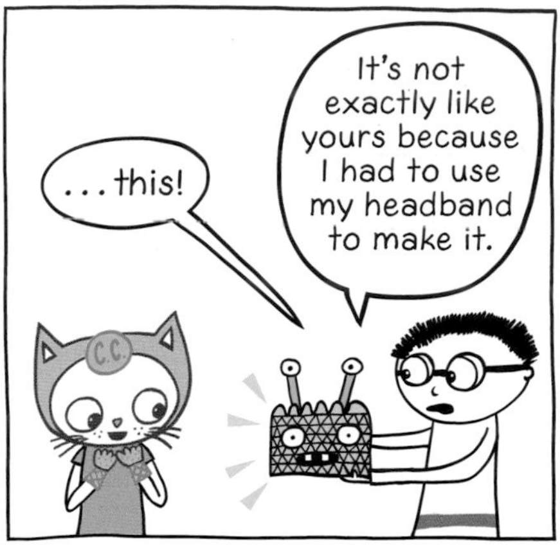
. . . this!
It's not exactly like yours because I had to use my headband to make it.

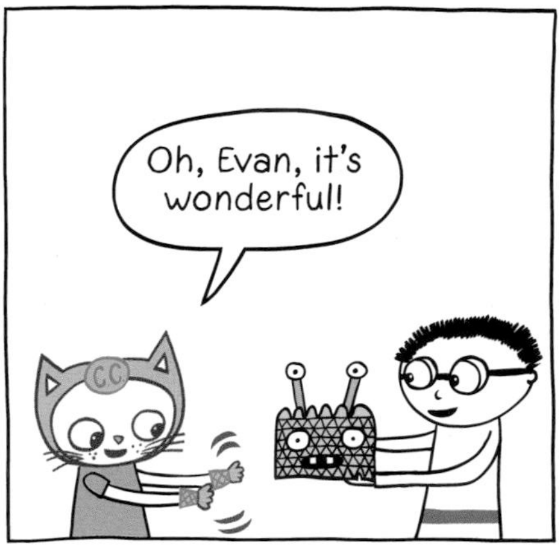
Oh, Evan, it's wonderful!

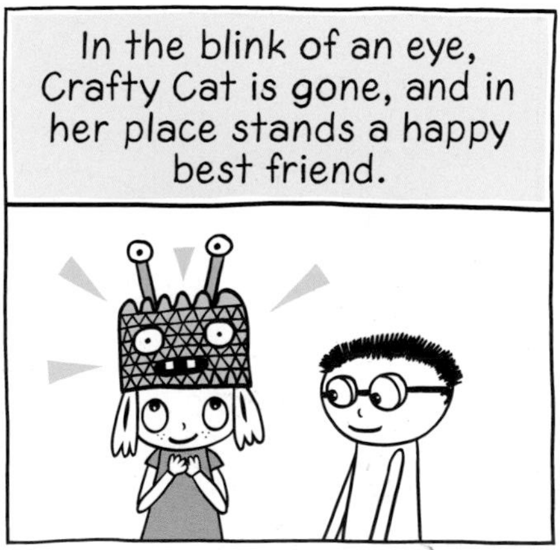
In the blink of an eye, Crafty Cat is gone, and in her place stands a happy best friend.

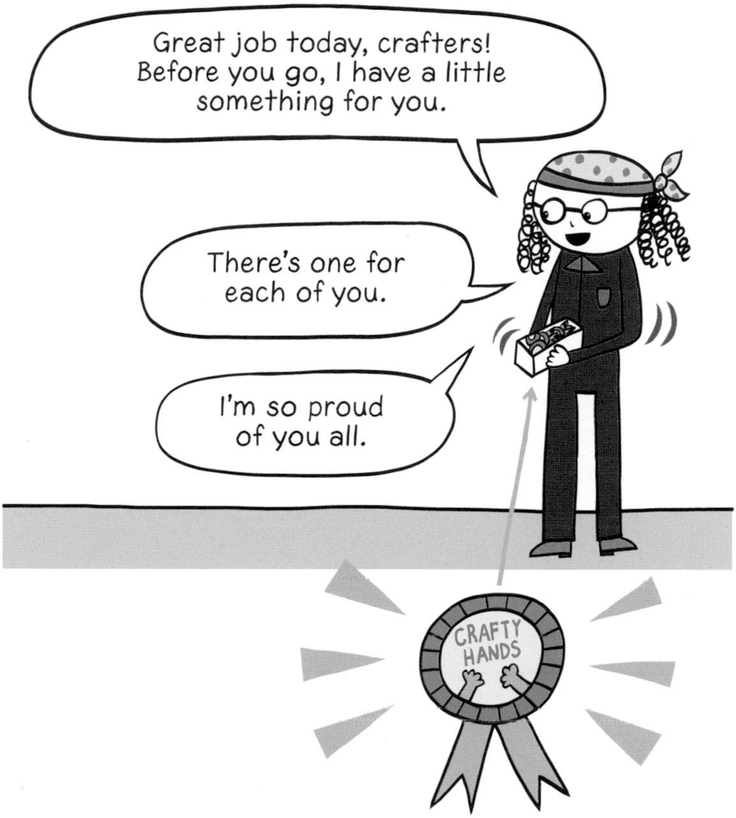
Great job today, crafters! Before you go, I have a little something for you.
There's one for each of you.
I'm so proud of you all.
CRAFTY HANDS

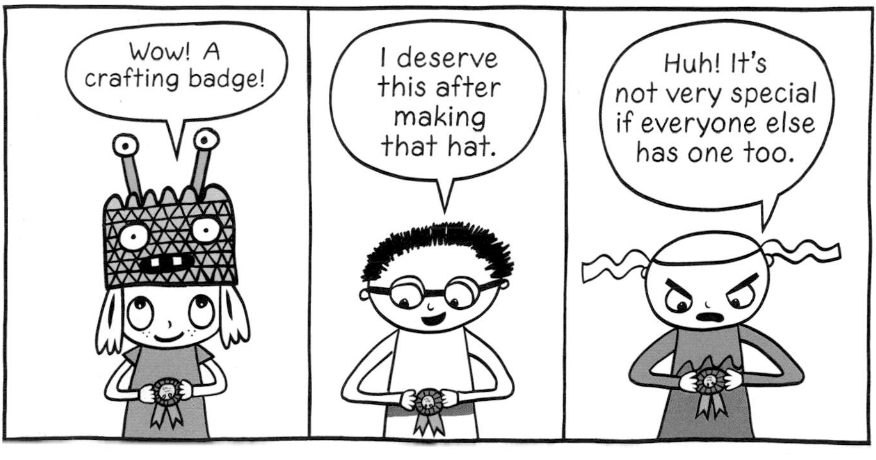
Wow! A crafting badge!
I deserve this after making that hat.
Huh! It's not very special if everyone else has one too.

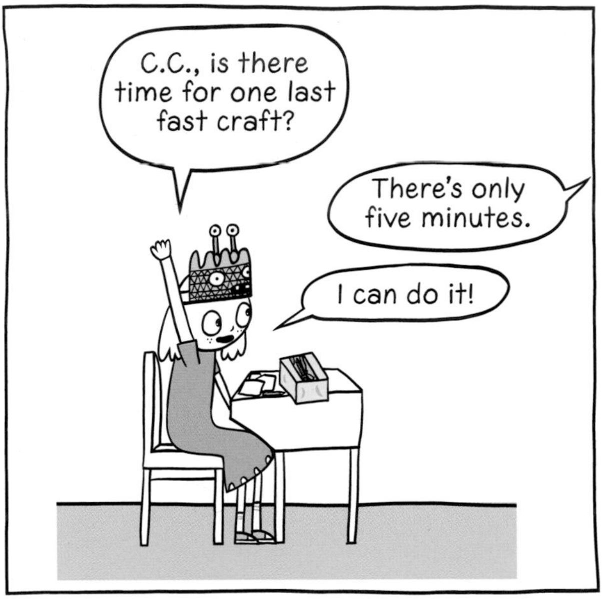
C.C., is there time for one last fast craft?
There's only five minutes.
I can do it!

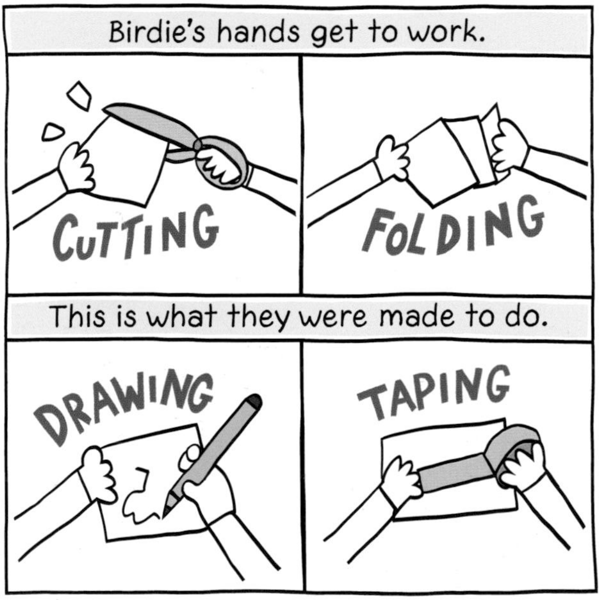
Birdie's hands get to work.
CUTTING
FOLDING
This is what they were made to do.
DRAWING
TAPING

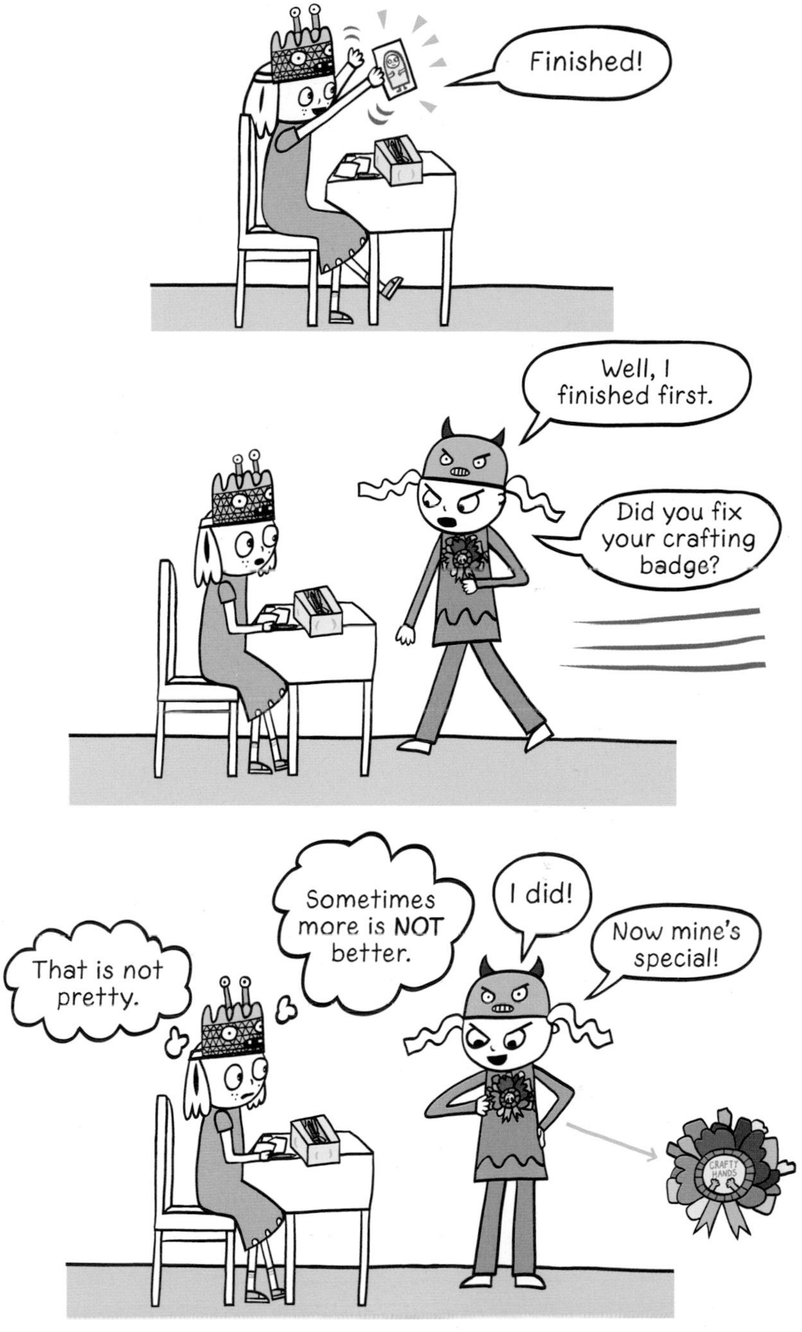
Finished!
Well, I finished first.
Did you fix your crafting badge?
I did!
Now mine's special!
That is not pretty.
Sometimes more is **NOT** better.
CRAFTY HANDS

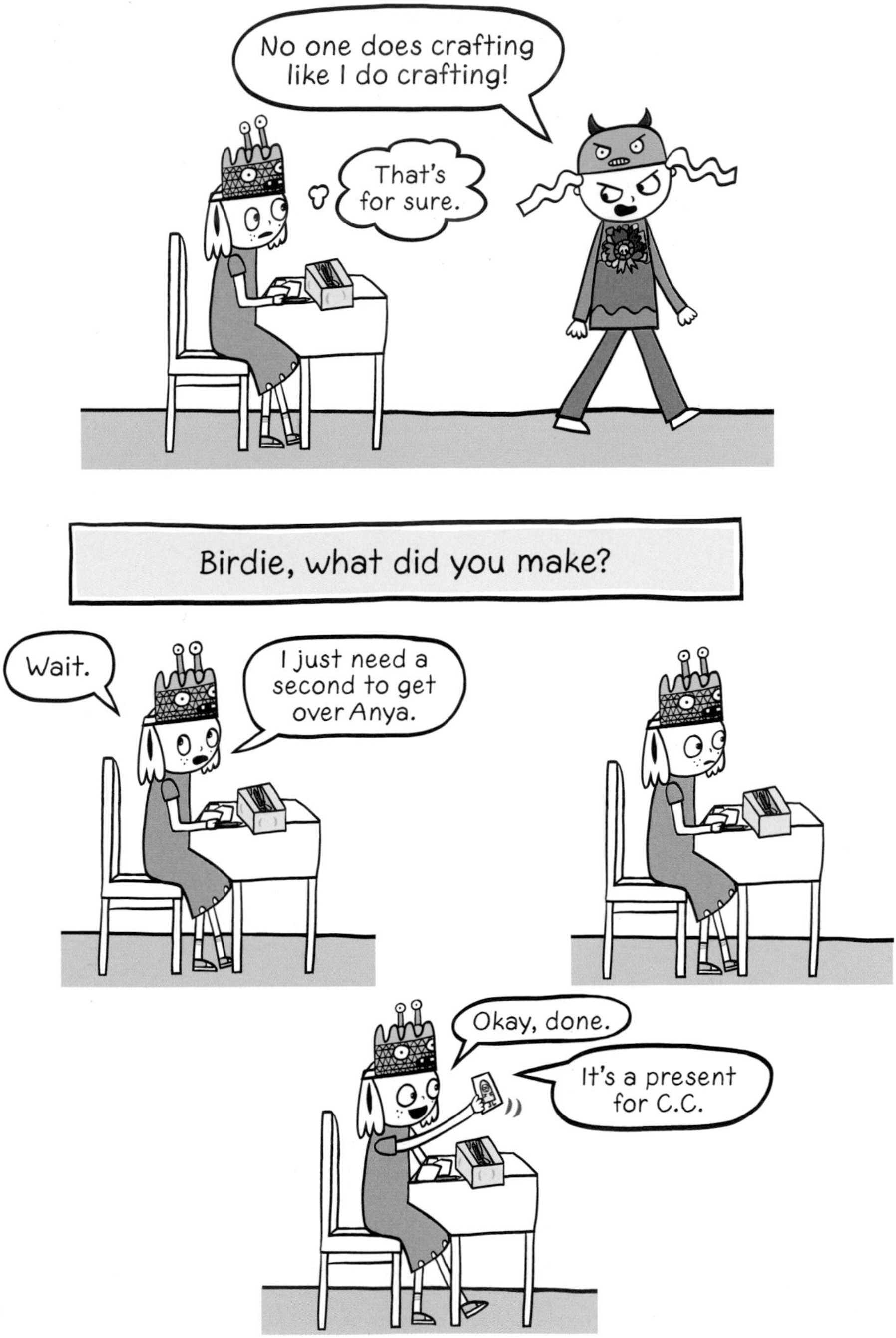
No one does crafting like I do crafting!
That's for sure.
Birdie, what did you make?
Wait.
I just need a second to get over Anya.
Okay, done.
It's a present for C.C.

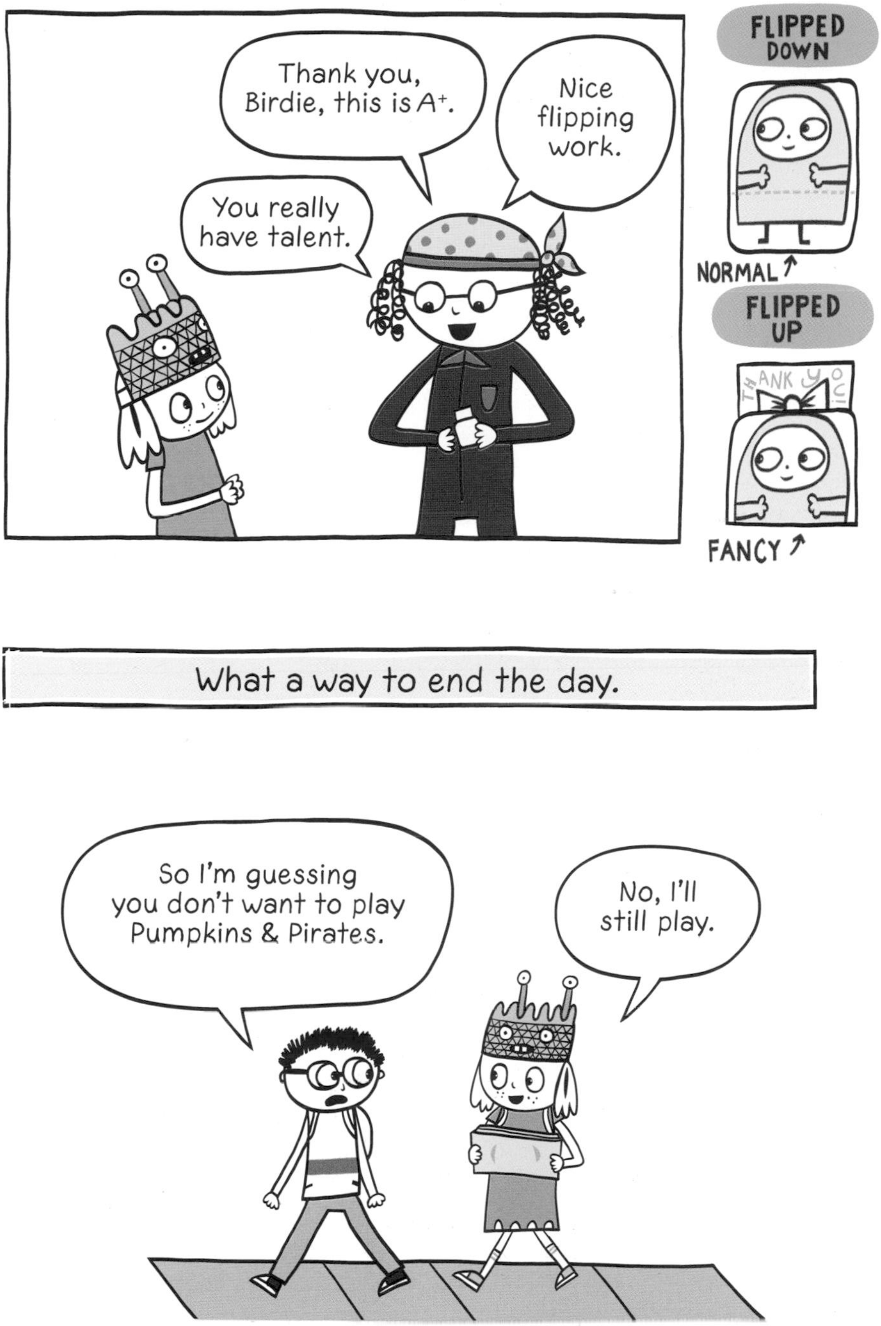
Thank you, Birdie, this is A+.
Nice flipping work.
You really have talent.
FLIPPED DOWN
NORMAL
FLIPPED UP
FANCY
What a way to end the day.
So I'm guessing you don't want to play Pumpkins & Pirates.
No, I'll still play.

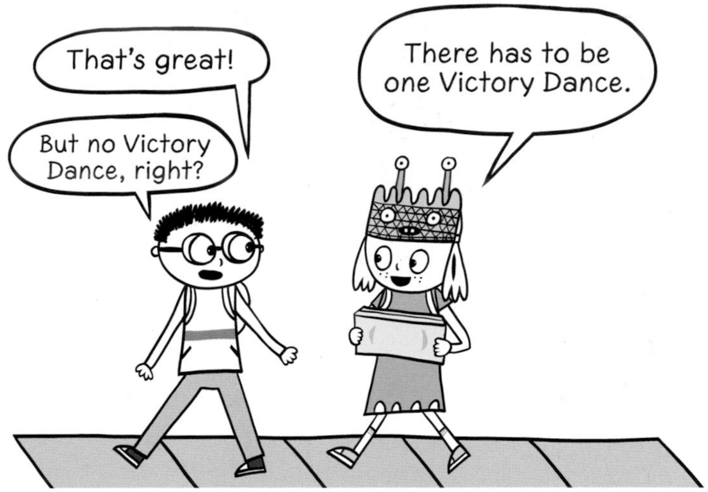
That's great!
But no Victory Dance, right?
There has to be one Victory Dance.

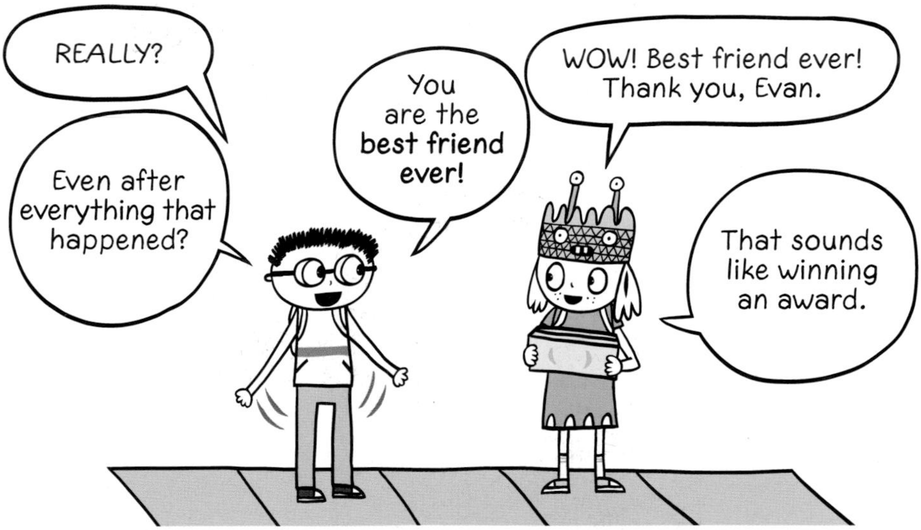
REALLY?
Even after everything that happened?
You are the **best friend ever!**
WOW! Best friend ever! Thank you, Evan.
That sounds like winning an award.

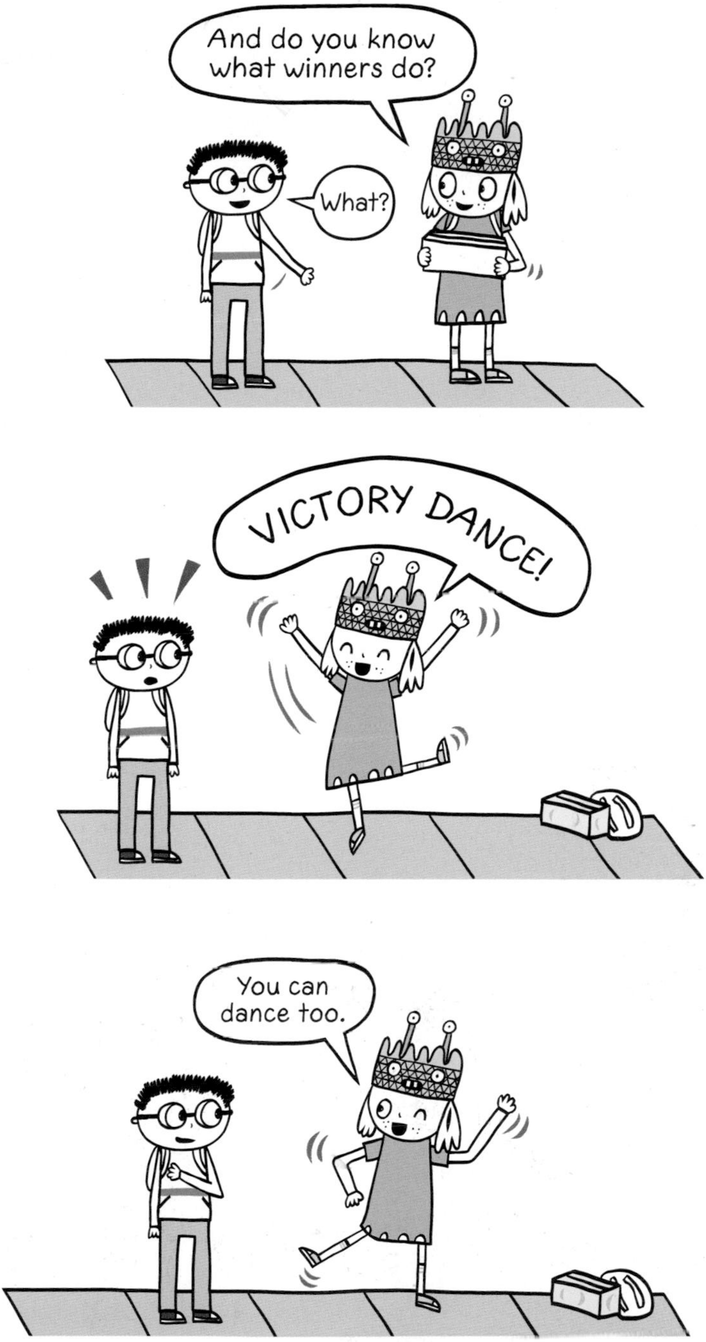
And do you know what winners do?
What?
VICTORY DANCE!
You can dance too.

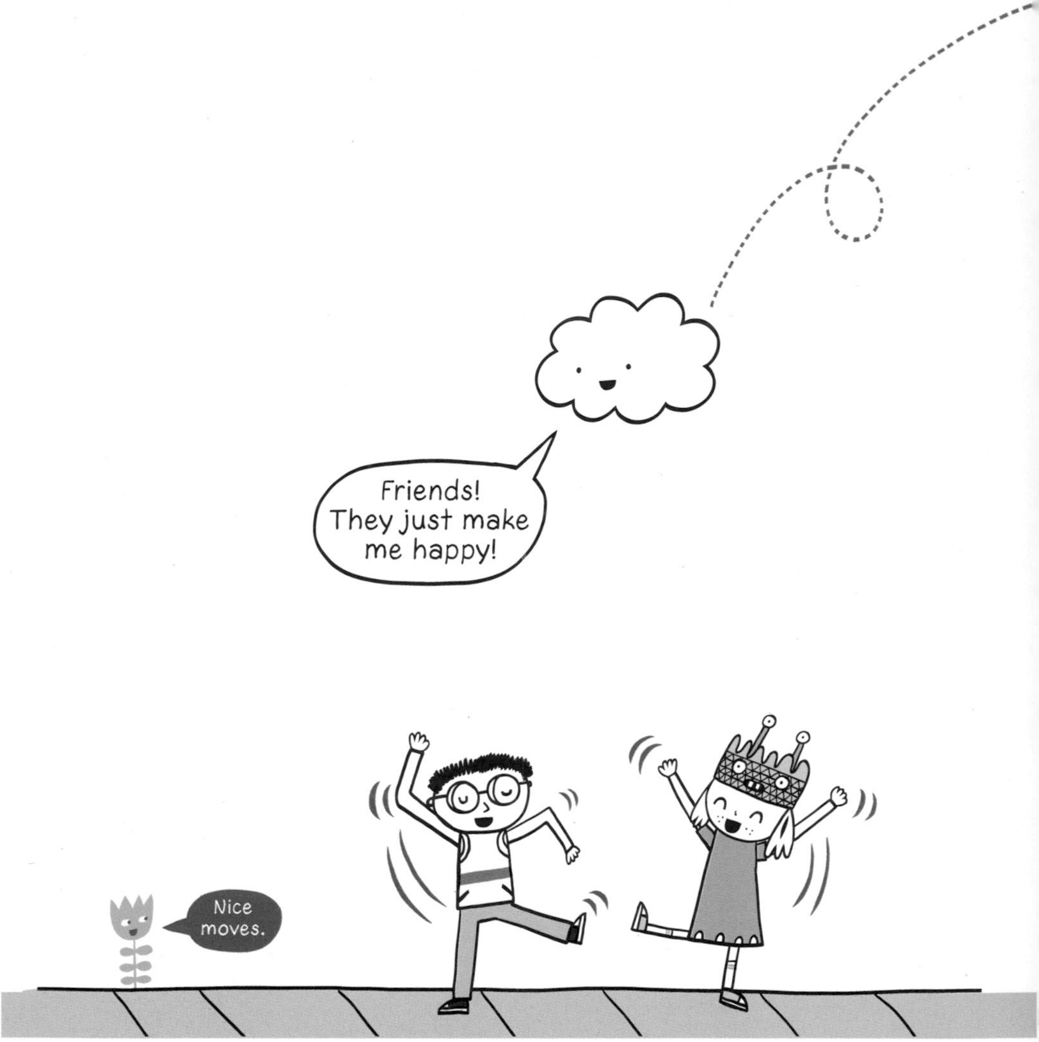
Friends! They just make me happy!
Nice moves.

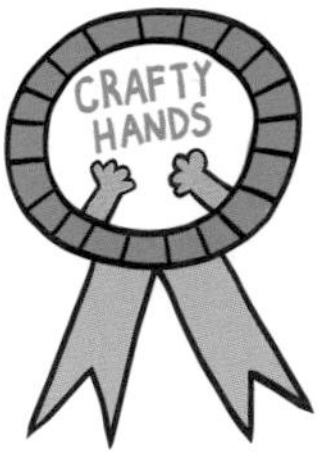
CRAFTY
HANDS

GET YOUR PAWS READY IT'S CRAFTY TIME

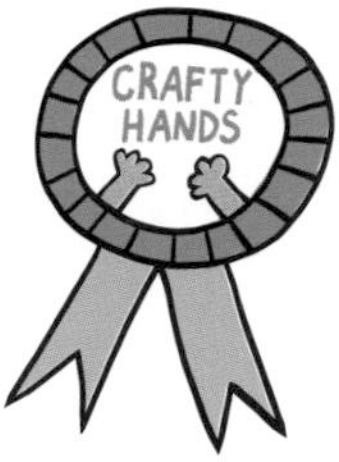
CRAFTY
HANDS

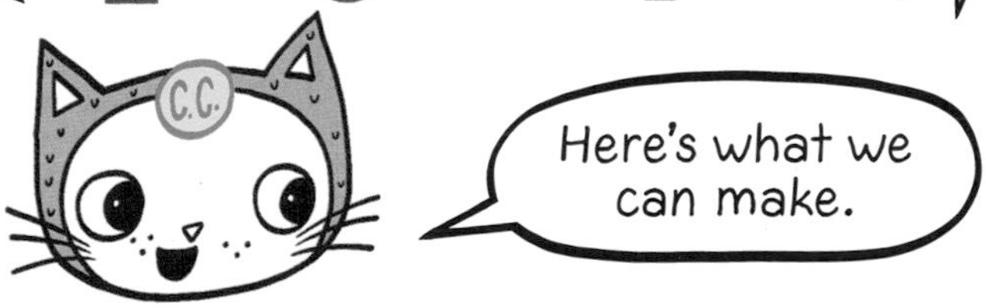
C.C.
Here's what we can make.

MONSTER MASH-UP

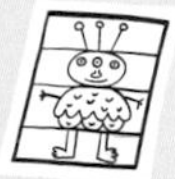

SUPPLIES

- 1 or 2 friends
- Paper
- Pencil

YAY MONSTER BANNER, MINI-MONSTER, and CLOUDY

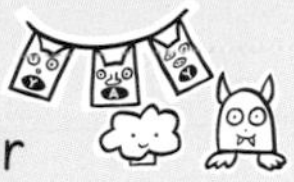

SUPPLIES

- Cardstock
- Scissors
- Markers
- String
- Clear tape
- Photocopier
- Glue

MOODY MONSTER BADGE

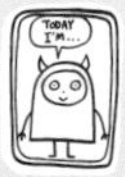
TODAY I'M...

SUPPLIES

- Cardstock
- Scissors
- Markers
- Clear tape
- Wire brad
- Pin back or safety pin
- Photocopier

SLEEPY MONSTER WITH TONGUE OR BOW

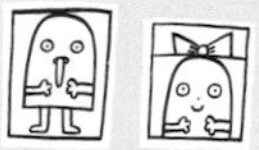

SUPPLIES

- Cardstock
- Scissors
- Markers
- Tape
- Glue stick
- Photocopier

MONSTER HEADBAND

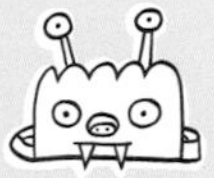

SUPPLIES

- Paper
- Black marker
- Clear packing tape
- Scissors

MONSTER MASH-UP

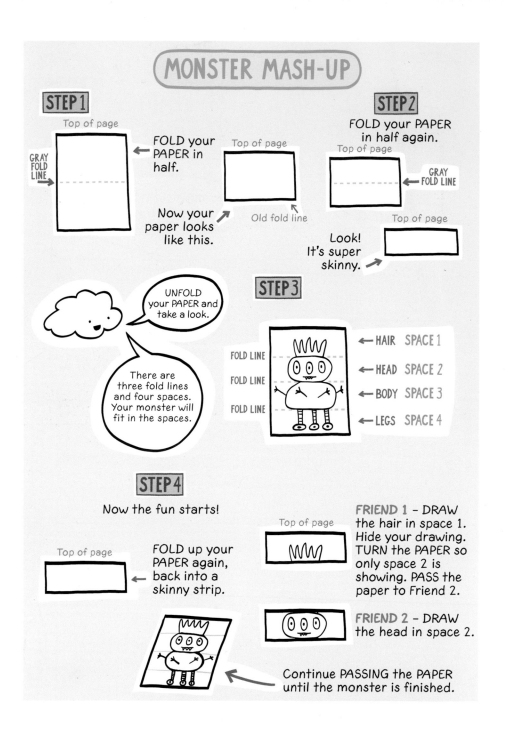

STEP 1

Top of page

GRAY FOLD LINE →

FOLD your PAPER in half.

Top of page

Now your paper looks like this. ↗

Old fold line

STEP 2

FOLD your PAPER in half again.

Top of page

GRAY FOLD LINE ←

Top of page

Look! It's super skinny. ↘

UNFOLD your PAPER and take a look.

There are three fold lines and four spaces. Your monster will fit in the spaces.

STEP 3

FOLD LINE

FOLD LINE

FOLD LINE

← HAIR SPACE 1
← HEAD SPACE 2
← BODY SPACE 3
← LEGS SPACE 4

STEP 4

Now the fun starts!

Top of page

FOLD up your PAPER again, back into a skinny strip.

Top of page

FRIEND 1 – DRAW the hair in space 1. Hide your drawing. TURN the PAPER so only space 2 is showing. PASS the paper to Friend 2.

FRIEND 2 – DRAW the head in space 2.

Continue PASSING the PAPER until the monster is finished.

YAY MONSTER BANNER

1

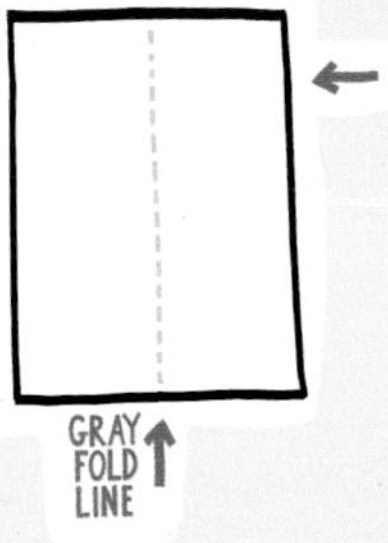
GRAY FOLD LINE

FOLD your PAPER in half.

2

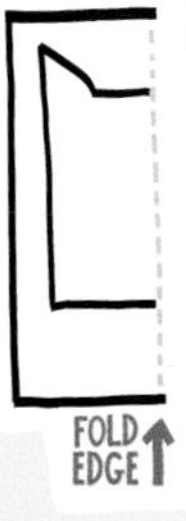
FOLD EDGE

DRAW a monster flag outline in the size of your choice.

3

CUT out the monster flag with the paper still folded, then UNFOLD your first flag.

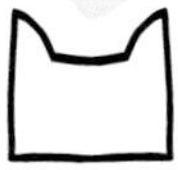

4

Repeat directions

1 2 3

to make two more monster flags. Now you have three monster flags.

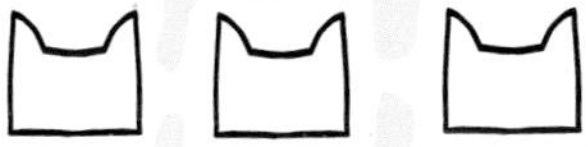

5

ADD monster faces to your flags. Be creative. They can all be the same or different.

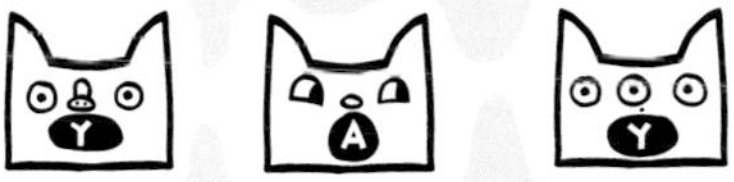
Y
A
Y

Don't forget to WRITE YAY in the mouth spaces.

6

TAPE string to the backs of your flags.

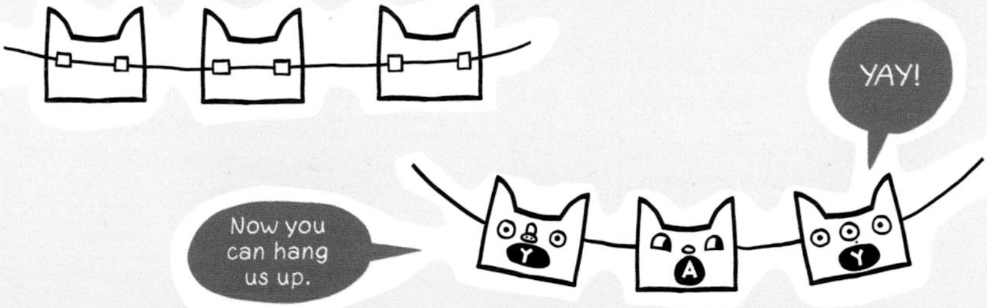
YAY!
Now you can hang us up.
Y
A
Y

MINI-MONSTER AND CLOUDY

1 FOLD your PAPER in half.

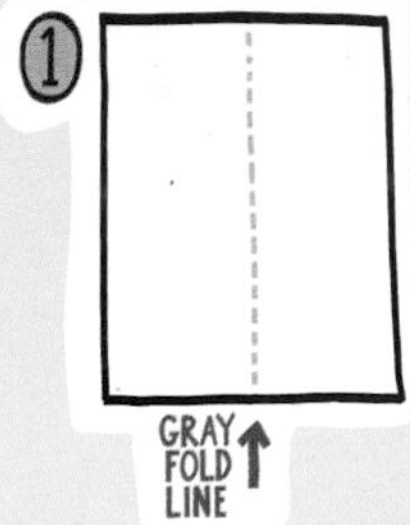
GRAY FOLD LINE

2 FOLD your PAPER in half again.

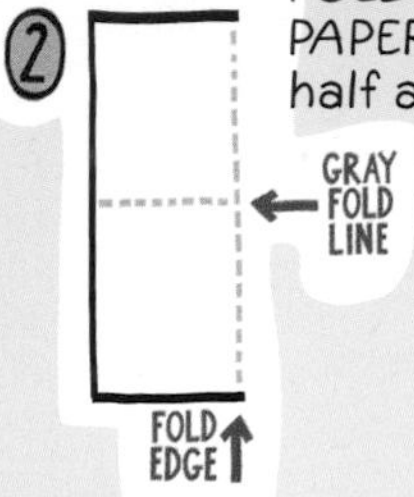
GRAY FOLD LINE
FOLD EDGE

3 DRAW a mini-monster outline and a horn outline.

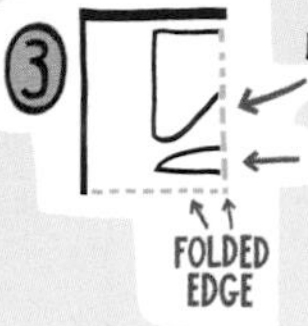
FOLDED EDGE

4 With paper still folded, CUT out your mini-monster and horn.

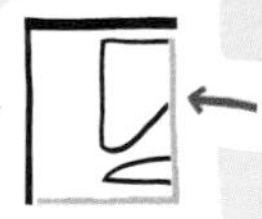

CUT along your drawn outline. Do not unfold while cutting.

Now you can UNFOLD.

You have two mini-monsters and two horns. FOLD the horns and GLUE together.

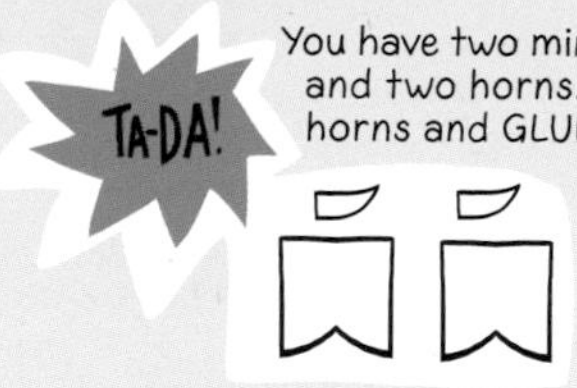
TA-DA!

5

DRAW your mini-monsters' faces.

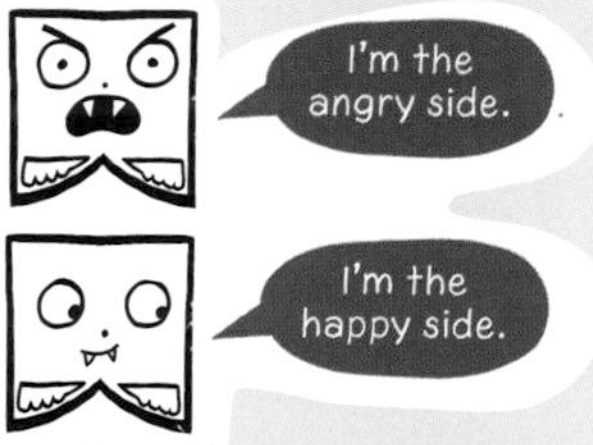
I'm the angry side.
I'm the happy side.

COLOR both sides of the horns.

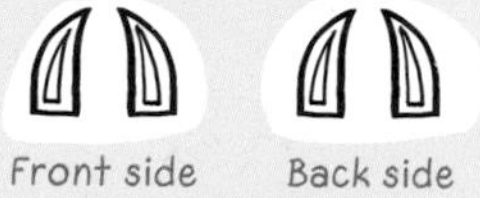
Front side
Back side

6

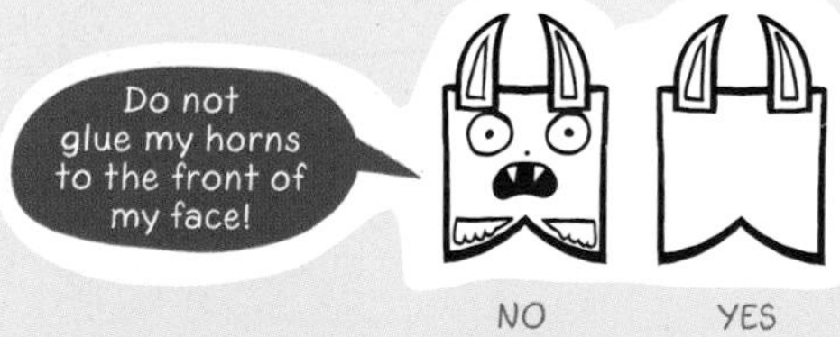
Do not glue my horns to the front of my face!
NO
YES

TAPE or GLUE the horns to the back of the angry monster.

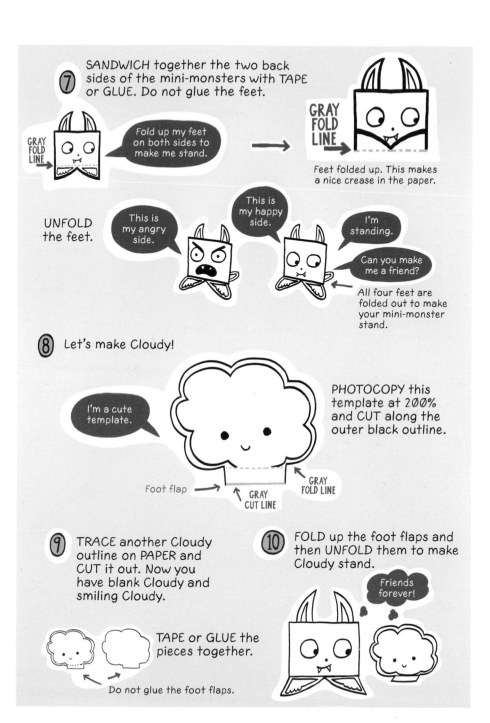

7 SANDWICH together the two back sides of the mini-monsters with TAPE or GLUE. Do not glue the feet.

GRAY FOLD LINE

Fold up my feet on both sides to make me stand.

GRAY FOLD LINE

Feet folded up. This makes a nice crease in the paper.

UNFOLD the feet.

This is my angry side.

This is my happy side.

I'm standing.

Can you make me a friend?

All four feet are folded out to make your mini-monster stand.

8 Let's make Cloudy!

I'm a cute template.

PHOTOCOPY this template at 200% and CUT along the outer black outline.

Foot flap

GRAY CUT LINE

GRAY FOLD LINE

9 TRACE another Cloudy outline on PAPER and CUT it out. Now you have blank Cloudy and smiling Cloudy.

10 FOLD up the foot flaps and then UNFOLD them to make Cloudy stand.

Friends forever!

TAPE or GLUE the pieces together.

Do not glue the foot flaps.

117

MOODY MONSTER BADGE

① PHOTOCOPY and ENLARGE these three templates at 15Ø%.

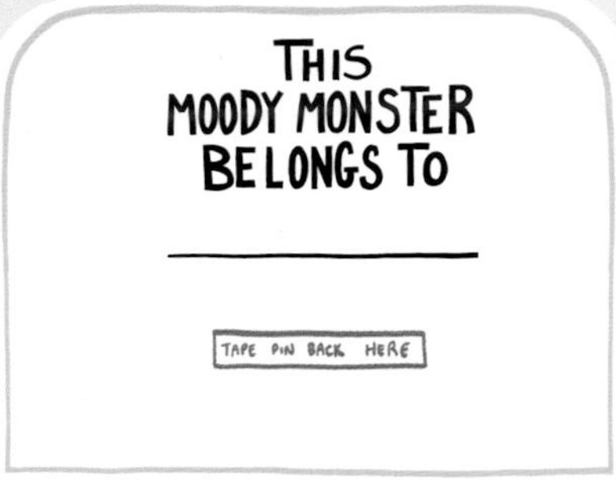
THIS MOODY MONSTER BELONGS TO
TAPE PIN BACK HERE

Back template

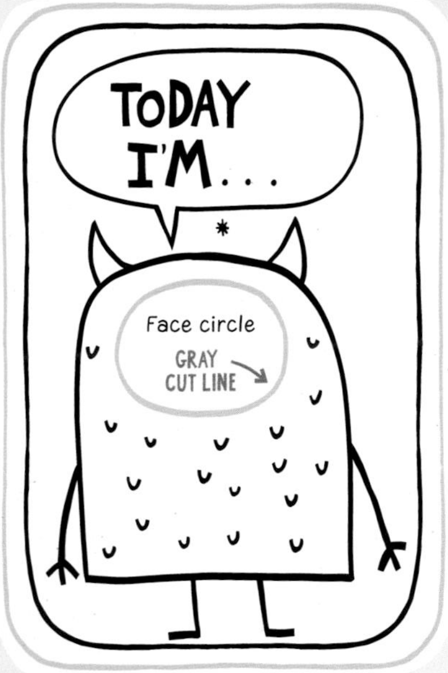
TODAY I'M...
Face circle
GRAY CUT LINE

Front Template

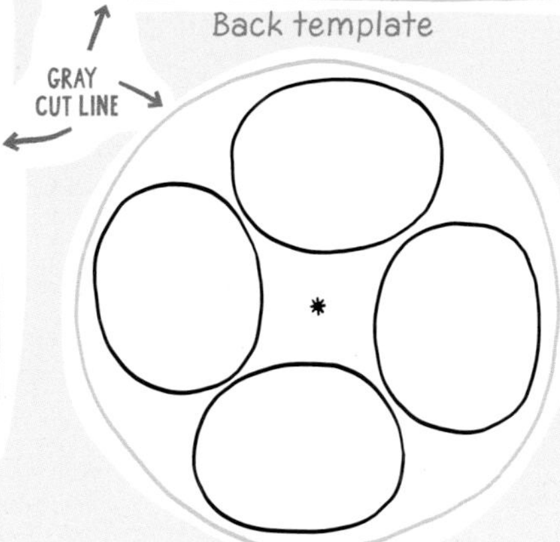
GRAY CUT LINE

Face dial template

② CUT out the three templates along the gray cut lines.

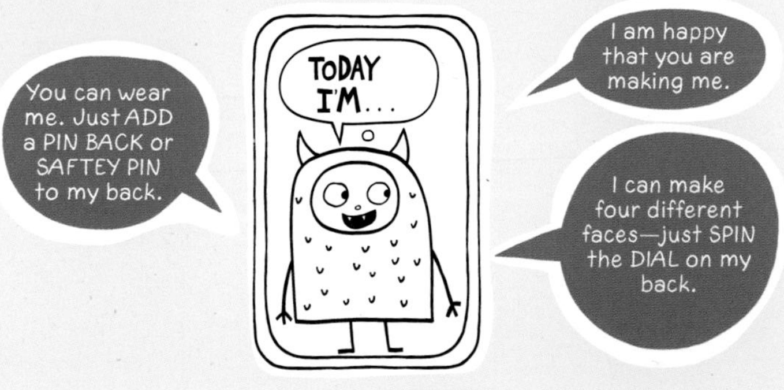
You can wear me. Just ADD a PIN BACK or SAFTEY PIN to my back.
TODAY I'M...
I am happy that you are making me.
I can make four different faces—just SPIN the DIAL on my back.

3. Carefully FOLD the front template in half, and CUT out the face circle.

TODAY
I'M
FOLD
EDGE

This is a temporary fold, so try not to crease the paper too hard.

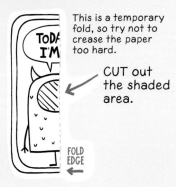

CUT out the shaded area.

4. DECORATE the front template, and DRAW four faces in the spaces on the face dial template.

I can't wait to get my face.
TODAY
I'M...
Draw us with the eyes near the middle.
Face dial

5. POKE holes in the two BRAD stars. Now your brad will be able to hold the face dial template in place.

Hi, my name is Brad.
I am a metal brad.

6. Use the BRAD and ATTACH the face template behind the front template.

I have a face.
TODAY
I'M...

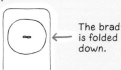

Front view

Back view

The brad is folded down.

7. TAPE the back template to the front template.

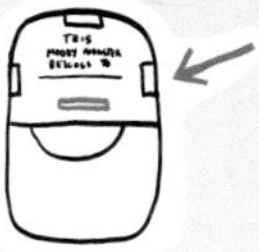

Be careful to tape only the edges.

8. If you want to wear your Moody Monster Badge, ATTACH a PIN BACK or SAFETY PIN with TAPE.

TODAY
I'M...
Crafty.
Let's make more crafts!

MONSTER WITH TONGUE

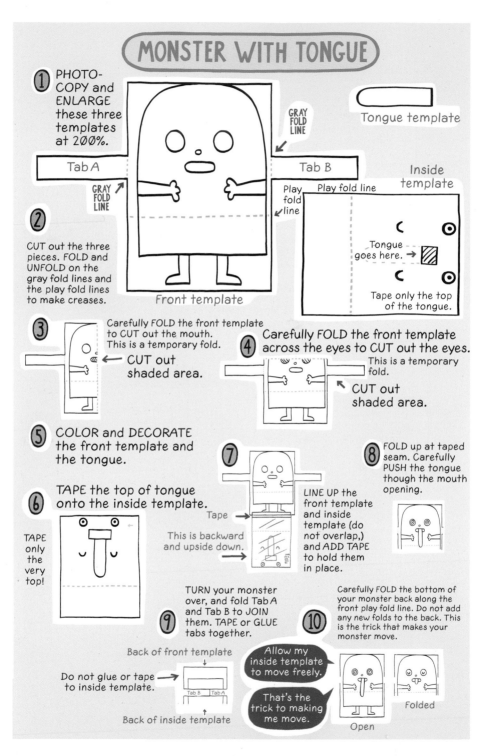

① PHOTO-COPY and ENLARGE these three templates at 200%.

Tongue template

GRAY FOLD LINE

Tab A

Tab B

Inside template

GRAY FOLD LINE

Play fold line

Play fold line

② CUT out the three pieces. FOLD and UNFOLD on the gray fold lines and the play fold lines to make creases.

Front template

Tongue goes here. →

Tape only the top of the tongue.

③ Carefully FOLD the front template to CUT out the mouth. This is a temporary fold.

← CUT out shaded area.

④ Carefully FOLD the front template across the eyes to CUT out the eyes.

This is a temporary fold.

↖ CUT out shaded area.

⑤ COLOR and DECORATE the front template and the tongue.

⑥ TAPE the top of tongue onto the inside template.

TAPE only the very top!

⑦ Tape →

This is backward and upside down. →

LINE UP the front template and inside template (do not overlap,) and ADD TAPE to hold them in place.

⑧ FOLD up at taped seam. Carefully PUSH the tongue though the mouth opening.

⑨ TURN your monster over, and fold Tab A and Tab B to JOIN them. TAPE or GLUE tabs together.

Back of front template

Do not glue or tape to inside template →

Tab B   Tab A

Back of inside template

⑩ Carefully FOLD the bottom of your monster back along the front play fold line. Do not add any new folds to the back. This is the trick that makes your monster move.

Allow my inside template to move freely.

That's the trick to making me move.

Open

Folded

120

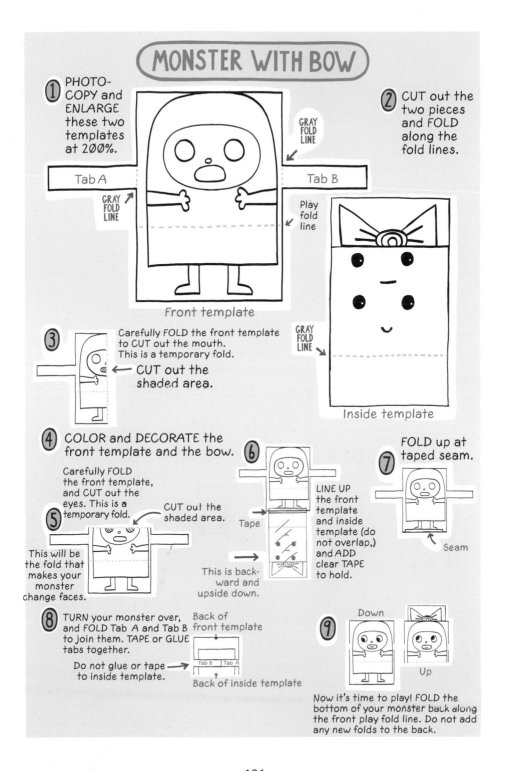

MONSTER WITH BOW

① PHOTO-COPY and ENLARGE these two templates at 200%.

GRAY FOLD LINE

Tab A

GRAY FOLD LINE

Tab B

Play fold line

Front template

② CUT out the two pieces and FOLD along the fold lines.

GRAY FOLD LINE

Inside template

③ Carefully FOLD the front template to CUT out the mouth. This is a temporary fold.

← CUT out the shaded area.

④ COLOR and DECORATE the front template and the bow.

⑤ Carefully FOLD the front template, and CUT out the eyes. This is a temporary fold.

CUT out the shaded area.

This will be the fold that makes your monster change faces.

⑥ Tape

This is backward and upside down.

LINE UP the front template and inside template (do not overlap,) and ADD clear TAPE to hold.

⑦ FOLD up at taped seam.

Seam

⑧ TURN your monster over, and FOLD Tab A and Tab B to join them. TAPE or GLUE tabs together.

Do not glue or tape → to inside template.

Back of front template

Tab B Tab A

Back of inside template

⑨ Down

Up

Now it's time to play! FOLD the bottom of your monster back along the front play fold line. Do not add any new folds to the back.

MONSTER HEADBAND

1 FOLD CARDSTOCK in half.

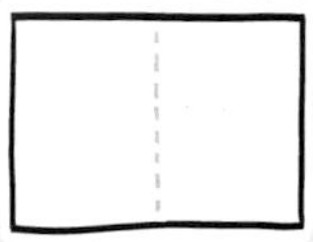

2 DRAW your monster outline and CUT it out. 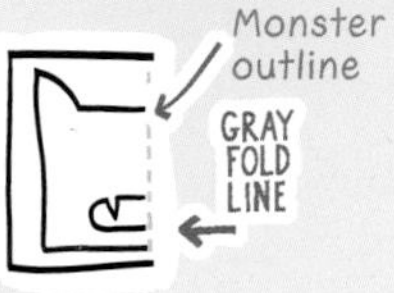
Here are some outline ideas.

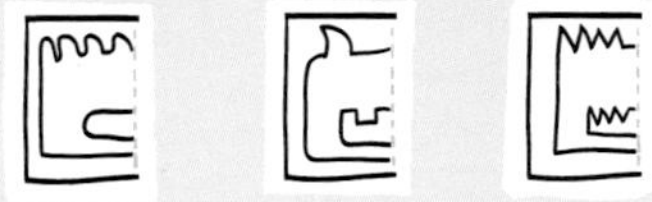

Monster outline

GRAY FOLD LINE

3 UNFOLD your monster head.

ADD details to your monster.

EYE-BALLS!

BIG TEETH!

LONG TONGUE!

Here are some detail ideas.

4 COLOR your monster.

Make fur.

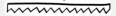

Long strips of paper with cut-out slits

Make scales.

Long strips of paper with cut-out notches

5 You can GLUE these to your monster.

Hey! Someone forgot my nose.

Monster with fur

6 To make the headband, GLUE or TAPE the cardstock strips to the back of your monster.

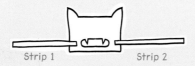

Strip 1   Strip 2

7 ADJUST the strips to fit the head, and TAPE or GLUE strip 1 to strip 2.

GRRR!

I will look good on your head.

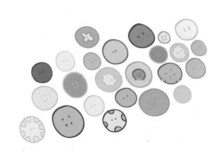

First Second

Published by First Second
First Second is an imprint of Roaring Brook Press, a division of
Holtzbrinck Publishing Holdings Limited Partnership
120 Broadway, New York, NY 10271

Library of Congress Control Number: 2016945549

ISBN: 978-1-62672-485-3

Our books may be purchased in bulk for promotional, educational, or business use. Please contact your local bookseller or the Macmillan Corporate and Premium Sales Department at (800) 221-7945 ext. 5442 or by e-mail at MacmillanSpecialMarkets@macmillan.com.

FIRST EDITION

First edition 2017
Book design by Joyana McDiarmid
Printed in China by Toppan Leefung Printing Ltd.,
Dongguan City, Guangdong Province

3 5 7 9 10 8 6 4

Sketched on an iPad Pro. Inked and colored on a Cintiq in Photoshop with a digital nib.

BY ART WE LIVE